Going Home

By

Elizabeth Castle

Name: Castle, Elizabeth, author

Title: Going Home

Publisher: In The Air Publishing

Cover Designer: Victoria Cooper Art

Chapter One

Tessa Harris slammed the tailgate of her rented pickup truck and glanced around the worn yard. It was strange being back here. The small town of Willow Landing in southern Utah was the last place she thought she'd ever set foot in again. The house she never expected to see the inside of as an adult, though it had remained a strong presence in her memory over the years, was even more worn than it had been during her childhood. The trees were overgrown, and several branches grew over and brushed the roof of the small ranch-style house. The grass, what little there was of it, was mostly brown. There had been little rain, so the rest of the dirt between the dead grass patches was cracked. The house itself was in only slightly better shape than the yard, but Tessa saw the potential of what the house could become.

Tessa picked up one of the boxes she had removed from the truck and headed for the covered porch, or at least that's what she thought it was called. The space was narrow, not much of a porch really, but a couple of rusted chairs sat under the overhang where one could sit, assuming the chairs would hold weight, which she doubted, and gaze out toward the dead lawn.

She remembered well back when flowers bloomed in front of the brick wall that acted as the porch railing. The house itself had always been the dull faded brown color it was now, but most of the paint had peeled and cracked. The roof needed new shingles, and she hoped nothing else. If the wood that held up the roof was rotted, then the cost to fix it would double.

But Tessa wasn't worried about fixing up the exterior of the house. Her brother Simon had a contractor lined up to handle residing the house in a pretty light blue she had picked out and putting on a new roof in light gray, so only the inside of the home remained her problem. And what a problem it was. She smiled, thinking about how it would all look when she was done.

As Tessa entered the house, she touched the old, worn walls that had once been painted white. They were dingy now, fingerprints and who knew what else stained them. The light fixtures were also old and dingy, their once-brassy shine a distant memory. The majority of the glass globes were broken, and many of the bulbs burnt out. The fixtures made the interior look even more worn than the old paint did.

The kitchen wasn't in much better shape, though the old cabinets made Tessa's heart race a little bit. It would take some work to get off the layers of paint, but they were original to the house, and once restored, would add some much-needed charm. And there were hardwood floors under the threadbare carpet, and they too, once restored, would be a major selling point. She had pulled up a few corners, and they seemed to be in good shape for their age.

While gazing around the forlorn kitchen where she had set the box, she heard a vehicle pull into her drive. Not bothering to even get upset this time, she headed for the front door. She had had several visits over the past couple of days from one Deputy Boyd Thomson. She supposed it had been too much to hope he had forgotten who she was. But she had not been that lucky. In fact, the knowledge that her old childhood nemesis was now a cop had come as a shock, as much as it had dismayed her. And while he had towered over her looking incredibly smug, he had made it clear that he wanted her gone. She had listened to him and had taken deep breaths until she was once again calm. By his fourth visit, she had barely blinked when he had written out a citation for disturbing the peace. She'd simply taken it and watched with relief as he left.

But it wasn't Boyd this time blocking her drive; it was the chief himself.

She watched dispassionately from the porch while the man unfolded himself from the SUV. She had known Mason Slade was Willow Landing's Chief of Police. His father, Donald Slade, had been chief before him. Word was Donald had retired a year ago and that was when Mason took over the position. It was one of the first pieces of gossip she'd heard when she hit town.

Tessa first noticed how tall he was. Mason had always had a good ten inches on her, but in his uniform and hat, it looked more than that. His chest was broader, his legs were wider than she remembered from her early teen years, and the belt wrapped around his waist showcased that he was one very fit man. There was no paunch or gut on him. The tailored fit of his uniform left very little to the imagination.

"Good afternoon, Tessa."

Tessa took a step off the porch and headed back toward the boxes she'd left on the ground by the truck. "Good afternoon, Mason. What brings you out here? Or should I guess which one of my many fans called you out here?"

Mason took off his hat and sunglasses to get a better look at Tessa Harris. She didn't look all that different from when she'd been fourteen, though she'd filled out into a more feminine shape in the hip and breast area. Definitely no mistaking her for a child any longer, despite her small stature. Her hair was still a shade somewhere between blonde and red, her skin still fair with prominent freckles sprinkling her cheeks.

Tessa sighed and leaned her hip against the truck when he didn't speak. "So I take it you want me to guess. I vote my neighbor Philip Degrassi called you again. What was it this time? More loud music? Did I vandalize his yard? Kidnap his dog?"

Mason took a step toward her. She had a sheen of sweat on her chest, and he watched as a droplet ran between her breasts. She was wearing an old tank top that had seen better days. Her long hair was tied back in a ponytail. Now that he was closer, he also remembered her bright blue eyes, the shade of a clear summer sky. They were currently glaring at him.

"No, not your neighbor, though his complaints have been varied over the past couple of days."

Tessa grabbed a box and started for the house, her voice trailing after her. "Well, then who?"

Mason picked up one of the boxes and followed.

Tessa almost bumped into him when she met him at

the front door. She took the box from him. "I didn't give you permission to enter my home."

"That you didn't. Just giving you a hand."

Tessa was forced to look up at him when he didn't take a step back. His dark brown hair was cut almost military short, and his dark brown eyes bore into hers. She remembered those eyes, eyes that she thought could see all her secrets. Not wanting to be intimidated by him, or those chocolatey eyes, she pushed past him.

Mason followed her back to the truck. "Deputy Thomson said he had to cite you for disturbing the peace. He also said you threatened old man Degrassi and his dog."

Tessa gritted her teeth and turned to face Mason. "His word against mine, though I suppose my word doesn't mean much. But I plan to fight that citation. I was nowhere near here when he claimed I was blasting music. I was two towns over at the bank. I guarantee you I'm on their security cameras. And as for him and his dog, I've got better things to do. His dog is a very large Rottweiler that weighs almost as much as I do, and Degrassi outweighs me by a hundred or more pounds. If anyone threatened anyone, it was him threatening me."

Mason had dismissed the threat accusations when Boyd had come in complaining loud enough for everyone to hear that Tessa Harris was a nuisance and should be run out of town. What did surprise him was hearing about the bank. That wasn't in the report Boyd filed. "Why didn't you tell Deputy Thomson you were at the bank?"

"Deputy Thomson and I go way back. He wasn't going to listen to me any more than you are. And even if he had, it wouldn't have mattered. He would have found a different excuse to write that citation."

That rankled. "I uphold the law, Tessa; I don't break it. Want to tell me your side of the story?"

Tessa's eyes narrowed as she saw Mason go on the defensive. She'd obviously hit a nerve, but really, what did he expect? She didn't trust him any more than she trusted anyone else in this town. But it also wouldn't do her any good to antagonize the police chief. "Fine. Degrassi came over the day I arrived. That was two days ago. He told me I'd be sorry if I didn't pack up and leave. I suppose he couldn't exactly pick me up and throw me out of town, so he's bent on either running me out or getting me arrested."

Mason nodded. Degrassi wasn't known to be the most honest of men, but he was known for holding grudges. Degrassi and her father had gone quite a few rounds back in the day, and Mason would bet Degrassi wasn't thrilled to have the daughter back. Honestly, no one was, including himself. He and his father had thought themselves rid of all the varied members of the Harris family, but here was little Tessa, the youngest of the clan, back and already the center of trouble.

Mason gestured to the boxes from a big box store. "The local hardware store could have supplied everything you need. Why did you go two towns over to get them?"

"Now see, I tried to do that, but I was thrown out of the hardware store about five minutes after I entered. Then I remembered that Degrassi and old man Baxter are friends. My money wasn't welcome."

Mason picked up the receipt from the box. She had

been an hour away when the most recent phone call came in. John Baxter, who ran the hardware store, said that Tessa had helped herself to some tools from his store without paying for them. At the alleged time, Tessa hadn't been there. But still, he had to make sure.

Tessa saw him frowning at the receipt. "What?"

Mason pulled a list from his pocket. "Do you have these things here?"

Tessa took the list, noticing he kept his hands clean and his nails trimmed. She shook her head. "I didn't buy anything from the store."

"John Baxter didn't say you bought the stuff. But he does say the items went missing."

Tessa paled, the paper slipping through her fingers. "He said I stole them."

Though not a question, he nodded. "I need to check the premises."

Tessa felt a flicker of anger, but the ember died out. She didn't have the energy left to fight. "Look around. You won't find the items. What's in these boxes will match my receipt."

Mason saw her energy fade, and her shoulders sag. For the first time, he noticed how thin she was and saw the faint bruising under her eyes that spoke to either a lack of sleep or a lack of nutrition. If her frayed jeans and worn shoes were any indication, he'd guess a little bit of both.

Mason picked up the paper from where she had dropped it. "I'm sorry, Tessa, but I have to look."

Tessa simply nodded and grabbed another box. Mason took the receipt and went through her purchases. He went through her rented truck, her worn-out dark blue Honda that sat on the gravel drive beside the house, and then followed her inside.

"Needs some work."

Tessa set the last box down while Mason finished searching the house. "Simon inherited the house after Aunt Sylvia passed. With all the nearby resorts and tourist traffic around these parts, Simon asked if I wanted to tackle a remodel. I think he'll get a pretty penny for it once it's spruced up."

Mason, who had gone through all the supplies she bought and didn't find a single stolen item, was curious. The supplies were not of someone doing a little home renovation, but of someone who knew what she was doing. "Is that what you do? Fix houses?"

Tessa wiped the sweat that had gathered on her forehead. The house had central heating and air, but the air conditioning hadn't worked for years. Simon had a man coming at the end of next week to take care of that. "Sort of. Mostly I do house painting. But I'm handy with flooring and other minor repairs. Simon has a contractor coming to do the roof and siding and to redo the baths. I can't seem to get the hang of plumbing."

Mason turned and leaned up against the kitchen counter. Her brother Simon was about his age, maybe a year or two younger. Back when they were kids, they were not what you'd call friends. Mason was surprised to hear Simon had the money for those kinds of repairs. The best anyone figured, he'd end up in prison like his father. "I haven't seen Simon since I left for college. How is he?"

Tessa's eyes narrowed, and her hands fisted at her side, prepared to defend her brother. "He's fine."

Mason decided not to pursue the conversation on her brother. "All right, Tessa. I don't see a single item on the list here. And I'm guessing if I call the bank, I'm going to find out you were there. I'm going to drop the citation. And I'll have a chat with Degrassi. Okay?"

Tessa gaped. She had half expected to be hauled in anyway. "You believe me?"

Mason kicked away from the counter. "Let's just say I understand. There's a lot of bad blood between your family and this town. People are not happy you're here. But you have as much right to be here as they do. Keep your nose clean, and you and I won't have any trouble."

Tessa didn't respond, but apparently Mason wasn't waiting for one. He let himself out of the house and headed back to his SUV. She watched as he put his hat back on. Tessa found her voice. "Thank you, Chief Slade. You won't have any trouble."

"Let's just keep it Mason. I always did like the way your cute Southern accent said my name."

Tessa stared after him as he got in the SUV and drove away. That had almost sounded like he was flirting with her. But since even the idea of that was absurd, she dismissed it. And she supposed her accent was a bit out of place. She'd been born in Alabama, and no matter how long she'd lived in the Midwest, the accent had remained with her, though muted with time.

Once he was out of the drive, Tessa turned to look through the trees. She could just barely make out Degrassi's house. He was on his front porch staring her way. She couldn't make out his expression, but she imagined he had been standing there hoping to see her hauled off to jail. Though tempted to wave at him, or perhaps flip him off, she turned her back instead and went inside. Right now all she wanted was to get something to eat and prop up her feet. She'd been running around since dawn, and she had a big day ahead of her tomorrow. Tomorrow she was going to start stripping paint off the cabinets. And from the looks of them, that was not going to be an easy feat. But since the kitchen was the heart of a home, that was the place she wanted to get started.

Hours later, she was curled up in the old bed in what was considered the master bedroom but found she couldn't sleep. Shortly after Mason had left, she had sent a quick text to her brother to let him know she had all the supplies purchased and was ready to get started. She also wanted to let him know that while he was doing the siding and roof, he should probably do the windows as well. His negative reply had been expected, but with persuasion, he had finally agreed to it. He trusted her judgment and told her to do what she needed to do but to take it easy on his wallet. She had smiled to herself, sent him a message back telling him no chance, and then had lain down to try to sleep.

Now staring at the ceiling where she could tell there had been some water damage, she thought about how strange it was to be back in the house she had spent a good part of her childhood in. Aunt Sylvia had been a saint, and Tessa hoped there was a reward for her in Heaven for having put up with all she had over the years. Tessa had been eight when her father, Randy, had lost his job, which in and of itself wasn't exactly significant. But because he'd been fired from almost every job he'd ever had, he found it impossible to find a new one. He had cursed up a storm, then informed his small family that they were moving in with his sister.

Her mother, Janine, had cried, which just angered her husband. She hadn't wanted to leave her home, which then sent Randy on a tirade. Her brother Simon had been silent about the move. He knew not to cross their father when he laid down the law. Tessa had cried, but she had done it silently in her bed. She and Simon had to share a room, so he had heard her tears. He had come over, picked her up, and let her sleep with him that night. She took comfort in his presence. And because Tessa adored her brother, she had believed him when he told her everything was going to be okay.

But things were not okay. They had lived with Aunt Sylvia for four years. She and Simon had continued to share one of the three bedrooms. It had been the smallest one in the house. Over the course of those four years, Simon had become a different kid. He no longer let his little sister sleep in his bed; he started missing curfew and had been caught drinking and vandalizing property.

When she turned twelve, her father had finally gotten tired of living with his sister and bought a small house across town, though to this day she still wasn't sure where he'd gotten the money to buy a house. Then things had gotten worse. Her father was drinking all the time. Her mother was a shell of the woman she had been and went about taking care of her family on autopilot; there but not participating. Simon went from vandalism to outright theft. He got into fights in school, one of the most notable fights being with Mason Slade. Chief Slade had arrested her brother for that fight, and many more times after that. Every time the chief called saying Simon had been arrested, her father cursed the chief, cursed his son, and cursed life in general.

Tessa rolled over on her side. She was grateful Simon had not ended up like their father, as everyone had predicted he would. But they didn't know the Simon she knew, the one who cuddled his baby sister. The one who held her when she cried. And while he might have gotten derailed for a time, he had eventually gotten back on track. It had taken their father's arrest to get him to see the error of his ways. For Tessa, it had been a blessing the day Chief Slade, accompanied by officers from the neighboring city, took her father away.

She, Simon, and her mother moved back in with Aunt Sylvia. It was Sylvia's influence that helped Simon get back on track, telling him he was the man of the family now and had a duty to them. Their mother let Sylvia take care of her children while she hid away from the world.

Tessa sighed and flipped onto her stomach. When Simon left to join the Army, Tessa had been left alone. Sylvia started spending more and more of her time with her boyfriend and was never home. Janine never left her bedroom, and Tessa had been starving for company. The day she turned eighteen, she ran off with her boyfriend. Timothy and she had been friends since shortly after she moved to town. He had been one of the other children who had been tormented by their classmates. Everyone knew her father was a loser who couldn't hold down a job. She wore old clothes that didn't fit, and she had been very unkempt. For Timothy, his father was the town's garbage man, and his mother worked in the school kitchen. The children were not kind to him.

In hindsight, her and Timothy's plan to move in together and start a new family wasn't one of her better ideas. And it had been her idea. But he had been the only person, besides Simon, who seemed to care about her. But life had beaten the two of them down pretty quickly, and what had started with such enthusiasm had turned into a nightmare.

Tessa punched her pillow and tried to relax. She supposed it was understandable that she would be bombarded with memories, lying alone in her aunt's house with the ghosts of those memories trapped in the walls of the old home. And seeing Mason Slade probably hadn't helped. Though where she expected hostility, she had gotten reasonable. He had listened to her side of the story, had done his job without destroying her property, and had dropped the citation against her.

She couldn't help but notice he had aged well. She was a few years younger than her brother, and Simon was only a year behind Mason. She had just turned thirty-one, so she knew Mason was thirty-six. Thirty-five would have been very young to become police chief, but she supposed having a father who had the job before he did made the transition easier. And Mason had always been a take-charge type of person. He played almost every sport in school, had gotten a full-ride scholarship to some fancy college, and studied law and law enforcement. Shortly after that, he'd entered the police academy. He had always been an overachiever, so being chief at thirty-five was probably inevitable.

She knew he had left town for a while and had been a detective at a major city police precinct before moving back home to take his father's job. She had to admit he looked the part. The short hair, the tall, muscular build, and his intimidating presence were probably all prerequisites for a police chief, even in a small town. Though the town wasn't so small anymore, what with the tourists and the nearby resorts to police. She imagined he was a busy man. So it begged the question, why had Mason shown up at her home today? Over the past two days, she had only seen Boyd, and he had been less than friendly since their history was long and colorful. In a school full of bullies, Boyd had been the ringleader. It still surprised her that anyone would let him wear a badge. But perhaps his unprofessional attitude and the threats he had issued had more to do with her than with his job.

But regardless of Boyd, or even Mason, Tessa was going to stick it out. She owed her brother, and this was a simple enough way to repay him. She would have to find some way to deal with Degrassi and keep her fingers crossed that she wouldn't find Boyd or Mason at her doorstep again.

Chapter Two

Mason finished reading the last of the reports on his desk. He had his own reports to type up, and he had a meeting with the mayor and the town council in a few days about budgets, but he was having a hard time focusing. Yet another report had come across his desk on Tessa Harris. This one had about as much credibility as the last ones. If this report was to be believed, Tessa had been seen drunk and naked on the road outside her home, disturbing traffic and making a nuisance of herself. Mason hadn't seen a single liquor bottle in her home; not even a case of beer in her fridge. And since the report came in from Degrassi, Mason was filing it away with the rest.

Hopefully, that would be the last one. Mason had had enough and made the promised visit to Degrassi just that morning, which was why he had been late getting into the office. He'd told Degrassi that it was illegal to file false police reports and to be sure he had his facts straight the next time he called in with a complaint. So unless Degrassi had photos of Tessa naked in the street, he had nothing else to talk to the old man about. Of course, Mason thought, a picture of a naked Tessa dancing in the street would be a sight to behold.

"What's that look all about?"

Mason jerked his head up, drawing his thoughts away

from a naked Tessa. He smiled at his dad. About two or three times a month, his dad popped into the office. Mason wasn't bothered by it; his dad missed being an active police officer, though if ever needed, his dad was ready and willing to lend a hand. Mason humored him when he stopped in, and his visits usually ended with a free lunch at the local diner, courtesy of his dad.

Mason tossed the latest complaint against Tessa on the desk by his dad. "Philip Degrassi has made it clear as day that he has a real problem with Tessa Harris moving in next door to him. His complaints have been plentiful and varied. They've also mostly been proven false."

"Naked in the street, huh? That would be a new one, and I guarantee that someone besides Philip would have noticed. But I can be your witness for this one. I was at Tessa's place when this complaint came in. And I can say with assurance that I didn't see her naked. I believe she was scowling at me right about this time and was fully clothed."

That got Mason's attention. "What were you doing at Tessa's?"

"Same thing you were doing when you went out there to see if she robbed John's store. I wanted to get a gauge on her. Let's just say Philip is not the only one who isn't happy to see her. I thought when Sylvia passed that we'd seen the last of the Harris clan."

Mason knew that Sylvia Harris had never caused any problems, but because of her brother, trouble had a way of circling around her. There had been one memorable occasion when Randy Harris had been arrested. Donald Slade had had plenty of people claiming Randy owed them money, or that Randy had stolen from them too. Rumors were that Randy had robbed a bank two towns over and stashed the money. But if Randy had stashed it, he had refused to tell anyone where it was. Eventually, he was released, and the charges were dropped because the money wasn't found in his possession. But in addition to the people claiming they deserved a piece of the stolen money, there were others who had shown up looking for it. It had been a long summer for the local police and for Sylvia Harris.

Mason felt a brief stirring of sympathy for Tessa. So far, she had not caused any trouble, and yet trouble was circling her. "I'll add your testimony to the report. The mayor is also interested in Tessa. If I remember correctly, he and Randy used to work for the same construction company. I'm pretty sure you arrested Randy for a bar fight the two had gotten into."

Donald and Mayor Griswold were good friends. "Alex had to file several complaints against him. Randy was constantly hitting on Alex's wife. Their last fight ended in Randy's arrest for public intoxication and assault. Several witnesses came forward and said that Randy had attacked Alex. Alex simply defended himself."

Mason pulled the file toward him and made a few notes. "Alex was elected mayor that next year. I think the town liked having a man in office who could defend and protect his family."

Donald took a seat and stretched out his legs. "That they did. And he's done a good job. He might retire soon. But that's not why I stopped in. I saw something while I was at Tessa's place."

Mason was almost afraid to ask. "All right, what did you see?"

"Someone vandalized her property. Someone spray-painted 'get out' all over the front and back of her house. Whoever it was also painted it on her car, though almost anything would be an improvement to that piece of junk. There were vile obscenities painted on her car too; the tires were slashed, and the interior was covered in what I imagine is animal feces."

Mason's gut clenched. "That sounds awfully personal. I didn't see a report filed."

Donald sat forward, his elbows on his knees. "I was under the impression when I left that she had no intention of filing a complaint. I hadn't noticed the car when I pulled up, and the words painted on her house were by her front door, so the porch shaded them. I came off a bit strong, and by the time I noticed, she wasn't in a friendly mood."

Mason rubbed his brow. "What exactly did you say to her?"

Donald made no apologies. "I told her what you probably told her. That she had better not cause any trouble or you'd see she was locked up. She paled but didn't say a word in response. Then she straightened her shoulders, thanked me for my concern for the town's well-being, and said to have a nice day. It was when she opened her front door that the sun hit the glass and lit the wall by her door. I came over and saw what was there. I asked her who did it. She looked me in the eye and said she did it herself. Then she closed the door in my face. So, I took a look around and saw the car. That, more than anything, has me worried. I figured I should come and file it for her."

Mason contemplated sending Boyd to take a look but dismissed it. He wasn't sure what was between Boyd and Tessa, but Mason got the impression that Boyd wasn't impartial when it came to Tessa. Even if Boyd hadn't ranted about the Harris clan and very vocally told everyone who would listen that she needed to go, he would have known. There had been an almost happy glint in Boyd's eyes when he brought in the last complaint filed against Tessa. And Boyd had said if Mason wanted her picked up, he'd be happy to do it.

"All right. Thanks, Dad. I'll make it a point to stop there later today. Right now, I think we could both use a fresh cup of coffee."

Donald slapped his son on the back and led the way out. "Now you'd be right about that. And your mother wanted me to stop in and say she's having everyone over on Sunday for dinner. She's hoping you can make it. She's excited about our trip coming up but is fretting about being away for so long."

Mason and his dad walked along the main road through town as they headed to the restaurant. "So you mean dinner tomorrow. She always frets. I think she thinks we'll all starve to death or forget all about her while she's gone. Never mind that all of us moved out years ago. But the two of you deserve this."

"I've got the motor home rented and I've got all the supplies stacked up in the mudroom. She's got the itinerary planned. And now that she's finished with planning the trip, she's fretting. So you and your sisters are all being asked to come for Sunday dinner. And then the next Sunday and the next until we actually leave."

Mason laughed; he couldn't help it. "So this is a command performance then. I think I can swing it. Since I got a new officer, I can take a day off now and again."

"How's that working out? I hear Officer Jackson did well in school and got high marks."

Mason nodded. "His instructor at the academy recommended him. He's green, but he'll do. I've got him training under Lawrence, so he'll do fine."

"Good choice. Lawrence has broken in a lot of new officers over the years." Donald could only approve of his son's choice. Deputy Alicia Lawrence had been with the police department almost as long as he had been. She'd retire in the next couple of years, and that would be a shame for everyone.

When they arrived at the restaurant, it was oddly quiet. Everyone was looking at the front of the restaurant. Mason saw Tessa at the counter. When she turned, she stopped for a moment and stared. He couldn't decipher the look on her face. She then rushed past him and his dad, the bell ringing over the door as she did.

The hushed room steadily grew in volume. Mason was tempted to go after her but figured that would just cause talk. If she had been causing trouble, he had no doubt Margie, the owner, would have called him over.

Donald pulled out the menu, though he already knew what he wanted. "Wonder what that was all about?"

Mason watched as Margie headed their way. "I think

we're about to find out."

"What can I get you two fine gentlemen today?" She pulled out her pad and gave them her biggest smile.

The very robust, red-headed Margie had owned the diner for years, having inherited it from her parents. She'd been married three times, and each of those husbands had worked there for a time. But the restaurant was one hundred percent Margie's.

Donald ordered the special and asked to have the coffee keep coming. Mason did the same. "So how are things going today?"

Margie huffed. "Well, they were going just fine until Tessa Harris showed up. She had the nerve to ask about a job."

Mason knew very well there was a help wanted sign outside. Margie's most recent waitress had left for college. "Aren't you hiring?"

Margie tucked the ticket in her pocket. "Not her kind. Rumor has it she applied at a couple of other places too. As if anyone in their right mind would hire a Harris. I wish she'd just pack up and leave. Our town was doing just fine without her."

Mason frowned at Margie's retreating back. "All right, Dad. Why is Margie in a huff?"

"Margie is pretty sure Randy Harris robbed her restaurant shortly before he was arrested for the bank robbery. What little cash that was left in the register was stolen, as was a lot of food from the freezer. Everyone knew Randy was out of work again, and so the general consensus was that he was the perpetrator. I agreed with her, but I couldn't prove it. There were no prints, and Margie didn't have anything in the way of security cameras like she does now. Randy didn't make any large purchases, so we couldn't trace the money. And the house the Harris family was living in was empty of anything remotely resembling a meal. If he stole the food, he didn't take it home to his family."

Sympathy tugged at him for Tessa. "I hate to say it, but Tessa really would be better off if she left. Though a lot of the new folks in town won't have known the Harris family, a lot of the old folks will be more than happy to share the tales."

"Something tells me little Tessa isn't one to run off easily. She's got spunk."

Mason took a sip of the coffee Margie had poured him. "You almost sound approving."

"Your sister Laine had taken a shine to Tessa. They're the same age and were in the same class in school. Laine used to put extra food in her lunch bag so she could give it to her. She brought Tessa by the house once. Tessa had been quiet and barely said a word. But eventually, we had to tell Laine she couldn't be friends with her anymore. Simon was becoming a problem, and I didn't want my daughter playing with Simon's sister. Laine came in the next day in tears. She had told Tessa they couldn't be friends, and Tessa had told her that it was okay. She understood. Laine was actually upset that Tessa hadn't hit her, or at least shoved her down. Laine told me what I did was mean and broke Tessa's spirit. It was the first and only time I was ashamed of what I had done."

Mason digested that story. He didn't remember Laine ever mentioning Tessa. "So why did you show up at her house today?"

Donald shrugged. "Tessa had never done a single thing wrong, but it didn't matter, not then and not now. She's guilty simply because of who she is. I guess I wanted to see her for myself. Give her the same warning I'm sure you gave her. She's been gone a long time, and I told her I wouldn't let her cause trouble and to mind herself. I may not be chief anymore, but this town is still mine."

Mason figured one day when he retired, he'd feel the same way. "As far as I can tell, the only one causing trouble is the town's reaction to her. She said John refused to sell her supplies to fix the house. Margie has made it clear she's not welcome. And Degrassi, well, if he doesn't stop filing false reports, I'll have to arrest him."

"You'll have the town in an uproar if you do that."

Mason acknowledged the truth in his father's words. As the chief, he had to be careful. He had to answer to the mayor and the town council. If he let any infraction, no matter how small, slide when it came to Tessa, he'd hear about it. And if he sided with her if it came down to someone's word against hers, he'd have to justify that decision. And arresting one of the town elders would definitely get him in hot water.

Donald smiled at the waitress who delivered their food, then pointed his fork at his only son. "You have that look on your face."

"Which one?"

"The one that says 'just try messing with me.'"

Mason scooped up a bite of his eggs. "I'm not happy Tessa is here. But I'm also not going to let the town bully her. If Degrassi crosses the line, I'll haul him in. And anyone else."

"Just make sure you keep your temper under control when you see the house and car. It ticked me off, and I'm not chief anymore. A simple 'get out' note would have sufficed, but they took it too far. Slashing tires and writing obscenities on her car went way beyond a bit of snubbing or bullying."

Mason and his dad finished their meal and talked of much more pleasant topics. His youngest sister, Cyndi, had gotten married last year, and shortly after, she and her husband Tyler announced they were having a baby. It was hard to imagine his baby sister having a baby, but it was exciting for the family. She was the youngest of the bunch and had always been the nurturer. His sister Laine had been married a couple of years, but she said she wasn't ready for a baby, though their mother had been hinting at it not so subtly for a while. She hadn't started in on Cyndi yet when Cyndi had surprised everyone. Her husband was ecstatic and very much the nervous father-to-be.

Mason left his father at the car his dad had parked outside the station. Mason had a few more housekeeping items on his to-do list before he headed over to Tessa's. Part of him had hoped she would trust him enough to call and report the vandalism, but that hope died at four in the afternoon when she still hadn't called. He let his secretary and part-time dispatcher know where he was headed. She simply wished him a good night. Mason doubted Hailey knew who Tessa was, other than what she had heard from Boyd.

Mason waved at people he knew as he headed for his vehicle. The town had paid for the new SUV last winter and was a proud sight for the folks. The old sedan he had been driving was hardly more than an eyesore on a good day. The town had finally gotten tired of paying for the repairs and voted for the new, bigger SUV. The town's name was painted in bright blue letters against the white paint.

Mason took the time to stop and grab a sandwich and say hello to a few more people before he made his way to Tessa's. It was almost six by the time he got there. She lived on the outskirts of town, but not so far out that you hit the local ranches. Beyond her property was a small wooded lot that backed up to the Jackson ranch, one of the biggest ranches in the area. Her property wasn't that far from his own, which was maybe twenty minutes closer to town. But being the chief, he needed to be close by if he was needed. His parents had lived in town since his father had been chief for so many years, but now they were contemplating selling their house. They didn't need to be so close to town anymore, and they said it was time to downsize. It was on their list of things to do when they got back from their month-long trip.

Mason was tempted to buy it himself, but it seemed like a lot of house for a bachelor. And despite his mother's wishes, he didn't see himself marrying anytime soon. Being chief made it hard to date. If he dated too much, people would talk. If a relationship went sour, there was bound to be talk. When he did date, it was never a local woman, which made dating a lot more difficult than it should be.

Mason pulled the SUV up behind Tessa's car. Thinking about marriage, he thought about Tessa. He was surprised Tessa wasn't married. She was more than pretty enough to have attracted lots of male attention, and she was more than old enough. He didn't know where she had been living all these years but figured it had been far away from here. The license plate on her car said Indiana. He'd been tempted to run a background check on her. He knew the town would have applauded him for it. But she hadn't done anything wrong, yet, and it seemed wrong.

Mason stepped from the SUV and walked to her car. Obscenity was a mild word for the filth written on her car. There was no way Tessa was getting the bright orange spray paint off her car, and in some places the words were scratched into the paint. All four tires were not just slashed but shredded. And the smell that was coming from inside, from having baked in the sun all day, was foul.

Heading to the porch, he saw the "get out" message in spray paint, this time in black. It was stark against the dingy brown siding. It looked like Tessa had scraped some of it off that had been on the peeling paint. Taking a calming breath, he knocked on the front door. When there was no answer, he banged again. Still nothing. Scowling, he banged again. Cursing her, and with visions of what someone might have done to her similar to what they had done to her car, he kicked in the door.

Chapter Three

Tessa almost screamed as the front door flew toward her. Mason was standing there, gun drawn.

Finding her voice, she yelled at him as he stood scanning the room. "Have you lost your mind?"

Mason came further into the room to make sure there was no one else with her. "Are you alone? Are you okay?"

Tessa stuttered. "Yes, I'm alone. You broke down my door."

Mason holstered the gun. "And it was quite a flimsy one. You should add that to your list to replace. And you should know better than to not answer the door when the police chief comes knocking."

Tessa wrapped her arms around her waist. "I didn't know the chief of police was knocking at my door. I was lying down in the back. What did you think was going on here? I don't want to talk to you."

Mason pointed in the direction of where her car was parked. "Given what happened, there could have been someone inside with you. I had to be sure you were safe."

Tessa dropped onto the worn sofa. She supposed his father had told him what happened after his unpleasant visit. "Is that what you're putting in your report? Never mind. I'm perfectly fine, as you can see."

Feeling a bit sheepish now that he was coming down

from his adrenaline surge, he picked the door up off the floor. It was beyond repair, but he leaned it against the open space so it would at least keep the bugs out.

Tessa rubbed the tension from the back of her neck. Her belly was still in knots from the fear of having someone kick in her door and a gun pointed at her. She had been living with, but trying not to give into, fear. She knew people wouldn't be happy she was in town, but she hadn't expected this level of violence against her. Maybe some vandalism, or perhaps some veiled threats, but the destruction of her car was something else entirely.

Calm now, Mason pulled a notepad from his pocket. Just like his father before him and cops over the years, he preferred to take handwritten notes in the field. "I want to talk about what happened here. You need to file a report."

Tessa shrugged, showing a nonchalance she didn't feel. "Like I told your dad, it's nothing to get in a lather over."

Mason struggled not to snap the pen in his hand. "What he said was that you told him you did it yourself."

Tessa had been startled when Donald Slade had shown up. He had been less than friendly, at least at first. Her car was parked in the shade, and the words spray-painted on the house were in the shade of the porch, so he hadn't noticed either of them at first. He had been in full lecture mode as he strode toward her. He had been telling her that she had better think twice before causing any trouble, that the town wouldn't tolerate it, or her, if she got out of line. Even when he had come upon her, his height intimidating as he towered over her, he hadn't noticed the paint all over the house. It wasn't until she got to her front door that he had gone silent, and his attitude shifted. He had come up to the door to take a closer look. When he had casually asked her what else had been done, she had not been in the mood to answer him. She had simply pointed at the car. And at some point, she remembered she had told him she had done it herself, in hopes he would just go away.

"Well?"

Tessa realized he had been talking to her, and she had not been listening. "Well, what?"

"Why did you tell my dad you did this yourself?"

Tessa, who had been fighting tears, rose angrily to her feet. "Because that is what people will tell themselves. I might as well make it official. See, no one will believe that any of the good townsfolk would do something like this. And if it weren't for a Harris on the property, nothing bad would have happened. I must have done it myself. Maybe I did it to stir up trouble, and then maybe file a false report with my insurance company to get the money. And why not? I'm just like my daddy, right? The Harris family is bad news, and everyone knows it."

Mason pulled a cloth handkerchief from his pocket. It always paid to keep one handy. He handed it to Tessa. He didn't think she even realized she was crying, so great was her anger. And he supposed in a way she had a point. A lot of people in town wouldn't believe one of their own would do something like this. And yes, her father ended up in prison, at least the last time that Mason knew of, for insurance fraud. Of course, he had claimed something bigger than a car.

While his wife was at the laundromat doing her family's

laundry, and his kids were in school, Randy had very carefully set his house on fire. He claimed all sorts of things of value were inside as he ranted and raved to the police. But in the end, arson was proved, and Randy Harris went to prison. It had been the talk of the town for months. And everyone had breathed a sigh of relief. And it had also been the last time the town had seen Randy Harris. Mason didn't know where he was now, and he didn't care as long as it wasn't here.

Everyone had thought Janine Harris would pack up her kids and move, but she had stayed. But as time passed, first Simon left, then Tessa, and then Janine. Sylvia had remained until her death a short while ago, and she had never had so much as a speeding ticket. But the bad blood between the town and the Harris clan was thick, and even the law-abiding Sylvia had felt the brunt of it for most of her life.

Tessa took the handkerchief and wiped her cheeks. Hating the weakness of tears, she got herself back under control. "Look, I appreciate the visit, but there isn't anything you can do."

Mason took her arm, surprised by his reaction to the warmth of her skin and the slightly sweet smell of her hair. He helped her back to the sofa and had her sit down. He had to take a deep breath before he spoke. "The first thing is you file a report. I'll take pictures before I leave, and I'll send someone over to brush for fingerprints, though I'm guessing whoever did this was smart enough to wear gloves. And yes, you'll need the report to file a claim with your insurance company."

Tessa tucked her hands between her knees, the handkerchief between them. "Did you get a good look at the car before it was trashed? I can't imagine it had any value left."

"Either way, I need you to file a report. I can't help you unless you do."

Tessa was speechless for a moment at the thought of a Slade helping a Harris, even if that Slade was the police chief. But Mason had been nicer to her than anyone else in town, and she didn't want to antagonize him. "I don't have a car to drive to the station."

"What about the truck you had?"

"It was a rental. I was returning it when this happened. The guy who drove me home from the rental place offered to drive me to the police station, but I figured it would be a waste of time. It's not like you're going to catch who did this."

Mason laid a hand over hers. "I can at least try. Why don't I drive you in? It's early yet."

Tessa looked over at the clock. "It's already after six."

"That's early for a police chief. On a good day, I'm lucky to get into bed by midnight. Come on, let's get it done. I'll send someone out here to dust for prints, and then I'll see about getting a new door and a deadbolt. I'll feel better if you're locked up nice and tight."

Tessa shivered at the small touch of his hand on hers. "Sorry, but I'm not a fan of the 'locked up nice and tight' part. And besides, I told Simon he should replace the windows. A deadbolt on the door isn't going to make the house any safer."

Mason looked around. "You might have a point. There's a small hotel in town where you could stay until the windows and doors are replaced."

Tessa pulled away. She barely had enough money for food, much less a hotel. "I'll think about it. But if you insist on doing this tonight, we should get going."

Tessa let Mason help her into the passenger seat of the SUV. She tried to keep her heartbeat under control, telling herself that she wasn't under arrest, that she would be free to go. What she didn't want to admit to was that she hadn't wanted to call Mason, or the local police in general, because she knew she'd have to go down to the station. She kept telling herself over and over that this wasn't Dallas, that she hadn't done anything wrong. Of course, her last memorable ride in a police vehicle wasn't because of something she'd done, but because of something her boyfriend had done. In the end, it hadn't mattered. She was the one found guilty.

Mason pulled onto the main road that led into town. "So besides painting houses, what have you been up to since you left? If I recall correctly, you and Tim Dawson took off right after graduation."

Tessa glanced at him from under her eyelashes. The question had sounded innocent enough, but she didn't trust Mason's motives for the question. But like before, she could either answer him or risk antagonizing him. "Yes, Timothy and I ran off after graduation. He had a brother who was living in Dallas who said we could crash with him. As you can imagine, things were hard for a couple of headstrong kids who hadn't any idea what they were getting themselves into. A couple of years after we arrived, Timothy and I split up. The next few years were rough, but then I decided to head to Indiana where Simon was living. Then I started painting houses. Not much else to tell."

Mason glanced at Tessa. Her hands were in her lap, her fingers clenched so tight that she was cutting off the circulation to her fingers. "What about Simon? What does he do?"

Tessa relaxed. She was so incredibly proud of Simon. "He's a pediatrician at a hospital in Indianapolis. He's married, and he and his wife, Sarah, have a four-year-old son and a two-year-old daughter."

"A pediatrician?"

Tessa heard the disbelief in his voice but didn't take offense. "When he joined the army, he ended up on a medical detail. It fascinated him. As soon as his tour was up, he took the money he had saved and went to a junior college for a while. Then he got a scholarship to go to a full university, then medical school. That's when he decided to specialize. Sarah was a secretary at the first clinic he worked at. It was love at first sight."

Mason shook his head. "It's hard to imagine Simon Harris, M.D."

"I imagine most people here wouldn't believe me. You can look him up; he's on the hospital website."

Mason heard Tessa's defensive tone. "I believe you, Tessa. It's just amazing to think."

"Well, I think he surprised himself, but I had no doubt he could do whatever it was he wanted. You have to understand that our father was not an easy person to live with. And whatever Simon did or didn't do growing up, he's not the kid you once knew."

Mason reached over and tugged Tessa's hands from her lap. She was once again strangling her fingers. "I bet he's not. And the more I talk to you, Tessa, the more I bet you're not the woman I would have pictured you to be either."

Tessa pulled her hand from Mason's. He would lose that bet.

Tessa remained silent the rest of the ride, except to answer Mason's random questions with one- or two-word answers. When they pulled up in front of the police station, she realized the building was not the one she remembered from her youth.

"Nice, huh?" Mason came around and opened her car door.

Tessa kept her eyes on the building as she slid to her feet next to the SUV. "I remember the old building. About once a month or so, my mom would have to pack me and Simon into the car to go down to the police station to bail out my dad. His weekends weren't complete without a bar fight or two. When he lost, he'd end up locked up, usually with a black eye and busted knuckles."

"We've come a long way since then. Our new police station boasts four individual cells and one large holding cell instead of a single holding room. We have two conference rooms, three interrogation rooms, and a break room that has real coffee and a real vending machine."

Tessa couldn't help but be impressed by the building. Even though it was a police station, the town had built it in a way that maintained some of the old town charm many of the other buildings in town had. Unless you noticed the sign out front declaring the building the town's police station, it could be anything. But once inside, it looked much like the previous police station, though newer, with nice bright paint, and it was bigger than the old one.

Tessa followed behind Mason as he greeted the woman at the front desk and a couple of other people she didn't recognize. She cringed when she heard a loud, familiar voice behind her.

"She finally went too far, huh? What are we booking her for, Chief? Disturbing the peace, vandalizing private property, or maybe prostitution? Yeah, I can see that."

Tessa whirled on Deputy Thomson. "Why don't you watch your filthy mouth before someone shuts it up for you?"

Boyd drew himself up. "Now, that sounded like a threat. We can add threatening an officer to the charges, Chief."

Mason laid a hand on Tessa's shoulder, holding her in place. "Boyd, you have ten seconds to apologize to the lady."

Boyd glanced at Mason and realized he was serious. "For what? Nothing but the truth."

Mason drew Tessa next to him. "Five seconds, Boyd."

Boyd stuttered and muttered an apology. "Sorry, Tessa."

"That's Miss Harris to you. Go make yourself useful and get Miss Harris a bottle of water. I need to take her statement. And then go find Deputy Jackson and tell him to come see me."

Tessa glared at Boyd as Mason led her away, and Boyd stalked off into a different part of the office. "I don't want him anywhere near my house, Mason."

Mason led Tessa to the smaller of the conference rooms and pulled out a chair for her. "Seems to be some seriously bad blood between you two."

Tessa scooted the chair closer to the table and steepled her hands. "We were in school together. He flunked a grade in school, so we were in the same classroom. He took an instant dislike to me. Used to put bugs in my lunch bag, pull my hair, stuff like that. Then when we got to junior high, things got worse. He used to make vulgar comments to me all the time. Simon got arrested for getting into a fight with him when Boyd cornered me in the girls' bathroom after school."

Mason's fist clenched at his side. "Did you report him?"

Tessa glared at him. "No, your daddy came and arrested my brother. I doubt my brother got a word in edgewise as good old Boyd made up stories about what happened."

"You should have told him what happened."

"And what good would that have done? Do you think Chief Slade was going to believe me and my brother? I don't think so."

"Just like you think I wouldn't believe you, Tessa? You had and still have a lot of preconceived notions about my family."

"Yeah, sure, like when your daddy told your sister she couldn't be my friend anymore. I knew everything I needed to know about Chief Donald Slade that day."

Mason leaned back and watched as Tessa struggled against anger and tears. Again, he supposed she had a point.

She had no reason to trust his dad any more than she had to trust him. "I promise, Tessa, that I'll do what I can to find out who vandalized your home and car. And I promise Boyd won't get within ten feet of you again."

Tessa calmed at the soft tone in Mason's voice. Despite knowing she shouldn't, she found herself believing Mason. Thankfully she was saved from having to answer when a young man came into the conference room.

"Officer Walter Jackson, ma'am. My family owns the ranch that adjoins your aunt's property."

Tessa took the bottle of water from him and gave him a slight smile. "Raise horses and cattle, right?"

"Yes, ma'am. My daddy still runs the show, but my brothers and I help out."

"Seth Jackson, right?"

Walter nodded and turned his attention to Mason. "Boyd said you needed me. He seems bent out of shape over something."

"He'll get over it. I need you to get over to Miss Harris's place and see if you can find any evidence of who vandalized her home and car."

Walter's eyes hardened. "Yes, sir. I'll get right out there."

Tessa watched as Walter gave her a nod and headed out of the room. "He seems very earnest."

Mason smiled. Like he'd told his dad earlier that day, he liked Walter and had high hopes for him. "He's as green as they come, but he's good at his job. If there is anything to find, he'll find it. Now we need to go over your statement; I'll have you read and sign it, and then I can take you home."

It sounded easy enough, but it was a couple of hours before Mason was satisfied with her statement and had her sign it. She hadn't seen anything because she hadn't been there. She'd had confrontations with Degrassi, John Baxter at the hardware store, and Margie at the restaurant, though she wouldn't call that a confrontation exactly. She'd been thrown out of the hardware store and the local diner and had been denied the chance to apply for a job at the local feed store and consignment shop. She hadn't bothered to go anywhere else after that. Mason wrote down everything she said. He then left for a while and came back with a typed-up copy.

Tessa read it over and signed it. "That's it?"

"For now. Walter should be finishing up his work soon. It's getting late; I should get you home."

The station was quiet as Mason led her out. She let Mason take her empty water bottle and toss it in a recycle bin. How odd, Tessa thought; her hometown had a recycling facility. Would the wonders never cease? But she had a more pressing issue. "Mason, I need the ladies' room before we go."

"Yeah, sure." Mason led her to where the bathrooms were.

Once inside, Tessa took a deep breath. She didn't hold out any hope that Walter would find anything. And no one in town was going to own up to the vandalism. And while after spending time with Mason she believed he would try, she didn't have faith he'd get far. After using the facilities, Tessa took a minute, splashed a little water on her overheated cheeks, then dried off. Mason was waiting right outside when she stepped out. She couldn't help but feel flustered when he cupped a hand under her elbow and led her to the SUV.

She stopped outside the door of the SUV when he held it for her. "Thank you, Mason."

Mason stopped and stared down into her pretty blue eyes. The lights outside the station burned brightly. Tessa's face was flushed, and her lips parted. "You're welcome."

Tessa wasn't sure how long she stood staring up at him, but when she realized what she was doing, she pulled her gaze away and climbed in. Struggling to get her emotions under control, she kept her gaze on the street as Mason pulled out of the parking lot. Despite her wishes, she found herself watching Mason as he drove. His hands were competent on the wheel. His broad chest and shoulders filled most of her view. It had been so long since a man had held her attention the way Mason did. And when she realized what she had just thought, she forcefully pulled her gaze back to the landscape as it sped by. The last thing she needed was to develop a crush on the local police chief, the absolute last man she should find fascinating.

When Mason pulled into her driveway, she saw Walter was gone. The porch light was on, its soft glow lighting the barren lawn. Tessa didn't wait for Mason to come around and opened her door. She was halfway to her porch when he called out to her.

"Don't hesitate to call, Tessa, if you have any more problems. I'll start asking around tomorrow if anyone knows anything about the vandalism. If nothing else, it will warn whoever did it that I'm on the lookout."

"Good night, Mason." Tessa halted but didn't turn around.

"Good night, Tessa."

Tessa went inside and set the door back into the jamb to stop the bugs and cool night air from coming inside.

Chapter Four

Awareness. That was the word Tessa had been struggling to find throughout the night. At some point last night, after she had given her statement, Tessa became aware of Mason as a man, not the police chief. As she'd gazed at him, she'd been aware of the square cut of his jaw, the unexpectedly soft fullness of his lips, and the way the faint light from the dash highlighted his long lashes. Then her gaze had lingered over the fullness of his chest and shoulders, the way his uniform pants hugged his thighs as he sat in the driver's seat. Everything about him had become etched in her memory and had haunted what little sleep she'd gotten. She had rediscovered desire, and she was none too happy about it. A man, though really not more than a boy, had done his best to ruin her life. And she had vowed to stay away from the male of the species, with the exception of her brother, for what was left of the rest of her life.

But it was hard to remember that vow when her body heated as she lay on her back, staring at the water-damaged ceiling, thinking of Mason.

When Tessa finally rolled out of bed, it was still early, the sun barely up. Though generally an early riser, she wanted nothing more than to pull the covers up over her head and try again tomorrow. But work called, and at some point, so would Simon. She wanted to be able to show him via video chat what she had done in the short time she'd been here.

By seven, Tessa had fixed a quick breakfast, drunk two cups of weak coffee, and had already started sanding the cabinet doors she had stripped of paint. The kitchen was small, so she wouldn't have much to sand, but it had taken a lot of elbow grease to get most of the paint off the doors. Sanding would remove the rest and smooth the doors. She was looking forward to putting on the stain and seal.

Tessa was relaxed and humming while she sanded when she saw a large pickup truck pull into her drive. She flipped the electric sander off and relaxed once again when she saw Mason behind the wheel. There was also a rather large dog in the seat next to him.

"Morning, Tessa."

Tessa felt her lips curl into a soft smile. "Morning, Mason."

Mason stepped from the truck and came around to the passenger door. "Are you afraid of dogs?"

Tessa set the electric sander down and used the back of her arm to wipe the sweat away. "I don't think so. Is that a German Shepherd?"

"Yes. He comes with the truck."

"What?" Tessa shook her head as if to clear it.

Mason opened the truck door and the dog jumped out. Tail wagging, the dog waited for direction. Mason rubbed the dog's head between his ears. "Go play."

The dog came over to Tessa and gave her a thorough sniffing. Once satisfied, the dog went over to the grass nearby.

Tessa watched the dog for a moment before turning to Mason. "The dog comes with the truck?"

"Yep. I borrowed my dad's truck. Rexford has to come along for the ride. Otherwise, he sulks."

Tessa craned her neck so she could watch the dog. "Rexford?"

"Don't know. It's what Dad came up with. Anyway, he'll be fine. He'll sniff everything and eventually go lie down in the shade."

Tessa walked over to where Mason was standing. "So what brings you here? You're not in uniform."

Mason looked down at his jeans and black t-shirt. "It always feels odd when I'm out of it. There are times when I practically sleep in my uniform. But what brings me here is your door. I owe you one."

Tessa watched as Mason slammed the passenger door and went to the bed of the truck. He dropped the tailgate and started pulling out a door.

Tessa vaguely remembered him saying something about replacing her door, but she never imagined he was going to show up with one. "I can't take that."

Mason grunted as he finally got the door to the ground. "Sure you can. I didn't buy it from John Baxter's store."

There went one argument, she mused. Others came to mind but most of them were not ones she could say out loud. Like *I don't want you here because you kept me up all night. Or I don't want you here because you look way too appealing in jeans and a t-shirt that look like they were custom-made to contour his legs and chest.* "Look, I appreciate the gesture and all, but there's no need. I can put in a new door."

"Of that, I have no doubt. But you are not the only handy one here. And you might as well just say yes and let me get on with it. I'm not leaving."

Tessa had seen a similar look on her brother's face when he became stubborn and was determined to get his way. Sometimes Tessa would argue with Simon anyway, and other times she would relent. Right now, the wisest course of action seemed to relent. "Well, then you know where it goes."

Mason smiled and wrestled with the door. "Right decision. I'll get to it then."

Tessa went back to sanding her cabinet doors while Mason very competently removed the old trim and casing and went about installing the new door. It was a simple door, but it suited the design of the house. Her heart warmed a bit that he took the time to pick one that fit the design of the home.

Mason was sweating a bit by the time he finished. In addition to the door, he'd bought two new locks. One for the front door and one for the back. He didn't know who Sylvia might have given a key to, so he felt better with Tessa getting new keys. It only took him half an hour to get the new locks on her back door.

As he came back through the house to the front, he realized it was quiet. He'd been listening to the drone of the electric sander most of the time he'd been working. Tessa now had a sanding block to finish with a softer grit. He came over and ran a hand over the smooth wood.

Tessa blew some of the dust off. "All done?"

He ignored her question in favor of his own comment. "You're very good at this."

"Just have to take time and do it right. Once they're done, I'm going to stain them a color similar to the wood floors in the living room. Unfortunately, there is no wood under all the ugly linoleum. Simon wants me to go ahead and tile the kitchen. The tile I bought will really bring out the tones in this old wood."

Mason had seen the other work she had done. She had pulled up the old carpet and padding in the living room. There was some damage, but seeing what she did with the cabinets, he bet she'd get them looking practically brand new. "Planning on doing any structural changes? Removing any walls?"

Tessa set the door she finished sanding to the side and grabbed the next one. "No structural changes. I like the house as it is, and Simon would never let me start tearing down walls and hiring someone to check the structure, even if I wanted to. Some of the drywall is going to need replacing, especially in the master. I can see some water damage. The roof probably needed to be replaced ten years ago, if not more. I'm hoping the guy Simon sends to do the roof and siding can help me get the drywall in place. It's a little too heavy for me to manage by myself."

Mason had to stop himself from offering to help. Not only did he not have the time, but it also wouldn't look right to have the town's police chief drywall a citizen's house. "If he can't, I know some guys who might be willing to help out. They're young, but if you're willing to give them directions, they'll do a good job."

Tessa bit her tongue on the comment she was about to make that she doubted there was a person in town who would be willing to help her. Unless of course, it was to get rid of her faster. "Thanks. I'll let you know."

Mason pulled the keys from his pocket. "The set with the red ring is for the front door. The set with the blue ring is for the back."

Tessa took the keys, careful not to touch him. "Look, I really do appreciate this, Mason."

"But?"

Tessa tucked the keys in her pocket. "No but. Just thanks. I forget that sometimes people just like to do good."

Mason took a step back. "I kicked in the door when I overreacted. This is the least I can do. And I'll feel better now that you have new locks on those doors. Be sure to tell your brother to get moving on the window install."

Tessa watched Mason go back to the truck and whistle for Rexford. The dog perked up and heeded the call from his spot under one of the nearby trees.

"Tessa?"

Tessa set the electric sander she had just picked up back down. "Yes?"

Mason closed the truck door when Rexford hopped in. From his back pocket, he pulled out a card. "This card has the emergency number to the station. The dispatcher can get ahold of me in minutes. If anything happens, use it."

Tessa tucked it into her back pocket. "I will. Thanks, Mason."

Satisfied, Mason got in the truck, gave her a small

salute, and backed out of her driveway.

Tessa took the keys he'd given her back out of her pocket and jingled them while she looked over at the house. The door was new and shiny, a great contrast to the worn siding. She glanced back at the keys. They were still warm from his body heat. He had surprised her once again when he'd shown up today. She hadn't been able to help watching him while he worked, though she told herself time and again to look away. But she kept looking his way. She'd been fascinated by the play of the muscles in his arms, back, and chest while he'd wrestled with the door.

Frowning, she tucked the keys back in her pocket. If she knew nothing else, she knew Mason Slade was not for her. And she had better not forget it. The only reason he had come today was guilt from destroying her door. And he was the police chief. It was his job to protect the citizens. It wouldn't do for her to forget for even a moment that he didn't like her. He hadn't come to impress her or show off. Now that his duty was done, he wouldn't be back. Unless someone came up with some new excuse to call the cops on her.

* * *

Mason pulled into the driveway of his parents' house. No doubt his mother had been cooking since he'd left. He watched with amusement as Rexford jumped from the truck, just as happy to be home as he'd been to go for a ride.

"Finish your business?" Donald came out and petted Rexford, who was now on his back, waiting to get his belly rubbed.

"Yep. Dinner almost ready?"

"Yeah. Your sisters should be here soon. You should go wash up. You look like you've been busy today."

Mason tossed his dad the truck keys. "I had to replace Tessa's front door."

Donald held the front door open for his son and the dog. "Why? Something else happened?"

Mason gave his dad a sheepish look. "I went over there last night, and when she didn't answer her door, I sort of kicked it in."

"You did what to a door?" Mason's mom, Eleanor, met him at the entryway to the kitchen and kissed her son on the cheek.

Mason went to the fridge and grabbed a bottle of beer his father kept stashed on the bottom shelf. "Tessa Harris had some trouble. When she didn't answer her door, I thought someone might have come back to hurt her. She was perfectly fine, and I overreacted. So I owed her a door, and I installed it for her."

"Tessa Harris? Why does that name sound familiar?"

Mason lifted the lid on the pan on the stove. His stomach growled. His mother was making chili, which meant there would be some homemade cornbread coming his way. "She was Randy Harris's youngest child."

Eleanor's mouth tightened. "I could have gone the rest of my life without hearing that name again. He gave your father nothing but trouble. You don't think he'll show up here, do you?"

Mason set his beer down after taking a large swallow

and went to wash the dishes that were piled in the sink. His mother refused to get a dishwasher, believing she could wash them better than any machine. "Don't think so. Tessa hasn't mentioned him. She's just here to fix up her aunt's house. Her brother is financing a remodel so he can sell it. I don't expect she'll be here long once she's done."

Donald poured him and Eleanor a glass of iced tea while watching his son. It bothered him a bit that he seemed a little too interested in Tessa Harris. "What happened to her brother? I seem to recall having picked him up more than once for vandalism and theft."

Mason kept his back to his dad as he scrubbed a pan. "You'll never believe it, but Simon Harris is a pediatrician at a hospital in Indianapolis. When she told me, I couldn't believe it. But sure enough, I checked it out, and she was telling the truth."

Eleanor handed him another pan. "Well now, that's something to be proud of. Don't guess anyone in town believed he had that inside him. What of Tessa? She had always seemed like a nice, quiet child."

"Tessa paints houses. She wasn't very vocal about what she did before that, but she seems to enjoy fixing up houses. Does good work."

Donald took a seat at the kitchen table. It was rare for the family to use the dining room; they all just crammed themselves into the kitchen. "Did you run a background check on her?"

Mason shifted his shoulders uncomfortably. "No. She hasn't done anything wrong. It seems like an invasion of her privacy."

That was one area he and his son disagreed. Mason didn't dig into the townsfolk's lives unless he felt he had a good reason to. Donald had always felt knowing people's skeletons before they came out of the closet was better. Because sure enough, most of those skeletons eventually reared their ugly heads. "Probably only a matter of time before you have to. Even if she keeps to herself, the mayor is probably going to demand one."

"And I'll tell him the same thing I'm telling you. Unless she gives me a reason, I don't see the point. She deserves the same treatment and respect I would show to any other citizen or visitor."

Eleanor came to stand beside her husband. "Well, we can only hope she followed in her brother's footsteps, and you won't have to worry about her. And it was very nice to install a new door."

Donald grunted at that. "Hopefully she doesn't lodge a complaint against the department. Did you get her to file a report on the damage to her house and car?"

Eleanor glanced down at her husband. "What damage?"

Donald gave her an abbreviated version of what he saw.

"That poor girl. Do you think she's safe out there all by herself?"

Mason had been wondering the same thing himself, but there wasn't much he could do. There had been no usable evidence at the crime scene. No prints or hair, or anything that could tie someone to the vandalism. "No one threatened her physically. I had my officers questioning her neighbors today. I haven't checked in, but they have instructions to call if they find out anything, and they haven't called. I'm sure it won't escalate beyond that. Whoever it was knows her, and I can't think of anyone who would physically attack her. But unfortunately, I can think of half a dozen people or more who might have vandalized her home. I'll be making some inquiries myself tomorrow."

"Don't hold your breath, son. I just hope this remodel goes quickly, and she hightails it out of here."

Mason wished he could second his father's sentiment, but he couldn't strum up the same animosity everyone else was feeling. If anyone would simply take a moment to talk to her, they would see what he saw. She was a woman who was very much alone. The righteous anger she'd displayed last night had aroused his sympathies. He knew he had to keep his feelings in check and his mind open to the possibility that she was not what she seemed. But what he really had to watch for was the lust she had aroused in him. Just watching her, the skin on her chest glistening with sweat and her breasts showcased in a tight tank top, had gotten his attention more than once today. And when she'd been in his SUV last night, he couldn't help but notice the softness of her lips, the long length of her pale eyelashes, and the fact that without a hint of makeup, she was a beauty.

Thankfully, the subject was changed when his sisters and their spouses joined them in the kitchen.

Laine entered first. "Dinner can be served. Your favorite child has arrived."

Cyndi gave an unladylike snort. "She still suffers from middle child syndrome. It's sad, really."

Mason dried his hands so he could give his sisters a hug. It still stunned him from time to time how beautiful his sisters were and how grown-up they were. Laine had long dark hair the same color as his, and it fell in long curls down her back. Her eyes were also the same color as his. It was the shade they shared with their father. His sister Cyndi shared the same dark hair, but hers was pin-straight, and her eyes were blue like their mother's. Cyndi also had their mother's slighter frame but was a lot curvier, though no one was sure where she got those curves. He and Laine were tall like their dad and were also both on the leaner side like their mom. Their mother had despaired that none of her children had inherited her dark blonde hair, though these days she kept it discreetly colored to cover the gray and maintain its previous tones.

Laine accepted her hug and tugged on Mason's earlobe. It was an old joke between them. Laine always told him he didn't listen to reason, so she thought she'd try opening his ears up for him. Cyndi always gave him a peck on the cheek.

Mason took an extra moment to look Cyndi over. "How are you feeling? Well?"

Laine rolled her eyes but was very much interested in the answer. "You'd think she was the first woman to ever have a baby the way everyone is fussing."

Mason gave her a big grin. "Just wait until it's your turn."

Cyndi hugged her husband, Tyler, to her. "I'm doing just fine. And Tyler fusses enough for two, so there's no need for anyone else to."

Tyler took the beer Mason handed him. "Hey, I'm entitled to fuss. I thought I'd have a few more years to get used to the idea, but you know Cyndi; she likes to do things her way. Kind of like Laine."

That got a laugh from the family. Cyndi wasn't known for her patience or her ability to keep a secret. Laine was worse.

Laine's husband, Russell, declined the beer and kissed his wife's cheek before going to the snacks. "Laine and I aren't in a hurry."

Cyndi patted her flat stomach. "Neither of you are getting younger, and all that. Or at least that's what Mom says."

Laine stuck her tongue out at her sister. "Why don't you give Mason grief instead? He's the oldest, after all."

Mason grabbed a handful of veggies from the tray Russell had opened. "Sorry, all, but the married ones get to have the babies first. And I'm too busy serving and protecting."

Russell elbowed Mason. "I take it you broke it off with what's-her-name?"

Up until a few months ago, Mason had been dating a woman from the next county over. Generally, he liked to keep his private life just that. His mother tended to nag him when it came to his relationships and how he needed to devote just as much time to his girlfriends as he did his job. Unfortunately for him, he found his job more fulfilling than his shallow relationships.

"What woman?" Eleanor glared at her eldest.

"It was just a couple of dates. Didn't work out. She decided to date someone who lived closer."

Laine bit into a carrot and grinned at her brother. "Ha.

I bet you broke it off and broke her heart."

"All right, enough. You guys still bicker the way you did when you were kids." Donald wagged a finger at his three children.

Mason figured their bickering secretly pleased both his parents. Made them all feel like the old days. But enough was enough. He turned to Laine. "So how's business?"

"The shop is doing great. Russell is a genius. We've sold more crap to tourists than I ever believed possible."

"I keep telling you, it's not 'crap,'" Russell admonished.

"At least it's nice crap. We've been so busy I'm thinking of taking on an employee for the summer. Russell's been busy with a new project at work and hasn't been able to help much lately."

The conversation during dinner drifted through several topics. Mason thoroughly enjoyed his mom's chili. She made it nice and spicy the way he liked it. And he loved cornbread, so it was always a guarantee that it would be served with her chili. Tyler and Russell chatted about work, while Cyndi and Eleanor talked about babies. Laine just kept shaking her head at all the baby talk and would change the subject.

Mason thought he'd gotten through dinner without being cornered about work, but he was wrong. He had to be careful at gatherings, even with family, to make sure he didn't say anything he shouldn't or let something slip. Surprisingly, it was Cyndi who brought up Tessa's name.

Cyndi finished her glass of milk and turned her attention to Mason. "So I hear things are getting pretty heated over at the Harris homestead. Margie said you had to arrest Tessa Harris."

Mason was popping his last piece of bread in his mouth when several eyes turned his way. He swallowed and took a drink of his beer. "No, I didn't have to arrest Tessa Harris. I brought her in to take her statement."

Laine's eyes narrowed. "Tessa Harris? She's in town?"

It was Cyndi who rolled her eyes. "You need to get out of your shop once in a while. Tessa Harris showed up almost a week ago. Rumors are she is fixing up her aunt's house. And causing quite the commotion too, from what I hear."

Mason's voice deepened. "You heard wrong."

Both Cyndi and Laine were taken aback by his tone. Cyndi found her voice. "Town gossip has been pretty rampant."

Eleanor started clearing the table. "You should know better than to listen to gossip. Hardly ever any truth to it."

Laine turned curious eyes on her brother. "So what is the story, then?"

Mason sighed. "Not much to it. She's in town remodeling her aunt's house. She's had some trouble with her neighbors, but nothing that can be substantiated. But someone vandalized her property, so I had to bring her in so she could file a report. I'll be asking questions around town tomorrow, so you'll hear about it anyway. But if anyone asks, you can set them straight. I did not arrest Tessa Harris."

The family watched in surprise when he left the house.

Laine came out to the porch to stand beside her brother. "You have to forgive Cyndi. She didn't mean any harm."

Mason bumped his sister's shoulder with his and settled back against the railing. Of his two sisters, Laine and he were closer. He loved Cyndi, but he and Laine were more alike. "I know. I've been fielding questions and allegations since she arrived. She hasn't done a single thing to deserve it, but the townsfolk are bent on driving her out of town."

Laine glanced up at the stars shining in the sky. "I always liked Tessa. Broke my heart when Daddy said I couldn't be friends with her. She was so quiet, as if part of her spirit had been crushed. And I felt bad because she never had anything to eat for lunch."

"Dad told me the story yesterday afternoon. He had your best interests at heart. And you can't hold it against him. He was doing what he needed to do to protect his family. That clan is bad news."

"Maybe her father and her brother were, but she wasn't. How is she? Is she cute?"

Mason didn't want to answer the question but found himself answering it truthfully. "Probably very much the same. She probably still doesn't have much to eat for lunch. She's too thin. A little too pale. Her freckles practically glow against the pale skin of her cheeks. And yes, she's cute."

Laine turned her body so she could see into Mason's eyes. "Well, I'll be. You like her, don't you? How much time have you spent with her?"

"You always were a nosybody."

"And you're not answering my question, which means

I'm right. You do like her."

"Look, Laine. I went to her house. I lectured her that she had better not cause any trouble. Then I had to go back when I found out her house and car had been vandalized. I spent some time there today to fix her door. That's it. I haven't been around her long enough to 'like' her the way you mean."

Laine wasn't buying it. "Whatever. I knew Russell was the guy for me after one date. I'd say given the amount of time you spent with her over a three-day span, you know if you like her or not. And I say you do."

Mason didn't respond, and Laine didn't push. Like her? Yeah, he did. She had spunk. And though he couldn't say the time they spent together was quality time, it was enough for her to have gotten his attention. But it didn't matter. He was the police chief, and Tessa Harris was high up on the list of women he should steer clear of if he wanted to keep his job.

Chapter Five

Tessa and the carpenter her brother hired had made some serious inroads on the house project. The man, who told her to just call him Pete, had arms almost as thick as some of the nearby trees. He had to be at least six feet two and a good two hundred and fifty pounds of muscle. She would peg him in his late forties, but given his job was mainly outdoors and the sun had definitely weathered his skin, he might be a little younger.

But Pete seemed more than competent, and in the week he'd been here, he had removed all the old siding, insulated the exterior, and was making impressive progress with installing the new siding. Next on the list was the roof, then the windows she had talked Simon into letting her order. He was mostly quiet while he worked. If it weren't for all the noise he made while working, she wouldn't even know he was around; she saw so little of him.

Tessa couldn't complain about her own progress either. She had finished sanding the cabinets, which hadn't been an easy task. She was sure there had been about four or five layers of different colored paint she'd had to remove. Now the wood was gleaming with fresh stain and a lacquer coat to protect the wood. She had decided to tile the counters instead of buying a slab and having someone else come in and install them. Given the neighborhood and the likely price Simon would get for it, tile seemed like a nice compromise. She had bought large neutral-toned tiles for the counters, with slightly darker ones for the floor. She planned to lay the floor straight but do the counters diagonally.

But today she needed to get started on the lawn. Pete had come with a trailer full of supplies, including everything she'd need to get the yard into shape. Sod would cost too much, so she was going to till up the bald spots and seed the lawn. The quick-growing seeds wouldn't take long to start filling in and transforming the barren space.

"Expecting company?" Pete joined Tessa in the kitchen to get a fresh bottle of water.

Tessa frowned. "No."

"Fancy car just pulled up."

Tessa washed her hands and headed to the porch. Thankfully no one other than Pete had visited her since the night she'd filed her report with Mason. Degrassi had been silent, for which she could only be grateful, and she hadn't spent much time away from the house other than to get groceries and a few extra supplies. And though she told herself she was glad, Mason hadn't made another appearance either. He had called her to let her know he hadn't made much progress on the vandalism, but that didn't surprise her. And so long as Boyd stayed away, she'd be happy.

She stepped out onto the porch and saw the car definitely fit the "fancy" category. The sporty car looked very out of place, not only on her property but for the town. She didn't see the driver clearly, as the sun was shining down on the windshield. Finally, the driver's door opened and a tall brunette with long curly hair stepped out. The black pencil skirt and white sleeveless blouse went with the sporty vehicle, and the bright red high heels she wore were just as out of place as the rest of her.

"I hope you don't mind my dropping in. I thought about calling, but I thought you might tell me not to come."

At the woman's voice, Tessa was taken back many years to the young dark-haired girl she'd been friends with for a short time. "Laine?"

Laine took off her sunglasses and studied the other woman. Then she gave her a huge smile. "Thank goodness you remember me. I was hoping you did; otherwise, this might have been a bit awkward."

Tessa certainly did remember Laine. The younger version of the woman before her had spunk, charisma, and charm. Three things young Tessa hadn't had. Nor did she now, but that didn't seem to faze Laine. The woman came to her and gave her a big hug.

"When Mason told me you were back in town, I wanted to come see you right away. But I was nervous, so it took me a few days to work up the nerve to come out. How are you?"

Tessa took a step back. "I'm fine. I've got a lot of work to do."

Not easily brushed off or discouraged, Laine headed for the house. "I remembered where your aunt's house was. I think I only visited here a couple of times."

"I recall just once." Sighing, Tessa reluctantly followed Laine indoors.

"Oh, hi. I'm Laine." Laine greeted the man in the kitchen. "A friend of Tessa's?"

"Pete, this is Laine. An old classmate. Laine, this is Pete. He's my brother's contractor."

Laine strode further into the kitchen. "Then it's very nice to meet you. For a minute, I was worried you might be her boyfriend or husband. That might discourage Mason."

"Ma'am." Pete glanced at Tessa before heading back outside.

"Discourage Mason from what?" Not much had changed; Tessa still had a hard time following Laine's train of thought. It had been a normal occurrence during their brief friendship.

"I love the cabinets. I would love to have cabinets like these in my kitchen, but Russell is a very modern sort of man. We have these dark, glossy cabinets, but they are not nearly as charming as these."

Tessa hesitated but then found herself asking anyway. "Who's Russell?"

"Oh right, you wouldn't know. He's my husband. He's a doll. And a hunk. I just adore him. And he mostly adores me, except when I get chatty. But I usually only get chatty when I'm nervous, so as you can imagine, I was really chatty when we first started dating, his being a hunk and all. But he fell in love with me anyway. Are you married? Seeing anyone?"

Tessa wasn't sure why Laine would be nervous, since Laine was the one who came over to see her. "No, I'm not married. And I'm not seeing anyone. Is that what you came over to ask me?"

"Sort of, yes. It's not the only reason I came over, but as I said, if you were, it would discourage Mason."

"Discourage him from what?" She hadn't gotten the answer the first time she asked.

"You, of course. Last Sunday we had a family dinner. Not uncommon, but Mason and our parents had been discussing your arrival. I asked Mason if he liked you, but he said he didn't know you well enough to like you, which of course means that he does."

Not sure she entirely followed Laine's logic, she went to the fridge hoping to distract her. "Water?"

"Yes, please. It's been so warm. I'm forever forgetting to bring water with me. Russell chastises me for it, but it doesn't help me remember to bring it."

Tessa handed Laine the water. Uncertain of what to say or do, Tessa went back outside, hoping Laine would follow.

Laine stepped onto the porch where Tessa waited. She looked across the yard and saw Tessa's car. She angrily headed toward it.

Tessa, somewhat shocked by Laine's sudden mood change, followed her. She was even more shocked by the expletive that came through Laine's lightly tinted lips. "That's what brought your brother out. One of them, anyway."

Laine's stomach clenched at the foul words written on the car. Her stomach turned a bit at the foul smell coming out of it. "Mason mentioned the vandalism. And I heard about it in town. I don't get to town much anymore. Russell and I moved to be closer to my business. What are you going to do with the car?"

"Scrap it, I guess. I doubt the car is worth the flat tires it sits on. And anyway, someone trashed the motor. I hadn't noticed, but the report Mason emailed to me to send to my insurance company logged damage to the exterior, the interior, and the motor. When I popped the hood, it looked like someone had taken a sledgehammer to it. The insurance adjuster came out a couple of days ago, so I'm still waiting to hear back. In the meantime, I figure there isn't much to be done with it other than getting rid of it."

"I'm so sorry someone did this to you. Does Mason have any leads?"

Tessa shrugged. "It's highly unlikely he'll find the vandal. Half the people in town are possible suspects."

Laine took Tessa's hand. "Don't let the small-minded people in town run you off. I'm glad you're here."

Tessa doubted it but couldn't come up with any other reason why Laine would show up on her doorstep. She tugged her hand from Laine's. "So why are you here?"

"I heard in town you were looking for a job. I have a job."

"Laine, you lost me. What does you having a job have to do with me looking for one?"

"No, silly, I have a job opening in my shop. Russell keeps telling me I work too hard, and the shop is doing well, so he suggested hiring some help during the busy season this summer, or at least someone part-time. I've interviewed a few people, but I haven't liked any of them. You appreciate fine craftsmanship, so I wanted to offer it to you."

Tessa's head spun. "You're offering me a job?"

"Yes. Rumors are in town you're renovating your aunt's house, and I figured if I liked what I saw, then we have a similar aesthetic, and then I'd know if you were the right candidate. I love the cabinets; therefore, I want to give you the job."

"Because of my cabinets?"

"Yes."

Tessa rubbed the ache in her forehead. "Thank you, but no."

"No what?"

Tessa glared at Laine. "No job."

"But you need one, don't you?"

Tessa came at it another way. "You like this shop of yours?"

Laine frowned in confusion at the question. "Of course I do."

"And if you hire me, all those people who come to shop at your store won't shop there anymore."

Laine realized her train of thought. "My shop isn't in town. It's near the lake. There's a super quaint shopping district there now where tourists come to eat and shop. Trust me when I say not many people from town make their way to my shop. A few did when it first opened because they were curious about what I was up to, but they stopped coming after a few weeks."

"And what would your father say? Or your mother? Or your brother?"

"I'm a grown woman. I'll do what I please."

Tessa just shook her head. "Look, Laine, it isn't that I

don't appreciate the offer. I do. But we both know it's a bad idea. My family and your family shouldn't mix."

"Is this because of when we were kids? Tessa, I've always regretted what I did."

Tessa saw the pain on Laine's face, and she felt bad about it. But she meant what she said; Harris's and Slade's had no business mixing. "Like I said, I appreciate the offer, but it's a bad idea."

"What can I do to change your mind? I want us to be friends, Tessa."

Tessa hardened her resolve. "We were never friends, Laine, and we never will be. Why don't you get back into your fancy car and go home where you belong with your hunk husband?"

Laine bit back her words and stared into Tessa's face. "You don't mean that."

"Like I said, I have work to do."

Laine gaped at her, then sighed. "Okay, fine. But if you change your mind, here's my card."

Tessa ignored the offered card Laine had taken out of her skirt pocket and watched as Laine set it down by the stack of tools. She then watched as Laine headed back to her car and waved at her as she backed out of the drive. Tessa felt tears sting her eyes but turned her back on Laine. She instead headed for the lawnmower. She had weeds to mow down and then some tilling to do. She didn't have time to make friends. And though she would have jumped at the job opportunity had anyone else offered it, she didn't want the Harris taint anywhere near Laine. Laine was sweet and life hadn't dumped all over her. Tessa wanted it to stay that way. She liked to think that some people had storybook lives, and Tessa was sure Laine was one of those people. She didn't need a very disillusioned Tessa ruining that.

* * *

Mason told himself a dozen times to stay away from Tessa. But the rational part of his brain had been absent lately when he thought of her. And then he started rationalizing, if a man who had that part of his brain absent could rationalize, that if any other citizen had had their home vandalized, he'd check in on them, so why would he not check in on Tessa? He hadn't made any progress in his investigation, unless negative results were considered progress, so he had nothing new to share with her. He'd ruled people out but had no viable suspect. The townsfolk who would normally turn someone in who did something this odious proved to be unsympathetic in this case, since it was the Harris house and property that had been vandalized.

The sun hadn't quite set yet when he pulled into the yard. He could see the house had all new siding, at least from the front, and that the yard had gotten some much-needed attention. The car still sat where he'd seen it last, the writing on it just as disturbing as it had been the first time he'd seen it. He went to the front door and knocked. The new door he installed looked great next to the new siding.

The front door opened, and a wide-eyed Tessa stared

out at him. Mason had to resist the urge to shuffle his feet like a kid on his first date. "I wanted to see how things were going and if you had any more trouble."

"I, uh, no. No trouble."

Mason tried to ignore the fact that Tessa wore nothing more than a pair of short cotton shorts and a matching nightshirt. Though the fabric wasn't see-through, he swore she wasn't wearing a bra. And the long, smooth length of her legs made him ache to touch.

Tessa took a step back and held the door open a little wider so Mason could enter. Taking a look down at herself, she blushed. "Let me get dressed."

Mason closed the door behind him. "You're fine. I see people in their pajamas all the time."

It was on the tip of her tongue to tell him he'd never seen her in hers, but it sounded juvenile to her ears, so she nodded at him and took a seat on the farthest end of the sofa. She was extremely conscious of the fact that she was not wearing a bra.

Mason took a seat on the opposite side. "No disturbances or intruders?"

"No. Their message was clear the first time, but I have a job to do. Simon can't be here to do it, so I am. Though to be honest, I'm glad I'm here and not him. The situation for him would have been much worse."

Mason silently agreed with her. "Just the same, I wanted to be sure."

Tessa sat quietly and watched Mason's face. "You look tired, Mason."

He bit back a yawn. "Long day. There's a town festival

tomorrow and we spent the afternoon setting up security and parking. We'll get a lot of tourists tomorrow checking out our quaint little town. And the carnival people arrived a couple of hours ago, so we had to finish coordinating the setup for that."

Tessa had few fond memories of her childhood, but the town festival was one. There was always good food to be had, stalls selling all sorts of wares, and the carnival rides appealed to those young and old. There had been a couple of years when her aunt had slipped her and her brother some money so they could enjoy themselves.

Mason's voice filled the silence. "You should come, Tessa. See that the town has grown some since you lived here, and not everyone is so quick to judge."

It was tempting, to say the least. But she had no friends to go with, no one she was anxious to see. "I've got a lot to do around here."

Mason scooted closer and took Tessa's hand. He held firm when she tried to pull away. "You can't stay cooped up here. You need to get out and have some fun."

Tessa stopped struggling. "Fun? Do you think having my property vandalized, having people accuse me of stealing, and who knows what else is fun?"

"Tessa. I'm sorry about all that. And I'm sorry I can't find out who did it."

Tessa looked down at their joined hands. "It's not your fault. You know as well as I do that no one is going to confess. And there are no witnesses. So unless someone has a sudden attack of remorse, you're not going to find them. You should get some sleep instead of worrying about my problems."

Mason turned her hand over in his. "It's my job to worry. And so long as you're here, you're my responsibility."

Tessa's heart beat a little faster at his tone. The words were low and gruff, as if he didn't want to say them but couldn't hold them in. And though the words themselves weren't ones to make a girl's blood pressure rise, the look in his eyes was. She pulled away and he let her this time. "You sound like your sister."

Mason looked up in surprise. "Laine?"

"Who else?"

"There is Cyndi, but you wouldn't know her. When did you see Laine?"

"Earlier today. When I saw you at my door, I thought maybe she was why you were here."

Mason forgot his fatigue. "What did she say? I should have known that after dinner on Sunday, she'd decide to come see you."

Tessa shrugged. "She told me about her husband, and then offered me a job."

Mason wasn't sure how he felt about that. If trouble followed Tessa, it could end up on his sister's doorstep. On the other hand, his sister didn't live in town, and it was doubtful anyone would know if she took the job. "What did you say?"

Tessa rose. "I said no, so you don't have to worry about it."

Mason saw her agitation and understood the cause. "I know you need a job, Tessa. You filled out an application at every place that was hiring. My sister's..."

"Just stop it, Mason." Tessa headed for her front door, ready to toss Mason out.

"She's just trying to help an old friend."

Tessa's fists clenched. "We were never friends. For a time, I thought we were, but I was wrong. And don't act like you care. You don't. You can't wait until the day you see my taillights heading out of town for the last time, and you know it."

Last week he would have said she was right. But something about her drew him, and Mason found that seeing the last of Tessa was no longer what he wanted. Mason came and took her fists in his hands. "I do care, Tessa. And so does my sister. You could do worse."

Tessa yanked herself away. "And you can do better."

"Better than you, you mean? Tessa, the past was a long time ago. People like Degrassi have long memories and hold a mean grudge. But not everyone feels the same. You should come out and see for yourself."

"You should go, Mason."

More than anything else, Mason wanted to kiss her. Her chest was heaving, her limbs were trembling, and there was pain in the depths of her eyes. But her breath hitched, and he realized he had already pushed her more than he should have.

Mason lifted one of her fists and kissed her knuckles before releasing her. "All right, I'll go. Don't forget to lock the doors."

Tessa closed and locked the door. She could hear Mason's SUV start up and pull out of her drive. She closed her eyes and leaned back against the door. For a brief moment, she thought Mason was going to kiss her. Her knees wobbled, so she went back to the sofa. It had been years since she'd wanted a man to kiss her. Years since she'd let one get close to her. But had Mason chosen to kiss her, she would have let him. She would have participated wholeheartedly. And it would have been a big mistake. And while Mason was right that some people wouldn't care who she was, there were plenty who did. And if Mason didn't keep his distance, at best, he was going to find himself the center of a lot of unwanted attention. At worst, he might find himself out of a job.

Tessa flipped the lights off and headed for bed. She felt a dull ache in the region of her heart. All she could do was keep reminding herself she was only here for a short while. She knew better than to become attached. And Mason was the type of man a woman could easily become attached to. But in the end, she could destroy his career. And while she might have told him she didn't care, she did. And it was because she did care that she needed to keep her distance.

Chapter Six

Tessa continued down Main Street, browsing through the various arts and crafts that were for sale. Mason had been right. She was anonymous in the crowd of mostly tourists. When she did happen to spot someone she thought she knew, she would simply blend back into the crowd.

Tessa adjusted the brim of her sun hat as she continued down the street. It was Simon's fault she was here. She'd made the mistake of mentioning the festival to him during their morning call. Simon, too, recalled some of the happier moments in their lives, and the two of them had swapped stories of festivals past. Simon told her she needed to take a break and have some fun. His words painfully echoed the ones Mason had spoken to her the night before.

Then guilt had set in. Mason and Laine had both been very kind to her. Laine hadn't deserved to be treated so rudely. And Mason, well, Tessa's feelings about Mason were complicated, to say the least. In the past couple of weeks she had been back, Mason hadn't discovered the secrets of her past. A part of Tessa wondered if during the short time she'd be here, she could keep her past just that. And maybe she could make a few more happy memories to add to those few from her childhood.

With guilt riding her and Simon's encouraging words bolstering her courage, Tessa had pulled a sundress out of the closet. The dress hung a little loosely on her frame, a testament to the fact that she'd lost weight again, but it flattered her arms and shoulders. Physical labor had given some nice definition to what would otherwise be puny muscles. Despite the weight loss, the bodice still mostly hugged her breasts and nipped in at the waist. The floral dress went past her knees, and when paired with a comfortable pair of sandals, it made her feel feminine. The sun hat added a bit of a country touch and was needed in the heat of the summer sun.

Tessa hitched her shoulder bag higher and made her way toward the stands that were selling various food items. Pete had dropped her off an hour earlier. She had mentioned the festival to him, and he had decided to give it a whirl. Her quiet contractor had surprised her when he'd chatted a bit about some of the festivals he'd attended in his hometown, a town he claimed wasn't so different from hers. They'd parted ways shortly after their arrival, agreeing to meet back up at six. Pete had offered to drive her back home before he headed to his hotel for the evening.

Tessa pulled out the water she had tucked in her bag and took a large swallow, but the smells from the nearby concession stand drew her in, and her stomach rumbled. She made her way through the crowd and bought a soft pretzel. It was always her favorite festival food as a kid.

"Tessa!"

Tessa turned as she heard her name shouted over the crowd. She saw Laine across the way waving at her. A tall man stood beside her, his hair a shaggy blond. She smiled to herself. This must be the hunk husband. She had to admit she agreed. It was hard not to find his tall, lean frame, with broad shoulders and a flat abdomen, attractive. He had an indulgent smile on his face as his eyes gazed adoringly at his wife.

Laine grabbed Tessa's hand and drew her over to where a group of people were standing. "I can't believe you're here. The festival is just the most fun. I want you to meet Russell."

Tessa shook the offered hand of the tall man with her free one. "Nice to meet you. Laine mentioned she had gotten married."

Laine released Tessa and wrapped her arm around her husband's waist. "Told you, right?"

Tessa couldn't prevent her laugh. "Yes, you were right."

Russell frowned at his wife. "Right about what?"

Laine lightly kissed him. "Nothing. Just something I mentioned to Tessa yesterday when I went to visit."

Russell kissed her back before turning to Tessa. "By yourself?"

"Sort of. I came in with someone and we're going to meet up later."

Laine frowned. "Who?"

"Pete, my contractor."

Laine felt relieved. "Oh, good. Then you need to join us. Mom and Dad are over there, and Cyndi and her husband Tyler are here too. Mason always has to work, so at some point we'll find him and make sure he's fed and hydrated. Do you know Cyndi?"

The whirlwind that was Laine swept Tessa up and brought her over to where her family waited. Chief Slade wasn't looking too pleased. She vaguely remembered the woman next to him. She couldn't recall having met Mason's mother, but she did remember seeing her around town. Her skin was lined but only slightly so. Her hair was a few shades darker than her own. A shorter brunette stood next to the couple with another tall man with dark hair and dark eyes.

"Let me introduce you to everyone. You know my dad, and this is my mom, Eleanor. And this is my younger sister, Cyndi, and her husband, Tyler."

Tessa greeted everyone, feeling very out of place. Then Eleanor gestured for everyone to come have a seat, and she didn't see that she had much choice but to follow.

Eleanor sat across from Tessa. "So Mason tells us you fix up houses."

Tessa set her pretzel down and folded her hands on the table. "I paint them mostly, inside and out. But I learned a bit of other stuff over the years. Simon asked if I would be interested in fixing up Sylvia's place for him."

Donald swallowed the large bite of his sausage before he spoke. "Mason said your brother is a pediatrician."

Tessa went on the defensive. "Yes, he is. A very good one. He became a medic in the army after he left town and afterward went to medical school. Both his wife and I are very proud of him."

"Simon got married? Any children?" Laine tried to lighten the tone.

Tessa took a deep breath. "Yes, Simon got married. Her name is Sarah. Sarah was a receptionist at the clinic where Simon did his residency. They have two children.

Lilah is two, and Adam is four."

"How about your mother? Is she well? She must be ecstatic to have grandchildren." Eleanor picked up where Laine left off.

Though it was starting to sound like an interrogation, Tessa answered. "Mom is okay. Simon helped her buy a small condo not too far from where he and his family live. She's as happy as she's capable of being. And before you ask, no, I haven't seen my father. No one in the family has since he went to prison. He was released about five years ago, but we haven't seen him."

"Just as well. That man never did anyone any good." Donald said before finishing his sausage.

Tessa stood. "No, he never did anyone any good. And neither did I. Thank you for the conversation."

Tessa slipped back into the crowd. She hadn't gotten more than out of sight of the group when a hand grabbed her shoulder and stopped her. She turned to see Donald Slade looking down on her. "What?"

"Look, Tessa, I won't apologize for protecting my family."

Tessa's back went rigid. "I won't apologize for protecting mine."

"And that's how it should be. You have every right to be proud of what you and your brother accomplished. Not too many people try to be more than what those before them were, especially when they grow up with men like your father."

Tessa glanced behind Donald and saw Laine looking at her with pleading eyes. "I think your daughter wants you."

Donald turned to see Laine watching them. He waved at her, then turned back to Tessa. "Actually, it's you she wants. Laine was always one to make friends and keep them. But for all her spunk and kindness, she doesn't have many friends. There were a few who just wanted to take advantage of her. She's very gullible and always wants to help those in need. And the friends she does have, a good number of them have moved away over the years. Our little town doesn't have much to offer the younger generations who are bent on living the good life. She was full of questions when she found out you were in town. And she told me about the job she offered you."

"You don't have to worry, Chief Slade; I turned her down. Is that all?"

Donald tipped his head and gestured for Tessa to follow him. "Rumors are you're looking for a job. You could do worse, though Laine might drive you a little crazy. She acts like she doesn't have a care in the world, but only second to her family and her husband, that shop is what she loves most. She did say something to the effect that she knew I wouldn't approve of her hiring you."

Tessa pulled the brim of her hat down and gazed at her feet. "We both know you don't. And like I said, I turned her down."

Donald used a knuckle to tip her chin up so he could look into her eyes. "Laine is a grown woman and can pick her own friends. And she can pick her own employees. And my son is a grown man. He, too, can pick his own friends. Like I said, I won't apologize for protecting my family, but if you would like, I'd like you to join us for the afternoon."

Tessa felt her throat tighten but swallowed her emotions. She glanced up to see Laine smiling at her from where she was still waiting. "I suppose we can't disappoint Laine."

Donald gave her a genuine smile. "I always find that giving Laine what she wants is the easiest way all-around. She gets what she wants eventually anyway."

Tessa found herself back with the family. She picked up her pretzel where she'd left it and found she was hungry again. Conversations drifted from one topic to another. She learned that Cyndi was pregnant with her first baby, and both the soon-to-be grandparents were beaming. It took a few minutes to get used to Chief Slade being simply a father and grandfather, but eventually, she was able to relax. He was even funny, telling silly stories about his children in their youth.

Over the next couple of hours, she found herself plied with lemonade, ice cream, and fried foods that were not recognizable but delicious. They made their way through rows of vendors and eventually ended up on the outskirts of where the carnival rides were set up.

"Oh, good, there he is." Eleanor urged the group over to one of the entryways.

Tessa stopped when she caught Mason staring at her. He was in his uniform, this time with a matching hat. She couldn't help the flush that came over her skin as he looked her over.

Mason dragged his gaze from Tessa and kissed his mother's cheek. "Everyone having fun?"

Eleanor handed him a bottle of water. "Of course. How much longer are you on duty?"

Mason uncapped the bottle and took a large swallow. "I'm on until seven."

Cyndi yawned. "This is where we came in. If everyone doesn't mind, I'm ready for a nap."

Tyler fussed a bit at the admission, and the family bid the couple good night.

Eleanor seconded that. "I'm about ready to put my feet up."

"All good, son?" Donald glanced around the grounds as a group of teenagers made their way to the carnival rides.

"Yep. Don't think I'll have to call in the cavalry tonight."

Donald thumped his son on the back and then clasped his wife's hand. "Then we're off to put up our feet. All of you behave now."

"Yes, Daddy." Laine kissed her dad's cheek, then her mom's.

Russell shook his father-in-law's hand and kissed his mother-in-law's cheek. "I'll keep her out of trouble."

Laine kissed him. "Hopefully not all of it."

Russell said something in Laine's ear that made her giggle. Laine then glanced at her brother. "Are we still meeting up for dinner after your duty is done?"

"Definitely. I'll be starving by the time seven hits."

Laine turned to Tessa. "You should join us."

Tessa felt herself wanting to say yes, but she was meeting Pete. "Sorry, my ride leaves at six."

Mason's eyes caught hers. "I'll drive you home after

dinner. Let your ride know you won't need it."

Tessa heard the demand in his words and knew she should probably protest, but couldn't find the words. "Meet back here at seven?"

Laine clapped her hands. "Yes, seven. Come on, Russell, you owe me a ride on the Ferris wheel."

Tessa found herself alone with Mason. She suddenly felt awkward. "Are you sure you're up for dinner? You must be tired after standing out here all day."

"Yes, I'm more than ready for dinner. It's not exactly hard work monitoring the event. I've got civilians doing double duty as security tonight, and the deputies are scattered throughout. I like to man the gate and make sure everyone gets in and out safe. Honestly, the hardest thing is making sure the tourists find their way back out to the highway after I've seen them all safely parked."

Tessa watched as the crowd walked by. She saw Laine at the top of the Ferris wheel, waving at her, and she waved back.

"I'm glad you came."

Tessa turned back to Mason. "I guess I'm still trying to figure out why I did. But I had a nice day."

"Did my dad behave?"

Tessa thought back to their conversation. "He did, but probably not the way you mean. Let's just say we came to terms."

Mason wanted to question her more, but she had her lips pinched. What he really wanted was to see her smile. But for now, he had a job to do.

Tessa stayed nearby, not wanting to walk around

anymore. Her own feet were getting tired, and she could only imagine what Mason's felt like. But if his feet hurt, he didn't show it. Mostly he monitored the crowd, waving and saying hi to different people as they walked by. There were many people who spoke to him that she didn't recognize, which made her realize again how much things had changed since she'd left.

Tessa glanced at her watch and realized she'd better head over and find Pete. She rose to go to Mason. Right before she arrived, a couple of teenagers stopped.

"Hi, Chief."

"Hi, Ray. Hi, Monty."

Mason's eyes caught Tessa's. "Hey boys, say hello to Miss Tessa Harris. Miss Harris grew up here."

Ray held out a hand. "Neat. We're headed over to the carnival."

Tessa shook his hand. "I actually need to meet someone myself."

Mason nodded. "Here at seven."

Tessa waved her hand as she headed off. "Seven."

"She's a looker, Chief. Your girlfriend?" Monty watched Tessa walk away.

"Nope. But you've got good taste, kid."

Mason waved as the boys strode away. Ray was headed off to college in the fall. Mason doubted he'd be back, except maybe for an occasional holiday. Monty was another story. He was smart; there was no doubt. He got good grades, and the teachers all loved him. But his father was Mayor Griswold, so he was a little spoiled, liked to think he owned the town. And Monty was not headed off to college like his friend.　Monty liked football, had even helped his high school team make it to the state championship.　But as far as Mason could tell, he didn't like much else.　But he didn't cause trouble, and that's what mattered.　Having to arrest the mayor's son wouldn't have gone over well, though Mason would do it in a heartbeat if he had to.

Mason looked back into the crowd, but Tessa was now out of sight.　He settled back into his spot and watched the crowd.

* * *

Tessa hurried so she could meet Pete.　He showed up right on time.　She told him Mason was going to drive her home.　He wasn't so sure at first, but once she told him that Mason was the town's police chief, he seemed satisfied and left to head back to his hotel.

She eagerly made her way back to Mason.

Dinner was at one of the tents where Mason downed enough food for two people.　Tessa, who had eaten way too much earlier, munched on some fresh tortilla chips.　The conversation was lively, and she found herself relaxing and joining in the conversation.　It was after nine when they parted ways.

"I like your brother-in-law."　Tessa walked beside Mason as he led them to where he had parked his SUV.

"I figure he must be the most patient man on the planet to live with Laine.　I love her, but I was happy when I went to college."

"Simon felt that way too, I imagine, when he left for the army. Older brothers take on a lot of responsibility for their siblings."

Mason thought about it. He supposed he had felt a lot of responsibility toward his sisters. "Older brother syndrome, I suppose. They were happy when I moved out, so then when they brought dates home, they only had Dad to contend with."

"Did they like your girlfriends?"

Mason helped Tessa into the passenger seat when they reached his SUV. "Not really. They told me they weren't too bright."

That got a giggle from Tessa. Then she sobered up. "Your sister is matchmaking, you know."

Mason held the door open and placed his body between hers and the door. "I noticed. Laine isn't subtle."

"No. I was surprised she didn't bring up the job again."

Mason leaned in. "She'll bring it up again. She also knows how to strategize and throw people off guard."

"Mason?" Tessa leaned forward.

"Yeah?" Mason brought his mouth closer to hers.

"This is a really bad idea."

Mason came a hair closer. "I'm the chief, and I think it's a great idea."

"Hey, Chief!"

Mason hit his head on the top of the SUV roof when he heard his name shouted. He turned to see Ray waving at him. This time Monty wasn't with him. "Be safe getting home. You need a ride?"

Ray waved him off. "No, my dad is parked over there,

but thanks."

Mason looked back at Tessa, who was sitting rigidly in her seat with her hands folded over her bag. Sighing at the lost chance, he closed the door.

She glanced at him while Mason started the engine. "Must be rewarding, being chief."

"Sometimes. But sometimes it's like living in a fishbowl. Everyone knows who you are and are watching everything you do."

"You know that people will talk. They saw us at dinner with your sister, people saw me with your family today, and now you're driving me home."

Mason learned to take it in stride. "Yes, they will talk. But not all of it is bad, Tessa. People talk. And in a small town, there isn't much to talk about other than your neighbors. And being chief, people watch me closely. Some want to see me succeed, while others want to see me fall on my face. But I can't live my life or do my job being what other people want me to be."

Tessa just hoped his reputation was strong enough to hold out against what people would say about him and her.

Mason made the drive back to her place in silence. When he stopped the SUV in her driveway, he climbed out to open her door and walk her to her front door. Alert to his surroundings, he didn't see or hear anything out of the ordinary.

"I had a nice evening, Mason. Thank you."

Mason took her hand, not ready yet to let her go. Despite the lectures he'd been giving himself to stay away from Tessa Harris, he found he couldn't, nor did he want to.

"You feel it, don't you?"

Tessa thought about pretending she didn't know what he meant but figured it was a waste of breath. "Yes. But Mason, it's wrong."

Mason shook his head. "It's been a while since it felt this right."

Giving in to the inevitable, Tessa raised her mouth to his when he bent down to her. Mason's kiss was soft, his lips brushing hers, teasing and tasting.

Mason raised his head to look into her eyes. She looked more confused than anything else. But he didn't know how to soothe her or how to reassure her that this was right. He folded his arms around her to bring her closer, his breath mingling with hers. When she didn't pull away from him, he kissed her again. This time he kissed her the way he'd been thinking about for days.

Tessa wrapped her arms around Mason's neck and lifted herself onto her tippy toes. Mason kissed her, his lips and tongue encouraging her to open herself up to his kiss. It had been so long since she'd been held, so long since she'd been kissed. And she couldn't remember anyone kissing her with such open hunger. And she didn't know how to respond to the kiss. To him.

Mason pulled back for a moment. He brushed a single tear that had escaped Tessa's control. He shifted and lifted her, so she sat on the edge of the porch railing. He straddled her legs, then tipped her lips back up to his. He gently coaxed her mouth open, showing her and guiding her on how he wanted her to kiss him back.

Tessa lost track of time. She lost track of herself.

There was nothing but Mason: the touch of his lips, the thrust of his tongue, the feel of his hands as they stroked her back.

Mason pulled back, his breath heaving. "As I said, it hasn't felt this right in a long time."

Tessa wrapped her arms around his waist, leaning against him. She felt his breath on her hair. His heart thudded under her palm. He continued the long, slow sweeping motion of his hands on her back. She sighed and relaxed against him.

Tessa opened her mouth to speak. She wasn't sure what she would have said to him if, in that moment, a loud crack hadn't rent the air.

Chapter Seven

Mason immediately went into cop mode. "There's someone out there. Get down and stay down."

Tessa slid off the railing and dropped to her knees. The sound had come from behind the house. She watched as Mason drew his gun and gestured for her to stay down. She lost sight of him as he made his way around the side of the house. She crawled on her knees to where the porch ended. Each end was open, so she eased her head around so she could see him. She caught his shadow as he slipped into the darkness behind the house. She had yet to install a new light fixture for the back porch.

Mason crept around back, keeping alert to any sound. He heard another cracking sound and made his way slowly in that direction. He saw a shadowy figure in black. "Stop!"

The figure dropped a bag and started running in the opposite direction. Mason took off after him. No shots rang out; no other sounds were heard as he pursued the man into the woods. Then suddenly everything was still. Mason pulled his flashlight out and scanned the area. Everything was quiet. He kept going further until he was sure he had lost his quarry. Cursing, he started heading back out of the woods. He found the bag the man dropped and hoped he would find fingerprints, if nothing else.

He didn't want to scare Tessa, so he made plenty of

noise as he made his way back. "Tessa, it's Mason. You can come out."

Tessa eased herself upright at the edge of the porch. He was alone. "I take it you lost him."

Mason took her arm, held out his hand for her keys, and unlocked her front door. He guided her inside, then locked it behind them. "He headed for the woods. I can say with some confidence that it wasn't Degrassi."

Tessa gave him a nervous laugh. "I suppose it was too much to hope you'd catch the old man red-handed."

"No, but your visitor dropped his goodie bag. I'll call it in, but there isn't much we can do in the dark. In the morning, I'll have Jackson come out and look for footprints or anything else he might have dropped."

Tessa took a look at the bag, but it was an ordinary duffle bag. It could belong to anyone. Mason excused himself, and when he came back, he had a pair of gloves. She watched as he unzipped the bag and removed the contents.

"More spray paint." Mason removed six cans of paint and was grateful that no foul odors wafted from the bag.

"I should probably call Simon. It might be best if he leaves Pete in charge, and I go home. Pete just finished the siding, and he's starting on the new windows tomorrow. All Simon needs is someone to spray paint the new siding or bust out his new windows."

Mason heard what she said and knew she had a point. Whoever it was, assuming it was the same person as before, wanted her gone. The less rational part of him wanted her to stay. "Why don't you sleep on it. I'll stay tonight in case he comes back. But both times your intruder showed up, you weren't here. That means you might recognize him and that's why he waits until you're gone."

"Do you think whoever it was saw me at the festival and figured now was as good a time as any?"

It made sense, but Mason was only half sold on his theory. "It's the most likely scenario."

"For some reason, I don't find that comforting. But I guess you're right; there isn't anything I can do tonight. But you don't have to stay. I'm sure you're tired after being outside all day."

"Forget it. I'm staying. I have a bag packed in the car. I always keep one handy just in case."

Tessa scowled. "I said I'm fine by myself. I think it's a bit above and beyond the call of duty to sleep here."

"There was this lady in town. She was an older lady. She kept hearing things in her basement. She called me more than a few times. Then one night she called really late. I spent the night on her couch. In the morning, I called her son so he could take care of her. She ended up moving in with him. And there was this other time I slept in the spare room of our reverend's house. His wife went into labor early and we were in the middle of a snowstorm. She gave birth to her baby at home, and I stayed the night with the kids once the road cleared enough that they could make it to the county hospital. So it's not outside of my normal work to stay the night."

"Did you help deliver the baby?"

Mason's eyes darkened. "Yeah. I think that might have been one of the most terrifying experiences of my life.

Thank goodness everything went without a hitch. It was their third child, so they pretty much knew what to do without my help."

Tessa sat down on the couch next to Mason. "Boy or a girl?"

Mason looked at Tessa. She had a small smile on her face. "Girl. Thank goodness or I have a feeling the baby might have been named after me."

Tessa leaned back. "I think it's sweet."

Mason took the moment to place a soft kiss on her lips. "I think you should go to bed."

It shouldn't have been a difficult decision to leave Mason in the living room, but it was. Sex would only make things more awkward between them and make her more attached. She didn't do one-night stands, and she didn't do flings. But at that moment, Mason made her wish she were a different kind of woman.

Tessa pushed herself to her feet. "I have some extra sheets and I have a pillow you can use. You're lucky I kept the couch, though I am going to bet it is not going to be a comfortable night for you. But it's better than the floor. I donated almost everything in the house when I first arrived. I had a charity come and collect everything. It just gets in the way of the remodel."

"Then I'll just be glad to not sleep on the floor."

Tessa left and came back after a few minutes with sheets, a blanket, and a large pillow.

Mason thanked her. "What time does Pete get here?"

"Usually around seven. He likes to get started early. I'm usually up around six anyway. I plan to work on the counters tomorrow."

"Wake me up when you get up, if I'm not already. I'll call Jackson, and he can come log the bag. I have a meeting with the city council in the morning, so I'll need to head home for a fresh uniform. But my meeting isn't until ten. The mayor doesn't like to get up early."

"The mayor is a friend of your dad's, right?" Tessa vaguely remembered the man she'd heard was now the mayor. He was not a friend of her father's.

"Yeah, he's been mayor for several years now. Rumors are he wants to retire, but I think he's holding out for his oldest son to finish law school. You met his youngest son Monty tonight. His older son, Landon, is Cyndi's age, I think, so a few years younger than you."

All Tessa could think was that small towns were usually run by one or two families. Mason followed in his father's footsteps and became police chief. She did not doubt that the elder Griswold son would one day sit in the mayor's chair. "I wish him luck with that. Good night, Mason."

"Good night, Tessa."

Tessa fled to the bedroom and shut the door before she was tempted to do something she'd regret.

* * *

Mason woke in the morning when he heard Tessa's soft voice coming from the kitchen. Glancing at his watch, it was a little after six. He didn't hear another voice, so he figured she was on the phone with her brother. He sat up and stretched, wincing at the tightness in his back. The couch definitely wasn't comfortable.

He rubbed his face and stood. He was pretty grungy from the day before. He grabbed the uniform shirt he'd tossed over the back of the couch but couldn't bring himself to put it on. He had spent all day yesterday in that shirt, and the sweat and grime of the day on it were enough to wrinkle his nose. He needed a shower and a change of clothes. He had grabbed his overnight bag before he'd gone to sleep and hoped Tessa wouldn't mind him borrowing her shower.

He was headed to the bathroom when Tessa came into the living room.

Tessa stopped in her tracks and stared at his bare chest. It looked much like she had imagined. There was definition in the muscles of his chest and abdomen, and they were covered in a light sprinkling of hair a shade darker than the hair on his head.

Mason gave Tessa a similar once-over that she was giving him. Her hair was wet and pulled back in a ponytail. And she was wearing a pair of shorts and a tank top. He couldn't help but want to run his hands over the length of those bare legs. She wasn't tall, but her legs looked amazing in her small shorts.

Tessa was the first to speak. "Can I get you some coffee?"

"I'd love some, but I'd really love to use your shower first."

Tessa nodded. "Feel free to use what's in there. And the towels are in the cabinet."

"Thanks." Mason headed straight for the bath.

Tessa sighed and went back to the kitchen and made a

fresh pot of coffee. She didn't drink much of it herself, mostly because it was an unnecessary expense, but Pete liked to have a cup with his lunch and had restocked her pantry. The coffee pot on the side table had belonged to her aunt.

She pulled out a carton of eggs and grabbed the loaf of bread. It wasn't much, but she could at least offer him some eggs and toast before he left.

When Mason came into the kitchen, he felt human again. He saw Tessa at the stove. "You don't need to do that."

She could smell the scent of his aftershave and knew the moment he came into the room. Instead of responding, she poured him a cup of coffee and handed it to him. "It's nothing fancy. There's milk in the fridge and a bowl of sugar in the cupboard next to the fridge."

"I like my coffee black." Mason rummaged through the cabinets and found plates. He went in search of the silverware.

Tessa slipped the omelet she made for him onto his plate. "Butter is in the fridge for the toast."

Mason went to the toaster and pulled out the bread. "Having some?"

"Yes. Please, put a couple in."

Mason drank his coffee and buttered his toast but waited until Tessa was done making her own eggs before digging into his meal. Breakfast was quiet but nice. It had been a while since he'd sat across from a woman at the breakfast table.

"More coffee?" Tessa finished the glass of orange juice

she had poured for herself.

"Yes. Thank you. And thank you for breakfast."

Tessa gave him a warm smile. "I appreciate you staying last night."

Mason accepted the fresh cup. "Talk to your brother?"

Tessa tucked her leg under her when she sat. "I did. But I didn't tell him what happened. He had some wonderful news, and I just couldn't tell him. He needs me here now more than ever."

"What wonderful news?"

Tessa gave him a huge smile. "Sarah is pregnant again. She was an only child and vowed to have a large family one day. Simon is cooperating with her plan. But with a new baby comes more expenses, and he wants the money from the sale of the house to put toward his school debt. He wants to buy a house for his family and get them out of the apartment they rent, but he doesn't want to do that until his school debt is paid down. It's a nice apartment, but he wants a yard."

"Well, congratulations, Aunt Tessa. But you should tell him what's going on. He needs to know."

"I know, but he's got so much going on. He doesn't need the stress. And it's not like he can do anything about it."

Mason finished his coffee. "No, I don't suppose there is much he can do. Are you remodeling the house for free?"

"Mostly free. Since I'm not working, he gave me some money for living expenses and food. I don't have much in the way of savings, so I can't afford to take off work without some financial help. But I don't need much, and I've been keeping the project under budget. With the increased tourist activity, I think he'll get a pretty penny for the house when it sells. If I can keep the vandal away."

Mason had an idea about that but didn't share it yet. He couldn't stay here with her; he had a job to do. And while spending his nights with Tessa was extremely appealing, he knew she would protest.

"Anyway, Simon has his hands full, and the quicker I get the project done, the better."

"With any luck, Jackson can get some prints off the stuff in the bag."

Tessa shrugged. "Something tells me it won't be that easy. But I appreciate the effort anyway. Pete should be here any minute. You don't have to stay. I know you said you have a meeting today with the mayor."

Mason helped clear away the dishes. "Just part of the never-ending duties as police chief."

Tessa followed Mason to the living room, where he started gathering his things. She tried not to notice the very large gun he wore as he fastened his belt.

"Call me if anyone else shows up or if anything else happens. I'll have a patrol swing by a few times tonight to make sure everything is okay."

Tessa followed Mason outside. She waved at Pete as he pulled up alongside Mason's SUV. "Thank you again, Mason. I do appreciate you staying."

What Mason really wanted to do was kiss her, but he wasn't going to do that with an audience. He gave Pete a brief nod as he climbed into his SUV and drove off.

"He was here pretty early. Trouble?"

Since Officer Jackson was going to be by to pick up the duffle bag in her kitchen, she couldn't exactly lie to him, which would have been her plan. "Mason stopped a would-be vandal. Unfortunately, all he got for his trouble was a duffle bag. Whoever it was probably thought I wasn't home. Mason spent the night on the couch."

"Did you talk to Simon?" Pete started unloading the fresh supplies he had picked up.

Fingers crossed behind her back, she nodded. "Yes, I talked to Simon this morning."

"Good."

Used to Pete's quiet ways, Tessa went back inside. She had the counters trimmed out and ready for grout and tile. Hopefully, the project would keep her mind off of Mason. Not for the first time, she wished she were someone else. But for the first time, she wished she were the type of woman a man like Mason would fall for. He might have kissed her last night, but that didn't mean anything. Not really. It was her experience that men would kiss any woman they thought they had a shot at getting into bed. She knew better than to take his kisses as a sign of any true feelings on his part. It was late; she was there. And she would be a fool if she told herself otherwise.

Still, it was a great kiss, and she let herself think back on it from time to time while she worked.

* * *

Mason made it to the City Hall meeting in plenty of time. He had donned his more formal uniform, digging it out from the back of his closet, the pressed uniform still in the dry-cleaning bag. Thankfully he only wore it on rare occasions, like city hall meetings. More times than not, his everyday uniform did the trick. But he always felt the fancier uniform made more of an impression on the town's politicians and businesspeople. It helped show his authority and garnered him a little more respect among the good townsfolk who held the town's purse strings.

The city hall meeting had started off well enough. Minutes from the previous session were read. New topics on the agenda were approved. Old business was attended to. It was agreed that the town festival had gone well; attendance was up, and there were no major issues. The nearby resort town on the lake had also benefited, with rooms fully booked at the hotels and inns. And other than a couple of fender benders, there were no real problems.

Mayor Alex Griswold waited until all other business had been discussed before bringing up one topic not on the agenda. "Chief Slade. There is one more thing. It has been brought to my attention that we have a problem."

Mason had a good idea of what was going to come out of Alex's mouth next. "Yes, Mayor?"

"What are you doing about Tessa Harris? I've had more than a couple of people call me very concerned about her presence."

Mason decided his best course of action was to deflect the negative impact Tessa's presence might have on the townsfolk. "Right now, I'm still investigating the vandalism of her home and vehicle. No one in town seems to know who damaged her property."

"That is not what I meant."

Mason ignored the grumbling in the crowd. "If you mean the unsubstantiated claims made against her? I found no proof. And the charges Deputy Thomson brought against her were dropped, as there was unequivocal proof that she was two towns over when the alleged crime was committed. She's on camera at a bank. Their timestamps don't lie."

More murmurs went through the room. "And the rest of the claims? There were many."

Mason nodded. "Again, I was unable to substantiate the claims. And since I had a few words with her neighbors, I have not had any other charges come across my desk. I made a personal visit, as did my father. As far as I can tell, she's here to fix up her aunt's old house. Once that is done, she'll be gone. So if the town will just let her get on with it, the quicker they will see her taillights leaving town once and for all."

There was a bit of dissent in the crowd, but Mason ignored it. When the meeting was finally adjourned, he started making his way out.

"Hold up, Mason."

Mason turned to see Alex heading his way. "Social call or official?"

"Unofficial. I'm not happy that Tessa Harris is in town."

Mason shrugged. "You and half the town. Look, I went out there. She's not doing anything wrong. My dad went out there too. Heck, even my sister made an appearance. As far as I can tell, she's the injured party."

"Good. Some people liked Sylvia, but many feared her brother would show up with news of her passing. The last thing we need is Randy Harris showing up here."

"Tessa says she doesn't talk to her father. And Sylvia left the house and her possessions to Simon."

Alex grunted. "Guess I should be grateful it was Tessa who showed up and not Simon."

"As to that, I did a check on Simon. He's a well-respected pediatrician at a medical center in Indiana. Very well-respected."

"Huh. Who would have thought? Well, as long as Randy Harris doesn't show up here, I can handle Tessa. Just be sure she keeps her nose clean."

"Yes, sir. I was at her house last night. The man who vandalized her property made another showing. Or I suppose it could have been a copycat. I figure it's best to let you know I was there all night in case someone brings it up. Officer Jackson is heading over there to bag the vandal's duffle. He got away, but I'm hoping for some prints."

"Keep that to yourself. The last thing I need is rumors that my chief of police is playing patty cake with Tessa Harris."

Mason held his quick surge of anger in. "If that's all?"

"Yes, that's all. And tell your dad we need to go fishing when he gets back from his trip. It's been too long."

Mason took his leave, happy that news of his having dinner with Tessa hadn't made it to the mayor's ear yet. He hadn't thought about it at the time, but being seen socially with Tessa wouldn't have gone over well at today's council meeting, even if it had been in the company of his sister and brother-in-law.

Either way, he'd worry about it later. He needed to get back to the office. With any luck, Jackson would have found at least one usable print on the bag the vandal dropped last night at Tessa's place.

Chapter Eight

Tessa followed the directions on her phone. Pete let her borrow his truck so she could drive to Laine's shop. The shop was a town over, the opposite direction of where she'd shopped for construction supplies, and the road she was on now was one of the busiest strips she'd seen. This one curved around the lake and was filled with cute boutique stores, restaurants with outdoor seating, and inns with cute little names that invited travelers to stay.

After finding the shop, she drove down the road a bit and parked the truck down the strip so no one would see her get out of the battered truck. These people drove fancy cars with foreign symbols on the hoods. The shoppers and tourists who filled these streets would probably be horrified by the thought of getting within a few feet of the truck, much less climbing inside it.

Tessa smoothed the wrinkles from the skirt of her sundress and grabbed the oversized satchel from the seat. The gingham dress was the nicest dress she owned, but as she looked around, it looked a little too country and a little too out of date. Swallowing one's pride was never an easy task, but it would have been nice if she could have done it in something that didn't make her feel like she had been out of touch with fashion for the past twenty years.

The walk was a short one, but she was already a little

sweaty when she opened the door to Laine's boutique. She had simply named it Laine's, and inside was a tourist's dream. Most of the items on display looked homemade, except for the items on the back wall that had the town's name stamped all over them.

"Be right with you."

Tessa heard Laine's voice coming from the back of the building. She wandered further inside. The walls were white, with accents of turquoise and sand. The overall effect was very cheerful. Paintings of the nearby lake and parks, Tessa assumed, were done by local artists and covered most of the walls, the price tags discreetly tucked out of view. There were also handmade soaps and candles on tables throughout the space. Those price tags were not as discreetly hidden.

"Amazing, isn't it, that someone will pay that much money for soap I make in my kitchen?"

Tessa turned to see Laine smiling at her. "I was thinking about something else, but yes, it is amazing. You must be doing well."

"I'm so glad you came. I'll show you around."

Tessa listened while Laine explained that everything in the shop was made by locals, even the tacky t-shirts and water globes.

Laine led Tessa toward the back of the store. "The jewelry is some of my favorite. There are a couple of local women who make the jewelry. I do love anything that sparkles."

Tessa touched a finger to a bright, multi-faceted crystal drop. It looked like it had a rainbow inside it and hung from what looked like a delicate, hand-hammered silver chain. "It is very pretty."

"If you worked here, I could give you an employee discount." Laine didn't believe in subtlety.

Tessa shrugged. "Still a little too steep for me. But that's why I came. The job, I mean."

Laine clapped her hands. "Wonderful."

Tessa wasn't sure what to say to that, other than the obvious. "I'm not sure why you're all fired up to hire me, other than misplaced guilt, but I can use a little extra money. But I'll only be here a few more weeks at most."

"Which is why you're perfect. We're heading into peak season right now. Things will start to slow down in a few weeks, and then I'll be able to handle it on my own again."

It didn't get past Tessa's notice that Laine didn't defend herself against the misplaced guilt part of her comment. "What days and what hours? A friend is letting me borrow his truck, so I can be here pretty early, but I would need to cut out mid-afternoon."

"How about Friday through Sunday from eight to three? You can help me straighten up the shop and get settled before I open at nine."

Tessa let out the breath she'd been holding. "That would be great."

"Good. Why don't you hang out this morning and we'll get the paperwork all set?"

Tessa let Laine settle her in the back and hand her the paperwork to fill out. She bit her lip as she filled out the employment application. Her hand hovered over the last question.

Laine popped in to see how she was doing. "Don't worry about that. Just a standard question. I highly doubt you have a felony conviction on your record."

Tessa kept her head down. She left the question blank and then filled out the rest of the tax papers while Laine tended to customers. She then rose and joined her behind the counter.

Tessa hung out a good part of the morning, observing Laine and learning about the products. Traffic in the shop picked up as the morning sped by. It was noon before she knew it.

Laine took a moment to sit when the shop had a lull around lunchtime. "Sorry, see what I mean about crazy. You didn't have to stay."

"I just wanted to see how things flowed. But I should head back. It's only Wednesday, so I'll see you in a couple of days."

"Let me get you logged for the time you were here today."

Tessa shook her head. "No, I didn't do anything. Just watched. I'll see you on Friday."

Laine started to argue but stopped. "Okay. Friday at eight."

Tessa gave Laine a genuine smile. "Thanks for being my friend, Laine."

Tessa left before Laine could form a response and swiftly headed back to the truck. The job was settled, and that was good. She could work on the house in the evening on the weekends and would have plenty of time during the week to tackle all the projects left. Borrowing Pete's truck wasn't the best option, but he didn't seem to mind. And it had taken her only half an hour to convince him not to tell Simon.

When Tessa pulled the truck back into the driveway, she was surprised to see Mason's SUV parked beside the house. Her car was now gone, courtesy of the insurance company that paid to have it towed. She glanced around but didn't see Mason or Pete. She parked the truck next to the SUV and went in search of Mason.

It had been four days since Mason had stayed the night at her house. Deputy Jackson had come by the house shortly after Mason left to collect the duffle bag. He had also called her a couple of times to check on her and let her know that the investigation was still underway. Her vandal had not made another appearance, so either he was lying low for now or had gotten bored. Either way, Tessa could only be grateful.

She stopped in her tracks when she noticed Mason was helping Pete shingle her roof. From the look of things, Pete had gotten a lot done. Courtesy of Mason? She stepped around to the side of the house and saw Rexford lying in the nearby shade.

Pete saw her first. From his perch above her, he shouted down. "So did you get the job?"

Tessa stared at Mason, who was now standing bare-chested next to Pete. She pulled her eyes away from his sweaty chest. "Yes. Friday through Sunday. I'll need the truck from seven till four if that's okay?"

"Not a problem. Just keep the meals coming, and I'm a happy man."

Tessa glanced at Mason, then looked away again, her cheeks flushing pink, partly from the sight of Mason's bare chest, and partly from feeling bad for borrowing Pete's truck. And because she felt bad, she offered to fix lunch for him in return while he worked on the house. But she didn't have much choice but to take the job Laine offered her. The insurance company hadn't given her much for her car. And even if she did get another one with the money they gave her, the chances of being able to afford one that would make it back to Indiana were slim. Not to mention, with her luck, the vandal would come back and strike again. The money from working at Laine's shop would help her supplement the money the insurance gave her so she could get something reasonable when she got back home. She'd simply rent a car to get her home when the time came.

Mason nodded at Pete and climbed off the roof. He grabbed his shirt that he had tossed onto a nearby bush and tugged it over his head. "What job did you take?"

Tessa hadn't planned to tell him, but Laine no doubt would tell him anyway, so it wasn't as if she could keep it a secret. "Laine's job."

"What made you change your mind?"

"When the guy at the local ice cream shop refused to even let me fill out an application despite the 'now hiring' sign in the window."

Mason glanced at her neighbor's house. "I'm sorry, Tessa. The guy who runs the ice cream shop is Degrassi's nephew."

Tessa shrugged again. "Doesn't matter. The restaurant didn't want me, the feed shop didn't want me, and neither did the other two places I applied. And let's be honest, it's not as if the town is so big that jobs are lying around. Nor are there that many people to fill them. Laine is the only one who will hire me."

Mason took Tessa's hand and led her inside so he could grab a glass of water.

Tessa leaned against her almost finished counters. "Why are you here? And why were you on my roof?"

"I had an idea. So I ran it by my dad. I'd have been by sooner, but things have been a little crazy. Jackson tells me you haven't had any other trouble, so I haven't been by. My parents are taking a trip; I think Laine might have mentioned it at dinner the other day. I was going to bring Rexford to my place. But then I thought it might be better if he stayed with you. He's a retired police dog, and he'll alert you to any intruders. Dad agreed to let him stay with you. They don't leave for a week yet, but Rexford is all set to stay here. I put his bed in your bedroom, and I've got his supplies in a box in the living room."

"My bedroom?"

"Yeah, Rexford doesn't like to sleep alone."

Tessa eyed the dog. She had never had pets and wasn't sure how she felt about having a retired police dog staying with her. Then again, she bet he could look pretty intimidating when he wasn't lounging in the shade. "And why were you on my roof?"

"Pete looked like he could use a hand and I'm off duty today. Plus, I wanted to see you before I left to explain about the dog. Gave me an excuse to hang around." He left out the part where he'd questioned Pete about his relationship with Tessa. It seemed Pete had a girlfriend back home who would skin him alive if he even thought about straying. That suited Mason just fine.

Tessa didn't know what to say to that, so she just nodded.

Mason finished his water, then gave Tessa the rundown on Rexford before turning his attention to the house. "I see you're almost done with the kitchen."

Tessa glanced around. The cabinets were done, and the counters looked great. "I'm going to patch and paint it next, then lay the new tile floor. It should take me the rest of the week to finish the kitchen. The windows will be here in a few days, so Pete and I will have those to tackle once he's done with the roof. Then he'll start the drywall so I can finish the rest."

"What are you going to do for a vehicle after Pete leaves?"

Tessa shrugged. Pete wouldn't be here as long as she would be. "I don't know yet."

"I have a car you can use. It's a sporty little thing I barely drive."

Tessa turned her back on him. "You have an answer for everything. I can't borrow your car."

Mason came and stood behind her. "Why not? I don't drive it much. When I'm in town, I drive the SUV. I use the car for occasional recreational use, and that's about it."

Tessa wanted to lean back into the heat of Mason's body behind her. She felt herself swaying toward him. "I can't."

Mason wasn't sure she was referring to the offer of the

use of his car anymore. He heard the increased rate of her breathing as his body brushed against hers. "You mean we shouldn't. I've been giving that some thought too."

Tessa wasn't sure she wanted to hear what he had been thinking. "Mason, please. I just can't. And you can't either."

Mason turned her to face him. He hated to see the pain in her eyes. "I've done a lot for this town, and I've given up a lot to serve the good people here. I've not regretted any of my decisions. But I've come to the conclusion that I can't live my life worried about what the townsfolk will think, not this time. I lie in bed at night thinking about you, Tessa. And I think you do the same."

"So you're willing to give up your future for what? A roll in the hay? A short-lived affair? I'm leaving when the remodel is done. There is no future for me here. And if you keep up with this, with me, you won't have one here either."

"Definitely not just a roll in the hay. And I can't make promises to you beyond an affair. But if the town fires me because of you, then I guess it's better to know now where I stand rather than later."

Tessa blinked the tears from her eyes. "That's easy for you to say now while you still have your job. And I guess I should be grateful to you for not lying to me and making me promises you can't keep. But let me assure you, you'll regret it."

Mason yanked Tessa against his chest. "Regrets? No, the only thing I'll regret is if I don't see where you and I will go."

Tessa would have argued, but Mason kissed her. And much like before, she had no defenses against him. She felt

Mason scoop her up and set her on the kitchen table. When he deepened the kiss, she wrapped her legs around his waist and held on to him with all her strength. She didn't have to think about what she wanted; her body did the thinking for her. She melted in his embrace, aching for more. She felt his hands as they cupped her bottom, bringing their bodies closer together. She whimpered as the length of his erection ground against her while his teeth scored the skin of her neck.

Mason spoke softly in her ear. "We have to stop. Pete could come in at any minute. Have dinner with me tonight?"

Tessa would have agreed with anything he had asked of her at that moment. She forced her arms and legs to release him as he stepped back. She stared at him while he took a moment to catch his breath and get himself back under control.

"Dinner. I'll be back at six."

Tessa nodded because she knew no words would form. And she couldn't refuse him.

"Good. Now walk me out."

Tessa slid from the table and let Mason take her hand. She walked with him to his waiting SUV. The town name on the side of the vehicle, a reminder of who he was, cooled her blood.

"After dinner, we'll stop at my place, and you can pick up the car. I prefer knowing you have transportation should anything happen."

Now that Tessa was thinking straight again, she was having doubts. She couldn't keep him in the dark about who and what she was. "Mason, did you run a background check on me?"

Mason brushed back a tendril of her hair. "No."

Tessa took a step back. "Maybe you should before we have dinner tonight."

"That's the first time a date has asked me that. Why?"

Tessa took another step back. "Just run it, Mason. It's better if you know the truth before dinner."

"You think I don't trust you?"

Tessa shook her head. "It's not about trust."

Mason would have argued with her, but Rexford came and whined at him. Mason pointed at Tessa. "You stay here."

Rexford sat on his haunches next to Tessa. Tessa kept her eyes on Mason as he climbed into the SUV and backed out of her driveway without another word.

"What do you think? Do you think dinner is a good idea?" Tessa glanced down at Rexford, who was now wagging his tail at her. Seemed the dog approved. Tessa went back into the house on wobbly legs and started pulling out her paint supplies. She had a few hours before Mason would be back. If he came back.

* * *

Mason went back to the station even though it was his day off. It wasn't unusual for him to come in, so no one would question his presence. He had a few hours to kill before he had to go home and dress before he went back to pick up Tessa. He was confused by her request to run a background check on her. He didn't need to run one to know the type of person she was. He didn't need confirmation that she was who she said she was. Relationships had to be built on trust. And though he wasn't sure where his relationship with Tessa would go, by running one he would be proving to her that he didn't trust her. He wasn't sure if this was some test he was supposed to pass or fail, but he wasn't going to do it. The temptation had been there before, and he had run a quick check on Simon, not because he didn't trust Tessa, but because he didn't trust Simon. But just as Tessa had told him, he had cleaned up his act and had become a well-respected pediatrician. There had been no more arrests or any other hits when he'd run the check on Tessa's brother. And his juvenile record was in the past. And he knew there wouldn't be any hits if he were to run Tessa's name, which he wasn't going to do.

Right now his only concern was where to take Tessa for dinner. She would be uncomfortable if they ate in town. Though on the other hand, he feared if he took her out of town, she would be suspicious that he didn't want to be seen with her. In the end, he figured her discomfort was the bigger consideration, so he called and made a reservation for dinner not too far from Laine's shop. The lake resort town boasted the nicest places to eat for miles, and for their first date, he wanted to take her someplace nice. And though he spent a lot of time at Margie's diner, he wouldn't take Tessa there.

Mason dug into the pile of files on his desk and let work consume him for a few hours.

Chapter Nine

Mason showed up on Tessa's doorstep at five minutes to six. Tessa could tell he'd taken the time to shave and change. He arrived wearing black dress slacks and a light blue button-down shirt that was open at the neck and the sleeves rolled up. His normal work boots were replaced with loafers. Tessa had also taken a moment to shower and run a razor over her legs. She had opted to braid her long hair in deference to the summer heat. She only had two dresses hanging in her aunt's closet, and since she'd felt so out of place in the gingham dress, she had opted for the one he'd already seen her in. And then, because she wanted to look nice, she took the time to apply a little makeup, glad she had packed it.

Her first words were not ones Mason wanted to hear. "I take it you didn't run that background check."

Mason strode across the porch to her front door. He grabbed her shoulders and kissed her soundly before releasing her just as quickly as he'd grabbed her. "No. Let's eat."

Tessa wanted to be upset but instead felt relieved. While working on patching and sanding the kitchen walls after he'd left, she secretly wished for this one night. Perhaps it was selfish of her, but it had been so long since she'd felt desirable. It had been even longer since she'd had a normal conversation with a man, other than her brother. And this was Mason, not Timothy. Mason stood up for what was right. And while he was sure to turn his back on her once he did learn of her past, for now, he wanted to spend time with her. And since no man's kiss had ever turned her inside out like Mason's had, she wanted to be selfish. There would be time enough later to deal with the repercussions.

"Where are we going?" Tessa fastened her seat belt and looked over at Mason as he started the engine.

"There is this Italian place, Bianchi's, not too far from Laine's store. I thought we'd try it."

Relieved they wouldn't be eating locally, Tessa relaxed in her seat. "I don't suppose you venture out of town to eat too much."

"Not usually for food. The last woman I dated lived pretty far out, so we usually ate near her home. But I didn't want to take you to any of those places, and Laine raves about Bianchi's."

"What was she like?"

Mason flicked his turn signal on and headed out to the main county road. "What was who like?"

"Your last girlfriend?" Tessa really wanted to know since he'd brought her up.

Mason realized what he'd said. He gave her a wry smile. "Guess that wasn't the smartest thing to say on a first date."

Tessa shrugged, her stomach knotting at his saying this was their first date. It implied more to come. "Honest, anyway. So what is she like?"

"Her name is Harper. She's funny and smart. I like her, but it wasn't meant to be."

"What does she look like?"

Mason glanced over at her but couldn't figure out why she was asking. "Red hair, blue eyes, lots of freckles. She's dating a banker now. Someone with steadier hours."

Tessa figured it was Harper's loss. "I guess it would be hard to date local women. Probably hard to date at all with your hours."

"Par for the course, and all that. And no, I generally don't date locals. Plus I know most of the women my age from school, and a good number of them are now married. Of course, I'm also one of the few single men my age in town too."

"I don't suppose you've dated anyone from Indiana."

Amused, he glanced back at her. "No, never anyone from Indiana. But you weren't born there."

"No, Simon and I were born in Alabama. After my dad lost his job and had already been fired from every other business in town, we came to Utah. I don't suppose any of us thought we'd stay as long as we did. Mom always held out settling in, hoping to go back home, even after my dad bought a house. But as you know, we never did."

"So, why Indiana?"

"I don't know. Sometimes I think Simon just closed his eyes and pointed blindly at a map. And because he was there, I eventually followed. And now, with Sarah and the children, Simon has planted some pretty deep roots."

Mason heard the wistfulness in her voice but didn't comment. "Do you think you'll stay in Indiana?"

"Like I said, it's where Simon is. So yes, I'll stay."

"I've never lived anywhere else but Utah. I went to college here, went to the police academy here, and I joined the police department in Salt Lake City. When Dad said he was retiring, it felt like it was time to come home."

Tessa thought about the places she'd been. If only she had remained in Utah, perhaps her life would have been different. "I think it's nice. Minus the fact that the townspeople hate me, it is a nice town. It's a good place to live, to raise a family."

"My sister Cyndi is increasing our family. She told us a few weeks ago she's pregnant. Still can't tell that she is. And I think Laine is starting to feel the pressure since she's the older sister and has been married longer."

Tessa saw the smile crinkle his eyes. "I bet you're feeling a bit of the pressure too. You're the oldest and the only male."

"I'm not opposed to the whole marriage and family thing. I think my family, or at least my mom and dad, understands the pressures my job holds. My mother says it takes a special woman to be married to a cop, especially a police chief."

Tessa, who had been on the other side of the law, understood. "She has to understand that sometimes she and the children can't come first. That sometimes someone else needs you more. It's a lot of responsibility, and you don't strike me as a man who takes it lightly. I bet they're proud of you."

"My folks?" Mason pulled into the parking lot of the restaurant.

"Yes, your folks."

Mason shrugged. "I guess it's not something I think about. They understand me and what I do. I guess that's always been enough for me."

Tessa supposed she understood that. Her mother had never understood her. Her father, well, he hadn't cared about anyone other than himself, and his opinion hadn't mattered to her. But Simon understood her. He didn't pass judgment or make her feel bad for the life she'd lived in her youth. He'd gone through similar, though not as bad, things in his own life. But Mason was the law, and her family had been on the other side. Could he understand her? Could he see beyond the surface, beyond the facts, and see the real Tessa?

"Are you cold?"

Tessa heard Mason's words and pulled back to the present. "What?"

"You shivered. Are you cold?"

Tessa got her thoughts back under control. "No, I'm good. Hungry."

Mason could tell she wasn't lying, but her mind had been miles away. He wanted to press her about what she had been thinking about, but didn't want to start dinner on a sour note. Because he could tell whatever it was she had been thinking about, it wasn't pleasant.

Mason placed a hand on her back as he guided her into the restaurant. Glancing around, he was pleased with what he saw. The tables had linens on them, and small canisters that held flickering candles inside graced each table. There was soft lighting throughout, giving the place a romantic feel.

A well-dressed hostess seated them at a table toward the back of the restaurant. Tessa glanced around and was happy when she didn't recognize any of the faces. "This is nice."

"I can always trust Laine. She hates to cook and knows the best places to eat. Thankfully Russell does like to cook. He teases Laine that she married him for his cooking ability, and if it weren't for the way Laine stares at him adoringly, I might be inclined to believe him."

Tessa defended Laine. "She would never use someone that way."

Mason raised an eyebrow but ignored the comment as he handed her the drink menu. "What will you have?"

Tessa glanced at the elaborate beer and wine list. She didn't particularly like beer, and wine, on the rare occasions she drank it, was the kind with a screw top. This place didn't look like it ran toward screw tops. "I don't know. I don't go out to eat much. And when I do, it's usually with Simon and his family. Those places run to plastic cups with cartoon characters on them more than wine."

Mason laughed, imagining her surrounded by her family. "I don't know much about wine either. When I drink it, I usually go for a sweet red. Never understood why I should want to drink sour grapes."

Tessa set the menu aside. "I like sweet."

Mason knew he would not have been able to resist making some sort of comment about her being sweet, so thankfully the waiter showed up to curb his tongue. The waiter came back with a couple of options for Tessa, and she settled on the Moscato. He ordered one of their domestic beers on tap.

Tessa watched Mason over the top of his menu while they looked over the selection. She already knew what she wanted: the four-cheese ravioli with marinara. "Know what you want?"

"I think the chicken marsala."

Tessa made a face. "Is that the one with the mushrooms?"

Mason didn't miss the grimace she made. "Take it that you're not a fan of mushrooms."

"Just never understood why people like them so much. Too squishy."

The waiter came and took their order, and Tessa relaxed in her seat, sipping the wine. "So what else do we talk about? I think we've exhausted the conversation about our families and where we've lived."

"I told you about my last girlfriend. Who was your last boyfriend? What was he like?"

Tessa never imagined he'd ask her that question. Though she supposed it was only fair because she knew who he dated last. But the problem was that she didn't date. She hadn't been on one in years. She'd attempted it a couple of times after she moved to Indiana, but she had been so uncomfortable with her dates that she'd given up the attempts. Simon still tried to convince her from time to time to get out more, but between his family and his career, he didn't have much time to nag her about it.

Mason laid his hand over hers. "You don't have to answer that."

Tessa realized she had been silent a little too long. "No, it's okay. It's just that there hasn't been anyone memorable or worth sharing. During the spring, summer, and fall, I'm busy with work. You never know how long the weather will last for outdoor work. And right before the holidays, I'm pretty busy with people wanting their houses pretty for family, usually painting living rooms and dining rooms. Then during the winter, I tend to hibernate instead of socializing. Simon chides me about it, but I guess it's not a priority for me."

Mason released her. "Well then, I guess I should be flattered that you made an exception for me."

Tessa tensed, then forced herself to relax. He was just teasing her, but the idea that he would be grateful for a date with her was hard to believe. "I don't remember you giving me much of a choice. I was a bit befuddled when you asked me."

Mason took a drink of his beer to hide his look of satisfaction. He'd enjoyed befuddling her and couldn't wait to try again.

As dinner progressed, Tessa relaxed more. They talked about their work mostly, and he seemed fascinated by the homes she'd painted and some of the clients she'd had over the years. They talked about television, movies, music, and all the other things people talked about on first dates. They both liked country music, but he liked action movies, while she preferred dramas. Mason had asked her what her dream home looked like, and he had been surprised when she admitted that she wanted to live in a small ranch house in the country. He didn't have much of an opinion on houses, though he admitted to thinking about buying his parents' house but figured it was too much for a bachelor.

After dinner, Mason drove her to his house so she could take his car. That was one topic they hadn't talked about during dinner because Mason had a feeling Tessa hadn't changed her mind about not wanting to borrow it. But the thought of her being alone with no way to leave wasn't sitting well with him. The car, if nothing else, would give him peace of mind.

Tessa was content to let the good food, the wine, and the rhythm of the car beneath her lull her. She didn't fall asleep but was content to sit beside Mason in the SUV. It wasn't until he was pulling into a driveway that wasn't hers that she realized where they were.

"Want to come in for coffee or something while I find the keys to the car?"

Tessa stepped down from the SUV and surveyed the house. It was small; large trees shaded the house, and it looked well kept. There weren't any flowers or other adornments, but the grass was green and lush. The shutters on the house were a nice touch, and the small porch added charm. "It's cute."

Mason glanced back at her while she surveyed his home. "I like it. But it's not big enough for a wife and kids, as my parents not so subtly point out. I rent it from one of our local teachers who inherited it after her grandmother passed. She doesn't have the heart to sell it, but she needs something bigger for her own family. She lets me rent it pretty cheaply, and in exchange, I handle any repairs or maintenance it needs."

"I rent an apartment a few towns over from where Simon lives. He lives in a three-bedroom apartment not too far from the hospital he works at, but I can't afford to live in the city as he does. I rent a small studio apartment, but I don't have much, and I don't need much. But the space has a nice little kitchen with a counter to eat at, and a bathroom with a nice tub. And the heat and air conditioning work, so I'm happy."

"Sounds cozy. Come on in. I'll get the keys."

Tessa didn't even try to curb her curiosity. The small living room had a fireplace off to the side with a couch and recliner circling the space. There was a small television on a stand, and a small collection of movies was tucked in the bottom of the stand. The bookcase nearby was full of books, so it wasn't hard to see what Mason did in his free time. The case was packed, and the books were haphazardly arranged.

Tessa wandered into an eat-in kitchen that had lots of counter space and cabinets. The kitchen table had a laptop on it, and a stand that held a printer and more books sat off to the side. Off the kitchen, she could see a good-sized bathroom. As she wandered back into the living room, Mason emerged from what she assumed was the master bedroom. A second door was a little further down toward the kitchen, but the door was closed, so she assumed it was a second bedroom.

Mason tucked the keys into the pocket of the slacks and gestured for Tessa to follow him to the kitchen. "I've got decaf if you prefer."

Tessa wandered over and sat at the counter. "Decaf is

better, or I won't sleep tonight."

Mason set the coffee to brew and turned to Tessa. "I'm glad you came out with me tonight."

Tessa shifted in her seat. Mason had an intense look on his face, one she had seen before, right before he'd kissed her. "Me too. It was nice. You'll have to tell Laine we enjoyed it."

Mason came around the counter to stand next to her. "So I'm allowed to tell Laine that we had dinner?"

"It was just dinner."

Mason took her hand and tugged her to her feet. "But it could be so much more."

Tessa had been thinking about what she wanted from him, with him. She had already admitted she was attracted to him. And despite his drugging kisses, if she hadn't wanted to have dinner with him, she wouldn't have. He hadn't run the background check she'd told him to run. It was probable he never would. So unless she gave him cause to look into her past, he seemed content to believe what he saw in front of him. No one in town knew her past. And as long as they didn't flaunt their relationship all over town, it was possible no one would find out. And perhaps she would become a fond memory for him.

No, she couldn't deny her attraction to him. When they were together, she didn't feel awkward. When he kissed her, he made her forget her past, forget what had once been. She trusted he wouldn't hurt her. And maybe she too could have a fond memory of a summer romance with a man she was not only attracted to but also admired.

Tessa wasn't sure what he saw as he looked down at

her, but he gave her plenty of time to protest his kiss. But instead of drawing away, she took a step forward, bringing her hands to rest on his shoulders.

Mason claimed her mouth with his, taking time to savor her taste. He felt her fingers curling into his shoulders when he traced her lips with his tongue. And when she once again opened her mouth to his, as she had done earlier in her kitchen, he scooped her up in his arms and carried her to his bedroom.

Tessa didn't protest when he set her on her feet beside his bed. She started to feel unsure until Mason bent his head and kissed her again. After that, there was no hesitation on her part. She let her tongue mate with his and curled her arms around his neck, leaning her whole body against him. She felt her nipples harden against his chest as the rest of her body went lax, letting his greater strength support her.

Mason pulled away; his breathing harsh. "Believe it or not, I only intended dinner. But seeing you in my home, wanting you as badly as I do, got the better of my intentions. Tell me you want me, Tessa. I don't want you to regret this tomorrow."

Regret? No, Tessa couldn't imagine ever regretting a moment spent with Mason. She was more afraid she'd regret walking away from him. "I do want you, Mason."

Mason's arms tightened around her. "You have no idea how happy I am to hear that. I don't know if I could have just let you walk out on me."

Tessa didn't need any encouragement when he reached for her again. She had never been kissed like this before, as if he were trying to absorb her into him. She lost track of time, of where she was. She fit against him as if she had been made for him. When he reached for the buttons that fastened the dress, he had to remove her arms from around his neck so he could let the dress fall at her feet. In the back of her mind, she thought she should feel self-conscious that he was seeing her in nothing but her underwear. But given that she wanted to remove the clothes he wore, she supposed it was only fair.

Mason's gaze followed the lines of her body as the dress fell to the floor. She wore a plain cotton bra that barely covered her. The fabric strained across her full breasts; her nipples visible through the thin cloth. The plain white underwear wasn't sexy, but what was beneath it was. She was still too slim, but her body was lean and muscled from the physical labor she did for a living. His fingers drifted under the elastic of her underwear as his hands cupped her curvy bottom and drew her against him. He smiled against her mouth when her arms came back around his neck in a vice grip.

Tessa wasn't sure how long they stood there kissing each other before kissing was no longer enough. She was very aware of his hands on her bottom, kneading and caressing her bare flesh, but now she wanted to do the same. She dropped her arms, but unwilling to move away from him, or to have him stop the arousing caresses, she managed to get her arms between them and tried to unfasten the buttons on his shirt.

Mason whispered in her ear. "Let me."

Tessa almost whimpered when he withdrew his hands,

but he was quick to remove not only his shirt but also to unfasten her bra. When he drew her back against him and his mouth sought hers once more, she moaned. The crisp hair on his chest was a rough caress on her nipples, and she arched her lower body against his.

Mason released her mouth and tried to catch his breath. Tessa placed a small kiss on his neck and then his chest. Once again cupping her bottom, he bent his head and took a nipple in his mouth. He bit lightly when Tessa leaned back and cupped her hand around his neck.

"Mason?"

"Mmm?" His tongue traced the underside of her breast, then moved to the other one.

Tessa lost what she was going to say when Mason took her other breast in his mouth and sucked hard against her. Her fingers tightened in his hair the same way her lower body was tightening with desire.

Mason released her and stripped her underwear down her legs. He lifted her out of them and laid her on his bed.

"I've been thinking about having you here like this with me since I first saw you." He looked down at her. She was everything he imagined and more.

Tessa just stared as Mason stripped the rest of his clothes off. She felt a moment of unease as she saw him naked for the first time, his erection quite impressive in the low light and a little unnerving. She repeated to herself that Mason wouldn't hurt her and lifted her arms to him.

Mason didn't need a second invitation. He once again found her breast with his mouth, this time kneading the soft flesh of her other breast with his fingers that rose eagerly for his touch. With his free hand, he stroked the rest of her body, learning her shape and the softness that awaited him. He saw her flinch when his fingers found the heart of her, but she slowly opened her thighs to him to allow a deeper touch.

Mason continued to kiss and stroke her body. He knew the exact moment when she completely relaxed and gave herself over to him. Her thighs opened wider and the fingers that had been curled into his chest fell away. Her lips were parted, and her breathing increased. And though he wanted to make sure she completely enjoyed their first time together, he wanted to be inside her when she did.

Tessa watched with desire-filled eyes as Mason leaned over to reach into the drawer of his nightstand. She saw the condom he pulled out of the drawer and watched as he ripped it open. But before he put it on, she wanted to know him the way he knew her. She sat up and touched him with a tentative finger. Then when he stilled and his body tightened, her touch became bolder.

Mason let her touch him until he couldn't take anymore. The innocent desire and intent expression on her face left him with the impression that this was the first time she'd explored a man's body so intimately. The longer he was with her in his bed, the more he was convinced she wasn't very experienced. But she was so incredibly sexy, so incredibly hot, and he had to have her now.

Mason's voice was rough when he spoke. "Enough."

Tessa wanted to protest, but the words lodged in her throat when his mouth took hers in a fierce kiss. She found herself once again on her back, this time with Mason between her thighs. He only pulled away long enough to roll the condom on before coming back to her. Her arms came around his neck, his chest crushing her breasts, the same way his body was crushing her into the mattress. He was a lot bigger than she was, but she didn't feel fear. She wanted him inside her, desperate for him. Her body was on fire, and she knew only he could put it out.

Mason fitted himself to her and slowly penetrated her body, not wanting to hurt her in any way. Her thighs gripped him, and he felt the tightening of her body around him. He completed his penetration and let out a slow moan. She was hot and tight, and whatever control he had left was gone in an instant.

Tessa felt one of Mason's arms slide under her bottom as he lifted her into his thrusts. She found the rhythm and kept pace. Her thighs gripped him harder as she tried to pull him closer. Her arms came around his neck, and she pressed her face into his throat. He began thrusting harder and faster, and she quickened her pace to match his. Barely aware that she was crying his name, she came apart in his arms. She felt her lower body tighten before convulsing around him.

Mason felt and heard every moment of her climax. He heard her cries and felt the dampness of tears on his neck. He grasped her to him, thrusting again and again until he felt his climax overtaking him.

Mason lay on her for a few moments, completely spent. He managed to get enough energy to roll them over, so Tessa lay draped on top of his, his body still nestled inside hers.

Tessa lay there, as spent as Mason, and tried to think of something to say. Nothing came to mind. She knew that sex was something many women enjoyed, but this was the first time she'd enjoyed it. She wanted to laugh and cry at the same time. But she did neither. Instead, she laid her head down on Mason's chest, her legs lying limply at his sides, her mouth pressed against his chest, placing small damp kisses where she could reach.

Mason savored Tessa's mouth on his chest, cupping her head to hold her close.

Tessa's voice was soft in the quiet of the room. "That was nice."

Mason raised his head to look down at her disbelievingly. "Nice?"

"Mmm. Yes, very nice."

Mason saw the very satisfied smile on her lips and felt a small burst of laughter rumble in his chest.

Tessa leaned up. She had felt, more than heard, his laugh. "What?"

"Let's just say I've never had anyone tell me it was nice. But you're right. It was nice. And sweet and satisfying. And I can't wait to do it again."

"But it was. And so are you."

Mason lifted her off him and laid her against his side, pulling a pillow under their heads. He knew if he stayed inside her a moment longer, he'd be taking her again. But she'd winced a little when he'd separated their bodies, confirming his earlier thought that it had been a while since Tessa had let anyone make love to her. He knew now was not the time.

Tessa draped a leg over his and placed a hand on his chest. He put an arm under her and pulled her closer. Contented, she felt herself drifting.

Tessa woke a short while later when she felt Mason leave the bed. She watched as he left the room. She sat up and clutched the sheet to her breasts. She waited a minute to see if regret would come, but it didn't. Mason had treated her with care, as if he cared, and had treated her as if he desired only her. It was more than she'd experienced before, and she wouldn't, couldn't, regret it.

Mason came back into the bedroom, sans the condom, and climbed back into bed. "You should get some sleep."

Tessa remained sitting. "I should go."

Mason dragged her down to him and kissed her roughly. "I think you should stay."

Tessa wanted to, but knew she shouldn't. What if someone were to see her leave his house? And besides that, there was a very practical reason to go. "I have to let Rexford out and feed him his dinner."

Mason groaned and dragged her closer. "I forgot about the dog."

Tessa probably would have too, had she not been looking for an excuse to leave. "I'm sure he'd be heartbroken to hear that."

Mason grunted but let her go and sat up. "Just let me get my clothes on."

Tessa saw her dress on the floor and awkwardly tried to pull it on without revealing too much of her body to him.

Mason saw her, smiled at her sudden shyness, and came around the bed. He took the dress from her, ignoring her unspoken protest. He pulled it over her head himself and helped her into it, fastening the button that held it around her neck. He then bent down to retrieve her bra and underwear.

She took them from him and blushed.

"You are so sweet." Mason bent and kissed her again, bringing her body flush to his. He felt his body's renewed interest but tamped it down.

Tessa's voice was a whisper when she pulled away. "I have to go. I just need the keys."

Mason swore under his breath. She meant the keys to his car, the one he told her to borrow. It didn't sit right with him not driving her home, but the sole purpose of her being here was to get the car.

"I can follow you. Make sure you get safely inside."

Tessa bit her lip and stepped away before she was tempted to kiss him again. "You're the one who's sweet. And it's silly to follow me back. I've got Rexford standing guard. And it's late. Pete will be at the house in a few hours. I'll be fine."

Mason kissed her and then picked his jeans off the floor. He pulled the keys out of the pocket but donned the jeans so he could walk her out. "I don't like it. Call me when you get there and let me know you're safe."

Mason led her outside to where his car was parked. He savored Tessa's moan when his body pressed hers up against the door of the car. He kissed her again, his lower body mimicking the movements he made with his tongue.

Tessa grasped him and lifted herself against him. She almost staggered when he suddenly released her.

Mason opened the car door and took a step back. His voice was husky when he finally spoke. "Call me. Promise."

"I promise." Tessa slid into the car with trembling legs. The car started up with a quick twist of the key in the ignition. Without another word or look, she backed out of the driveway and headed home.

Mason stood in his driveway until she was out of sight.

Chapter Ten

Tessa took a sip of coffee as she let Rexford out for his morning ritual. He sniffed every tree in the backyard before sniffing the ground until he found the perfect spot. When he came back to her, she patted his head and told him what a good boy he was. He licked her hand and bounded into the house, knowing breakfast was next on the list.

Tessa was exhausted but was feeling good. She'd left Mason's house and made the call that she was safe and sound as soon as she pulled into the driveway. They'd chatted briefly before they said a final good night. She had lain in bed, wondering if sleep would elude her, but it hadn't, and she had fallen into a deep, peaceful sleep. When she woke, her first thought was of Mason, and that thought made her smile.

"Morning." Pete's voice drifted through the house as he opened the front door.

"Morning. In the kitchen."

Pete came over and poured himself a cup of coffee. "Windows will be arriving today. We'll need to store them in the living room, just in case."

Tessa didn't have to ask in case of what. Though they didn't openly discuss it, neither of them was convinced they'd seen the last of the vandal. "We can shove the couch up against the wall. There should be plenty of room. And

Rexford should sound the alarm."

Pete patted the top of Rexford's head when the dog came up to greet him. "This here is one mighty fine dog."

Tessa poured the dog a bowl of food, then tossed in a little extra. "I'll be painting the kitchen today. I got the walls patched and sanded. They're as good as they're going to get. Next week I'll need help tackling the bathroom walls."

Pete downed his cup of coffee and poured a second. "I'll be done with the roof by tomorrow. I had to replace some of the rotted beams and had to shore up the back section. Gutters are up in the back but still need to be done in the front. We're getting there."

Tessa nodded but didn't reply when her cell phone rang. Her heart began to pound a little harder at seeing Mason's number on the screen. She hit the button and turned her back on Pete. "Hi."

"Morning. Just checking in on how you're feeling this morning."

Tessa felt her cheeks heat and was grateful Pete didn't seem to notice or care that it wasn't Simon on the other end. "I'm good. You?"

Mason leaned back in his chair, enjoying the sound of Tessa's voice. "Feeling pretty good myself. I don't know what time I'll get off work tonight, but we could shoot for a late dinner."

Tessa shuffled her feet. "Where?"

"I was thinking your place. I could bring something by."

Tessa cleared her throat. "Not too late. I have to work

tomorrow."

Mason smiled. "I bet Laine would excuse you for being late."

Tessa turned when she heard Pete make a small noise. His eyebrow was raised at her. She shrugged and put her head down. "I bet she would. But I think I can do dinner tonight and not have to call in late on my first day."

"Good. And I hope you'll be the dessert."

Tessa was glad she hadn't taken a sip of her coffee. She probably would have spit it out. She knew her voice was husky when she finally managed to get her words out. "I could probably arrange that."

Mason smiled again. It was going to be a long day, but she was something to look forward to at the end of it. "Good. I'll call you when I'm on my way."

"Okay."

"Bye, Tessa."

Tessa licked her dry lips. "Bye."

"Hot date?"

Tessa didn't know why she felt like the kid who got her hand caught in the cookie jar, but she did. "I, ah, Mason and I had dinner last night. He asked if I'd like to again tonight."

Pete washed his cup and set it in the drainboard. "Did you tell Simon you're dating the police chief?"

Tessa set her phone down. "It was just one dinner. Nothing to tell."

"It might not be my business, but that blush says it was more than just dinner."

Tessa felt her cheeks heat even more. "It can't be more than that. I'll be leaving. And there's no sense in worrying

Simon."

That got Pete's attention. "And why would that worry Simon?"

Tessa realized what she had said. "Simon and Mason weren't what you'd call friends back when they were kids. Mostly because Mason's dad was the police chief back then."

Pete knew enough of Simon's history to understand why the two boys would not have been friends. "Fair enough. But he seems all right."

"He is."

"And if at any time he's not all right, you let me know and I'll take care of it."

Tessa wasn't sure if she should be flattered or worried. But since she'd gotten to know Pete over the past couple of weeks, she decided to be flattered. "Thanks, I will."

"Good. I'm heading up."

And with that, Pete left. Tessa shook her head. That was probably the longest conversation she'd had with Pete the whole time he'd been here. The good news was he didn't seem inclined to tell her brother what was going on since she'd asked him not to; she felt confident he wasn't going to turn into a gossip.

Tessa got to work herself. She'd chosen a green that was so pale it was almost white. Almost but not quite. The slight hint of color was accented by the wood and the new tile. But it was not so bold that it would turn off buyers. She tackled the ceiling first and was happy with the results. She then tackled the walls. She was going with a tin backsplash, and she thought the antique look suited the home. And once the painting was done, she had new light fixtures to install over the sink, over the main floor space off the kitchen, and one in the area where a table would go.

"This looks amazing. You'd never know how old this house is." Mason's voice echoed in the empty space.

Tessa started and was glad when she didn't slosh any paint. "What time is it?"

"Getting late. About eight, I think."

Tessa vaguely remembered Pete saying good night. She had just wanted to finish the last section of the wall before cleaning up. She'd lost track of time. The light was getting faint outside. She then smelled Chinese food coming from the bag he was holding. "Did you call?"

Mason brought the bag to the counter and set it down. "Yep, about an hour ago. When you didn't respond, I decided to grab Chinese. I hope you like it. Other than the fact that you don't like mushrooms, I don't know what you do like."

"It smells good. Probably can't go wrong with rice and stir fry. Let me wash up and get the paint out from under my nails."

Mason leaned back and admired the view. She wore another tight tank top and shorts. It seemed to be her uniform. The top was damp with sweat and plastered to her body like a second skin. And now he knew firsthand what that skin looked like.

Tessa saw the look in Mason's eyes and her stomach fluttered. But she was sweaty and probably didn't smell too good. She had wanted to shower and change before Mason got here, but since those plans were shot, she could at least take a shower before they ate. "Don't even think about what you're thinking. I'm going to take a quick shower."

Mason strolled over and settled his hands on her hips. "Too late. We can shower together."

Tessa tipped her head when Mason started nibbling his way down her neck but found the strength to pull away. "I'm serious. I need a shower."

Mason nipped the skin where her neck met her shoulder. "I'm serious too, but I suppose I can wait."

Tessa took the time to clean up the kitchen first. She cleaned up her brushes and closed up the paint. When she bagged up the roller brush and put it in the fridge, she saw Mason's look of confusion. "If you wrap the roller in plastic and put it in the fridge, it won't dry out, and you can use it again."

"Oh, handy trick. Can I help?"

"Nope, I don't want you to get paint on your uniform. And that's the last of it. I'll be just a few minutes."

Mason dished up the meal while Tessa was in the shower. He was tempted to disregard her wishes and join her anyway. He'd spent most of the day thinking about her. She intrigued him, she fascinated him, and she really turned him on. Tessa was a pretty little package that he wanted to unwrap again and again.

When Tessa stepped back into the kitchen, Mason had dinner laid out on the small kitchen table she'd shoved into the living room that morning. The windows had been delivered on time and were now residing in the other corner of the living room. Rexford was lying at Mason's feet.

Tessa took a seat across from Mason. "Thank you; this looks great."

"Good. There is this Chinese couple that moved into town. No one thought a Chinese restaurant would survive in such a small town, but the food is excellent, and they don't skimp on the ingredients. They've been here for probably three years now."

"Times do change." Tessa scooped up a bite and let the savory flavors melt on her tongue.

"Yes, they do. Who would have thought I'd be having dinner with little Tessa Harris?"

"And who would have thought I'd be having dinner with Chief Slade's son. Simon would be having a fit if he knew."

"You didn't tell him?"

Tessa scooped up another bite and just shook her head at him.

Mason set his fork down. "Are you going to tell him?"

Tessa heard an edge in his tone. "No. What would be the point? I'm a grown woman, Mason. I don't answer to Simon, nor does he answer to me."

Mason didn't like it, but he didn't want to start an argument. "No, I guess not."

Tessa felt bad about being so abrupt, but this was not something she would be telling Simon about. "Look, Mason, this is between you and me. And this is not something I normally do. It would just upset him, regardless of who you are."

Mason considered that. He knew from the moment he'd taken Tessa in his arms last night that it had been a while since she'd been with a man. She'd been shy and hesitant in her affection at first. She'd built confidence as they'd gone along, but there had been a little fear in her still. "How long had it been, Tessa?"

Tessa kept her head down. "I'd rather not say."

Mason took her hand. "It's not something to be ashamed of."

Tessa turned and laid a hand over his. "It has just been a really long time, and the last time it wasn't good."

Mason's hand tightened on hers. "Did he hurt you?"

Tessa looked him in the eyes. "Not the way you mean, no. But our relationship was an emotional roller coaster, and I guess you could say I just wasn't ready yet to try again."

Mason rose and pulled Tessa up with him. He pulled her body against his, savoring the soft curves pressed up against him. "But you were ready last night?"

Tessa's eyes drifted closed as Mason placed soft kisses on her neck, like he'd done in the kitchen earlier. "I don't know if I was ready or not, but I do know that I wanted to be with you."

Mason nibbled and whispered in her ear. "How about now?"

Tessa's knees buckled when his hands slid under her shirt and caressed her stomach. "I think I'm ready now."

Mason scooped her up and carried her off to the bedroom. Having been in it before, he already knew she was sleeping in a full-size bed. And though it was too small for him, he was just grateful it wasn't a twin. He laid her down and took his time stripping her.

This time was much like last night. But this time, Tessa let herself be caught up in the moment and didn't stop to think or analyze what she was doing. And when her body was limp and satisfied, she curled up against Mason, and his arm came around her, snuggling her up tight against his long, lean body.

"Are you asleep?" Mason's voice was a whisper in the darkness of the bedroom.

"No. I just wanted to enjoy this until you left."

Mason couldn't help but feel slight anger at the men who had been in her life before him. How many men had taken the time to just hold her? Or how many of those men simply took what they wanted and left? He had a feeling a rare few stuck around. But he wasn't going to be one of those men. "In that case, enjoy it until morning. I'm not going anywhere."

Tessa propped her chin on his chest. Her eyes were troubled. "But people will see you leave if you stay until morning. It's dark enough now, and Degrassi is an early-to-rise and early-to-bed type, but he'll notice your police SUV in my driveway. It will be all over town."

Mason rolled Tessa onto her back. "I'm not worried about it getting all over town. How long do you think you can keep this affair a secret?"

Tessa tried to scoot away, but his hips settled against hers, keeping her in place. "Secrets can be easy to keep if no one is looking. I don't want this to come back on you. You're too important."

Mason settled firmer against her. "And you're not important?"

Tessa wanted nothing more than to open her thighs to him, but she had to make him understand. "That's right. I'm not important. In the overall scheme of things, in the overall path of your life, I'm insignificant. But the damage my reputation can do to you is not a small thing. And when I'm gone, people will remember how you shacked up with Tessa Harris. And then they'll wonder what other bad decisions you've made and will make."

Mason got off her and stood, his anger so great, never mind that he once thought the same thing. "Is that what you think, Tessa? That people will think the worst of me simply because of my relationship with you?"

Tessa felt tears sting her eyes, but she held her ground. "Mason, I care about you. But this can't be anything more. You know that. It's best if people think you simply took the opportunity when it was handed to you, and that I'm just a brief convenience."

Mason yanked on his underwear and uniform pants. "I'd better go before I say something I'll regret."

Tessa grabbed the sheet and wrapped her body in it. She kept her eyes on him while he dressed.

Mason grabbed his shirt and buttoned it up, but left his belt unfastened. Instead of leaving, he came and sat next to her on the bed, unable to hold his tongue. "You're not a convenience, Tessa. As a matter of fact, you're quite the opposite. But I do what I want with who I want. And I think this is more about you being ashamed of the fact that you stooped so low as to have sex with a cop than it is anything else. You're so ashamed you won't tell your brother about me. But I don't feel like I've stooped too low by sleeping with you, and I don't care who knows. You're smart, you're witty, and when you're not feeling threatened, really rather sweet. But until you can admit to me and to everyone else that you want me more than you want to protect yourself, then we shouldn't be doing this. Because I don't think this is about me; I think it's about you. And it seems to me you care more about what your family would think if they knew you slept with me than what other people might think about the fact that I slept with you."

Tessa wasn't sure how he had turned this around on her, but he was wrong. He was all that was good and right in the world. She was not. And she was foolish for thinking she could have a taste of the world he lived in without her life tainting his. But instead of arguing with him, she pulled the sheet higher. "Good night, Mason."

Mason cursed under his breath. "Fine, have it your way. Good night, Tessa."

Tessa listened in the silence as the SUV started and Mason left. She curled up on her side. She felt a tear trickle onto the pillow. She closed her eyes until she felt something cold and wet on her face. She opened her eyes, and Rexford had his paws on the bed, his head lying near hers. She scooted back and patted the bed. Rexford didn't need a second invitation. He snuggled up against her and went to sleep.

Tessa sniffled and wiped her tears away with the back of her arm. Crying wasn't going to fix anything, and well she knew it. She laid a hand on Rexford and petted his silky fur. It was almost dawn when her eyes finally drifted closed.

* * *

Tessa woke, startled when Rexford was scratching at her bedroom door, a low whine emitting from his throat. She stumbled from the bed and let him out. When he then scratched and whined at the front door, she took a moment to pull on her robe. It was barely light out and too early for Rexford to demand to go outside. When she opened the front door, Rexford barked and started sniffing around her porch and then the yard. He seemed to be following a path into the woods. Feeling scared, she called him back. He didn't look too happy about it, but he obeyed.

Tessa looked around, but she didn't see anyone. And she didn't see any damage to her house or Mason's car. But she couldn't help but feel like someone was out there. She looked down at Rexford. "Guess it's too bad I was a jerk and ran Mason off last night. I wouldn't mind if he were here right now."

Rexford whined at her in what she took as agreement. She went inside and pulled on some clothes and a pair of shoes. When she took Rexford back outside, he went about his normal business. Tessa walked the perimeter of the house, looking for signs of an intruder. When she got a few feet from the house toward the trees, she saw a few footprints in the grass where it looked like someone had dug in his feet. Perhaps as he was running away from Rexford's keen nose. She shuddered, took a quick look around, lost her courage, and ran back to the house.

She wasn't hungry, but she forced herself to eat a light

breakfast. She took her time in the shower and primping a bit for her first day on the job. She was dressed and going through paint samples when Pete arrived. He came in for his customary two cups of coffee before heading back outside. Rexford went with him, and Tessa figured having the dog on guard would keep any other intruders away.

When her phone rang around seven, she fetched her phone thinking it might be Simon calling before his shift. He hadn't called her in a couple of days, so he was due to check in. And though she thought he was checking up on her more than the house, she didn't mind his frequent calls. But it wasn't Simon. Her breath hitched when she saw Mason's number. She almost answered it before she set it back down. She had to leave for work, and she didn't want to talk to him. When a few moments later her phone beeped to tell her she had a voicemail, she didn't have the courage to listen to it. Instead, she tossed the phone in her bag and grabbed the keys to Mason's car. She waved at Pete and headed off to Laine's shop.

This time, Tessa parked closer to the shop. She wanted to be able to see the car. She still felt guilty about borrowing Mason's car, even more so since their fight last night, but she was grateful anyway. Laine was unlocking the front door of the shop as Tessa made her way over.

Laine looked around, then focused on Tessa. "Mason loaned you his car?"

Trust that to be the first thing out of Laine's mouth. "Yes. He said he didn't drive it much and felt better if I had transportation."

Laine waved Tessa inside and locked the door behind

them, keeping the blinds closed. "Mason always did have a soft streak in him. I think it would surprise people how nice he is, given his profession and all. He has to be tough and appear intimidating, you know, not easily moved. But he's really a sweetie."

Tessa wouldn't ever call Mason a "sweetie," but he did have a soft streak in him. Part of her wondered if he didn't enjoy helping damsels in distress. Of course, last night he hadn't been soft. When he'd left, he'd been angry, and there had been a hard streak in him. She had yet to listen to his voicemail, afraid she would hear the same anger in his voice that had been there last night.

Laine waved a hand in front of Tessa's face. "Are you okay? You drifted off."

Tessa came back to the present. "Sorry. Rexford woke me up a little too early this morning."

Laine waved for Tessa to follow her into the back, where she put on a fresh pot of coffee. "Dad said Rexford was watching your house. Any more signs of intruders?"

Tessa didn't even hesitate in her lie. "It's been quiet. No more spray paint or messages. Whoever it is probably got bored."

"That's good. At Sunday dinner last weekend, Mason was frustrated that he had no leads on who vandalized the property. Dad just said sometimes cases can't be solved when people don't want to talk. Mason wasn't too happy with that, but he agreed he was probably never going to find the guy who did it. It's too bad. He should pay for what he did."

Tessa wasn't going to debate the point. Sometimes

innocent people suffered for those who committed the crimes. Better to never know than to point the finger at the wrong person. And in a town full of suspects and people who wouldn't come to her aid if she were on fire, she had already given up any hope of finding the culprit.

"Coffee? You look like you could use it." Laine handed Tessa a cup already doctored with cream and sugar. She took a sip and ignored the too-sweet taste.

"Thanks. So what can I do?"

Laine leaned against the counter and sipped her coffee. "You can tell me what's up between you and my brother. I heard a rumor you had dinner at Bianchi's. Then I heard you were at his house."

Tessa held the cup between her suddenly cold hands. "Yes, we had dinner. And yes, I was at his house. But I was there because I needed to pick up the car."

"Look, I know it's none of my business, but I love Mason. And I like you. I've been hoping you'd tell me you're having the romance of the century."

Tessa set the cup down. "Actually, we got into a fight, and he stormed out. He came by my place with Chinese food last night; we fought, and he left. Sorry, not the romance of the century."

Laine's eyes lit up. "What did you fight about?"

Tessa was confused by the short-lived flash of glee that lit Laine's eyes. "You're supposed to be angry and tell me I'd better not hurt your brother."

Laine shrugged. "Sorry, Mason and I used to fight like cats and dogs. Probably because we're so much alike. We used to go a few rounds, though we've mellowed as we've gotten older. But Mason usually was the one to apologize. And I usually got some kind of favor or trinket from him. He'd do a couple of my chores or drive me to my friend's house or buy me my favorite ice cream. When I fight with Russell, I can usually extract a favor from him, usually of a more intimate nature."

Tessa felt her cheeks heat. "I don't think I'm in any kind of position to demand a favor from him. I sort of started it, or at least, it was my fault that he was mad."

Laine rinsed their cups and turned back to Tessa. "Then offer him a favor. Should do wonders to soften him up. But we'd better motivate and get the shop open."

Tessa let Laine guide her through the morning routine, helped customers, and ran the register. She even got to meet a few of the women who supplied Laine's shop. Laine left her to add the discreet price tags to the new inventory. The day flew by.

"Tomorrow morning we'll put out the new pieces. Saturdays are the busiest days for foot traffic, so I like to have something new in the windows to grab people's attention. If you want to hang around, we can go out to dinner tomorrow. Russell is going to be out of town, and I hate going home to a lonely house."

"Sounds great." And it gave her an excuse to not go home herself. Her phone wasn't far from her mind.

"Great."

"Hey Laine, is there somewhere in town where I can get a few new blouses and slacks? Nothing fancy."

Laine wrote the name of a small shop a couple of streets over. "You tell Mauve, the owner, I sent you. She'll see you get a good deal."

"Thanks. See you tomorrow."

Laine waved her off and went back to her customers.

Tessa drove the car a few blocks over and peeked in the shop window. She hated to spend any of her money, but she was going to need a couple more pieces of clothing if she was going to work in Laine's shop. The customers had all been dressed well, though casually. Laine was wearing a bright pink pencil skirt and a printed blouse. Tessa's jeans, though a dark wash, were too casual. And the blouse she'd worn was the only one she had.

Tessa tried not to cringe at the price tags too much. She quickly made her way to the sales rack.

"Can I help you?" A rather robust brunette came over.

Tessa gave the woman a friendly smile. "I'm a friend of Laine's. She sent me over and said you'd have some clothes suitable for working in her shop."

"Any friend of Laine's and all that. I'm Mauve."

Tessa shook her hand, one that was covered in a multitude of shiny rings and nails painted with a dark orange polish. "Tessa."

"I think I've got some things you'll love."

Tessa let the woman pick out a few items and tried them on. The woman certainly knew what she was doing. The cut of the blouses accentuated her narrow waist and fit well across her breasts. With the muscles she had in her back, shoulders, and arms from physical labor, sometimes clothes tended to be too tight at the top and loose at the waist. But these fit just right. The slacks Mauve chose fit her hips and waist, and the black pencil skirt, much like the pink one Laine wore, fit her just as well.

Tessa gathered the clothes and stepped out of the room. "These are all very lovely, but I can't afford all this. I'll take the black slacks and the black skirt. And these two tops."

Mauve took the clothes Tessa held out to put back. She took out the dress she'd had Tessa try on. "I'm guessing this fits you like a glove. No man you might want to wear this for?"

Tessa eyed the navy blue dress with envious eyes. She had tried on the dress, thinking it would be rather plain, but the dress had been beautiful on her. It had accentuated her shoulders, nipped at the waist, and draped over her hips in a beautiful layered design. Though dark navy, the fabric had a glossy sheen to it that made it look expensive. She had briefly imagined wearing it to dinner with Mason. But she doubted there would be another dinner with Mason.

"I'll give you the friends and family discount. Come on."

Tessa followed Mauve to the register. She rang up the four items Tessa had chosen and gave her the total. Relieved it wasn't as much as she feared, she couldn't help but ask how much the dress would be. When Mauve quoted a price, Tessa protested. "I know the dress costs more than that."

Mauve rang up the dress and printed out a new receipt. "I think I saw that blouse you're wearing in a catalog ten years ago. And those jeans have seen better days. I've been where you are now. It's nice to pay it forward. And one day, you can do the same for someone else."

Tessa gaped at the woman as she blindly tucked her

card into her pocket. "Pay it forward?"

"Yes. See, I do something nice for you, and then you do something nice for someone else. And then you tell that person to do something nice for someone else. Makes the world a better place."

"Laine didn't call you before I came, did she?"

Mauve immediately said no. "You just tell Laine I appreciate the referral, and if anyone asks you where you got your new clothes, you tell them you got them here."

Tessa tucked her receipt in her bag. "I certainly will. And thank you."

Mauve waved that off. "You just see that you wear that dress for a special occasion. And come on back."

Tessa promised to do just that. She slid into Mason's car, tucking the garments on the floor of the passenger seat. Before she started the engine, she got the feeling she was being watched. She glanced around but didn't see anyone who stood out. People were walking along the pathways outside the shops, but no one was looking her way. Feeling paranoid, she headed back home.

Chapter Eleven

For her second day at Laine's, Tessa decided to wear the black pencil skirt and the pleated teal blouse. The cute pleats ran vertically down the front and had discrete ruffles on the sleeves and hem. Her sandals were black and simple enough to wear with her new clothes. As soon as she'd gotten home, she'd run a load of laundry and laid her new outfit out. It had been so long since she'd owned anything half as nice. She owed Mauve for this, and she promised herself that she would pay it forward to as many people as she could, as soon as she could. And for good measure, Tessa took a few minutes to put a little makeup on before she bid Pete good morning and left.

Tessa would have felt lighthearted and ready for the day had Mason not left her another voicemail that morning. She had yet to get the nerve to listen to his first one. She bet his second one was less pleasant than the first. But she pasted a smile on her face when she walked into Laine's shop.

"I see Mauve hooked you up. You look amazing." Laine took Tessa's hands and looked her over.

"Yes, she did. I can't thank you or her enough."

Laine waved her off, much as Mauve had. "You're going to earn your money today, and we'd better get cracking. You take the box on the left and put those items in the left window. I've got the right."

Tessa was in her element as she arranged the new items in the front window. It was a lot like staging a house. The trick was to make everything look like it was purposely left there and not cluttered.

"I think I'm putting you in charge of window displays next Saturday. You made that look effortless." Laine opened the shades and unlocked the doors.

Tessa blushed a bit and finished stocking the last of the items Laine had taken out of the back room. Once that was done, she barely had time to take a small break. The shop was busy all day, mostly window shoppers, but Laine had a gleam in her eye that told Tessa sales were going well. With the prices Laine charged, Tessa couldn't help but wonder what Laine paid for the items.

Things lulled around noon, but only slightly. Tessa took a moment to run to the bathroom and freshen her makeup. When she came back out, Laine was sitting behind the counter talking on the phone. She briefly heard her name and took a small step back.

Laine saw her and waved her over. When Tessa hesitated, Laine waved a little more forcefully. "Look, Mason, I don't know what you want me to say. Tessa is here; she's working. And if she wanted to talk to you, she'd call you. Yeah, yeah, you can chew me out at Sunday dinner. It'll be the last one before Mom and Dad leave for their trip. Bye, Mason."

Tessa rested her hands on the counter. She could feel heat crawling up her cheeks. "I take it he was checking up on me."

Laine set the phone under the counter. "He wanted to make sure you were okay. He says you haven't returned his messages, and he's left you three of them."

"I guess I should call him later."

Laine jumped off her stool. "Call him tomorrow. Let him stew. We're going to finish up the day, then we're having ladies' night."

Since lady's night sounded better than a confrontation with Mason, she agreed to call him tomorrow.

"One more thing, I was thinking you should help sell the merchandise." Laine headed toward the case that held the jewelry.

Tessa slowly followed. "Isn't that what I've been doing?"

"Yes, but we can do better." Laine lifted the crystal necklace that Tessa had admired on her first day in the shop.

Tessa balked when Laine went to put it on her. "I can't wear that."

Laine pushed her hands away and put the oversized chain over Tessa's head and lifted her hair out of the way. "And I think one of the silver rings too. I'd say earrings, but we don't want them to overpower the necklace."

Tessa glanced at the oversized earrings Laine was wearing. "I take it those earrings are inventory."

"I wear the perfume, I light the candles, wear the jewelry, and the accessories. I love the belts that one of my vendors makes. The buckles are one of a kind."

Tessa stood still when Laine slipped a pretty braided ring on her finger, then grabbed a nearby glass bottle. Tessa protested. "I don't like perfume. Makes me sneeze."

Laine set the bottle down that she was going to spritz Tessa with. "Okay. The necklace and ring it is. But you should try the hand cream. It's fabulous."

When Tessa wasn't busy, she found herself fussing with the necklace. It sparkled like a diamond. But she had seen the price tag, and she had already bought clothes. There was no way she could justify the necklace.

"I can put it in the back for you. I could take the cost out of your paycheck in installments."

Tessa sighed and released the chain. "Thanks, Laine, but it's still too rich for me."

"All right, I'll stop. Tomorrow, I think you should wear the topaz bracelet. I've been trying to sell that thing for a month. Maybe if someone sees it on, they'll realize what a gem it is."

Tessa glanced at the bracelet in question. The stones were huge and pretty gaudy, in her opinion. "I think Mauve would wear it."

Laine considered that for a moment. "You know, you could be right."

Tessa shook her head at her friend when Laine went to the phone and called Mauve.

Laine came back over after ringing up a couple of customers. "Mauve is going to join us for dinner. She's going to stop by after she closes up and come look at the bracelet."

The rest of the afternoon and evening went by quickly. Tessa's feet hurt by the time the store closed, but it was a good feeling. And though she wouldn't want to make retail a permanent job, she could see why Laine liked it so much. In her shop, people left with a mostly one-of-a-kind item to commemorate their trip. Laine told her it was perfect because even if someone decided they didn't want the item, or they had a complaint, they were too far away to come back and tell her about it.

Laine was positively gleeful when Mauve bought the bracelet. While Mauve admired it on her wrist, Laine put her arm around Tessa's shoulder. "I owe you a drink for that. Come on, happy hour calls."

Tessa grabbed her bag. She slipped off the silver ring and reluctantly pulled the necklace off and hung it back up on the display rack.

"Come on, ladies. I'm single and ready to mingle." Mauve was the first one out the door.

Tessa waited while Laine locked up. "Whose car?"

Laine ended up being the one to drive. Tessa wasn't comfortable driving Mason's car around town, and Mauve's car was back at her shop.

Dinner was a raucous affair. Mauve helped herself to a couple of drinks before their meal came. Tessa sipped some fruity drink Laine had ordered for her, and Laine had a taste for rum punch. They dined at a seafood place before heading to a local hot spot.

Tessa declined another drink, as did Laine. But Mauve had another and found herself a few men to dance with.

Laine took a drink of her sparkling water. "I had no idea Mauve could move like that."

Tessa tapped her foot to the music. "I didn't know anyone could move like that."

"Since neither of us is single, do you want to dance with me?"

Tessa's stomach clenched at the single comment. Laine had a point; she didn't feel single. "I'm probably rusty."

"Russell hates to dance, so I'm rusty too. We'll get Mauve to show us her moves."

Between Tessa and Laine, they managed to figure out the dance moves. Mauve was mostly occupied for the rest of the night. Tessa was breathless and laughing by the time the three women headed back to Laine's car.

Laine drove them back to Mauve's. She glanced at the woman sprawled in the back seat. "I think it's going to take both of us to get her inside. She lives above the shop, and those stairs will be tricky."

Tessa was able to rouse Mauve and get her out of the back seat. She ducked her head when Mauve went to plant a wet kiss on her mouth.

"I just love you guys so much." Mauve draped herself over both women's shoulders.

Laine wasn't as lucky to duck Mauve's kiss and ended up with a wet lipstick kiss on her cheek. "We love you too, Mauve. Just pay attention to the stairs."

Between Tessa and Laine, they got Mauve in bed. Tessa pulled the very tall heels off Mauve's feet, while Laine got her out of her jacket.

Laine took a step back. "I don't know that we should leave her alone. She's pretty out of it."

Tessa followed Laine out of Mauve's bedroom. "I need to get home; Rexford will need to go out."

"I'll drive you back to your car. She'll be fine for a few."

"No, it's fine. Stay with Mauve. Mason's car is just down the street from your shop and it's just a block over. And there are still plenty of people out and about. I'll be fine."

Laine looked skeptical. "Are you sure? I don't think you should walk back alone."

Tessa grabbed her bag and dug out her keys. "It's only ten. People are just getting started. I'll be fine. Take care of your friend."

"All right. Be careful and stay on the main streets. I'm going to call Russell and make him wish he were home."

"Okay, I'll see you tomorrow."

"Make it nine. I'm going to have to rush home in the morning to shower and change before we open."

"Nine it is. See you."

"Bye, Tessa. Be careful."

Tessa waved and closed the front door behind her. Her feet now really hurt from dancing, but the walk would help clear her head. She wasn't drunk, and she wasn't worried about driving home, but the club had been stuffy, and the fresh air would do her good.

The streets were still filled with people heading to restaurants and clubs. The resort town seemed to have a lively Saturday night. A couple of faces she thought she recognized from Laine's shop and the restaurant. She crossed the first road and turned down toward where the car was parked. The street Laine's shop was on had fewer people, but there were still a few people about. The shops were dark now, closed up for the night. In the distance, she could see lights from boats docked at the lake, many of them with twinkly lights adorning them.

Tessa saw Mason's car and breathed a sigh of relief. Her feet were now loudly protesting the workout she'd given them today. She passed the bookstore and a pottery shop before she thought she heard something behind her. She clutched her bag tighter to her side and held her keys like a weapon. She stopped and listened but didn't hear anything. She then chastised herself for letting her imagination get the better of her. Since the vandals had started showing up, she'd been on high alert.

She got past the souvenir shop when she heard another rustle. The car was just a block away. She hurried her steps and glanced around to see if anyone else was nearby. The street was deserted, and she quickened her pace. She was within a few feet of the car when she was slammed from behind. She hit the ground hard enough to knock the breath out of her and scrape her knees badly. She tried to scream, but her throat was closed off when a scarf came around her neck and tightened.

She clawed at her neck, choking and wheezing. She tried to thrash, but what she thought was a knee jammed into her back and pressed her into the ground.

"I warned you, Tessa. I told you to leave. You should have left. We don't want you here."

It was hard to hear the voice as the blood rushed to her head, her heart pounding. She felt the scarf loosen, but the knee was still in her back. She coughed as air tried to work its way past her bruised airway but couldn't quite take in a full breath. She tried to fight her attacker when he released her, but she could only struggle as she tried to get off the ground. She felt pain explode in her back and then a moment later in her ribs. She felt herself rolled onto her back.

"I told you, Tessa. Why didn't you listen?"

Tessa heard the voice, but it sounded like it was coming from a distance. It was odd, too, because the voice almost sounded like it was crying. In the dark of the street, she could see her attacker was male, but he wore a black ski mask. The white of his eyes stood out in contrast to the mask, and in them were not only tears but a fury she couldn't understand. She saw his fist coming at her, and she vaguely noted it was encased in a white glove. Then the man was on her, pinning her again. He hit her once, then twice. His words were no longer making sense, and his voice was fading. Confused and in pain, Tessa mercifully passed out as she once again struggled for breath.

* * *

Mason woke the next morning and called Tessa. He cursed when he got her voicemail again, but this time he did not leave a message. He'd had enough of this. It was Sunday, and he was on call, but so long as no one needed him, his day was free. He wasn't expected at his parents' house until three. He was going over to Tessa's and hashing this out. He'd been a jerk; he knew he'd been a jerk. Tessa deserved better from him than his temper. He'd let his anger get the better of him. His first message had been a lengthy apology, but he couldn't remember half of what he'd said to her because he'd not slept. It was amazing how clear things looked in the middle of the night when a man lay alone in his bed, when he could have been in bed with a beautiful woman had he not screwed things up.

His second message was much like the first. He apologized again and asked her to please call him. Fridays and Saturdays were busy for him, and he wouldn't be able to stop by, but he wanted to at least hear her voice and hear her say that she forgave him.

He was pretty sure his third message was not so nice. His temper once again got the better of him and he'd accused her of being childish. His fourth message had been another apology for calling her a child. His fifth and last message just said to call when she had cooled off.

Mason glanced over at the clock, and it was after seven. He knew Tessa was an early riser, earlier than he was outside of work, and no doubt she was already dressed and had eaten. She was probably on her way to Laine's shop. He figured he had two options: he could sit around and wait until she got off work, or he could go to Laine's shop and persuade Tessa to join him for lunch. He figured if he left now, he might meet Tessa there before the shop opened at nine.

Happy with that plan of action, Mason grabbed a pair of jeans and a pullover out of his closet. He'd already showered and shaved, so all that was left was to brush his teeth. He headed to his bath and grabbed his electric toothbrush. But before he could turn it on, his phone rang. Cursing and hoping at the same time that the call was just a friend and not work, he went and grabbed his cell. When he saw the number, he was left with just cursing.

Mason punched the call button. "Chief Slade."

"Hi, Chief. It's Alicia."

"What can I do for you, Deputy Lawrence?" Mason took the phone with him back to the bathroom and squeezed a glob of toothpaste onto his brush.

"We had a call come in this morning about a missing person. Normally, I wouldn't bother you and handle it myself, but I think you might want to know this time."

Mason felt his stomach tighten. Alicia Lawrence was his most trusted and reliable deputy. She wouldn't be calling him for something minor, even a missing person, unless it was a kid. "Is it someone in my family?"

"Oh, no, sir. Nothing like that. But we got a call this morning from a Pete Abernathy. He claims Tessa Harris is missing. Given what's been going on, I figured you'd want to handle it. But I can take care of it."

The knot in Mason's stomach tightened. "No, tell him I'll be right there."

Mason hung up the phone and tried to calm his racing heart. He knew better than most that most times everything turned out fine, and that the person wasn't really missing. He couldn't count the number of times he'd had calls like that, and it turned out that the person was just running late or had made different plans and hadn't shared. Tessa had probably just left early for work; that's all.

Mason took the time to brush his teeth but didn't bother to change into his uniform. Instead, he grabbed his badge, ID, gun, and holster. As a last thought, he grabbed a suit jacket. He didn't turn on his sirens on the way to Tessa's, but he broke some traffic laws.

When he pulled into the driveway, he only saw Pete's truck. His car was nowhere to be seen.

Pete stepped off the porch and met Mason halfway between the house and SUV. "Thank you for coming. When I got here this morning, your car was missing. And Rexford was whining at the door. So I went into the house looking for Tessa, but she wasn't here. I called her but just got her voicemail. I called the police station because I didn't know your number. I take it she isn't with you."

Mason patted Rexford, who had trotted over to see him as soon as he'd stepped from the SUV. "No, I haven't seen her for a couple of days."

Pete folded his arms across his chest. "I didn't want to call Simon and put him in a panic for no reason, but in the time I've been here, Tessa hasn't disappeared like this. And if she isn't with you, then she's missing."

Mason went past Pete and inside. He went to her bedroom. All her clothes and personal items were still there. Same with the bathroom. He looked around the place but didn't see a note or anything saying she was out.

Pete had followed Mason inside. "I did the same thing. Her things are still here. And she wouldn't bail on her brother. So what's next?"

Mason tried to use logic instead of emotion. "The next stop is Laine's shop. That's where she should be now, or at least on her way there now. Give me your number and I'll call you if I hear anything."

Once he had Pete's number, Mason ran back to his SUV and headed to Laine's. It was after eight when he got there. He banged on the door but didn't get an answer. He pulled up Laine's number and called her.

"This had better be good, big brother."

"Laine, have you seen Tessa?"

Laine yawned in his ear. "I was with her last night. We had dinner and went dancing. We're meeting at the shop at nine. I guess I should thank you for waking me. I need to get home and change."

Mason cursed. "Laine, listen carefully. I can't find Tessa. Her contractor said she didn't come home last night. What time did you see her? Where was the last place you saw her?"

Laine's voice came over clearly this time. She gave him a brief rundown of their night. "We had Mauve, a shopkeeper a couple of blocks from my shop, join us. She was pretty drunk, so we took her home. I didn't want to leave Mauve, and Tessa said she had to get home and let Rexford out. That was probably about ten last night. She insisted she was fine to walk back to the car. I told her okay but to be careful and to come in at nine, so I'd have time to get home and change before heading to the shop. What happened, Mason?"

"I don't know. That's what I'm trying to find out. Where did she park the car?"

"Just two blocks down. You can probably see it from my shop door if it's still there."

Mason took a deep breath and scanned the street. He didn't see the car. Its absence made the knot in his stomach tighter. "I don't see it. Was she sober when she left you?"

"Yes, she only had one drink before dinner. After that, she and I switched to water. We both have to work today."

Mason's next call would be to the local police. "Okay, Laine. Please come to the shop as soon as you can and call me if Tessa shows up."

"On my way."

Mason climbed into his SUV. "Can you tell me what she was wearing?"

Laine's soft tears came over the line. "She was wearing a teal green blouse with pleats and ruffles. And she had on a black pencil skirt. It was a new outfit she bought at Mauve's. And then she had black sandals, I think. And her shoulder bag."

"Thanks, Laine. I'll be in touch." Mason hung up before Laine could say anything else. He dialed the local police. They didn't have anyone by that name in custody, nor had any traffic accidents been reported under that name. He reached out to the county with the same answer.

Desperate, he dialed Tessa's number again. Still no answer. In a normal investigation, he'd reach out to her friends and family, except they didn't live here. He supposed he could make a visit to Degrassi's and see if he'd seen her, but he wouldn't trust the old man's answers. But knowing it was something that had to be done, he called Deputy Lawrence back and had her start talking to the neighbors.

With nothing else to do, he headed back to Laine's shop. It was almost nine. As he was walking up to the shop door, Laine opened it for him.

"No Tessa?" Laine hugged Mason tightly to her.

"No Tessa. I'm going to have Officer Lawrence talk to her neighbors. Right now she's not answering her phone. I also had her put out a BOLO for my car. At this point, all I can do is wait to see if she shows up or if my car turns up."

Laine went and fixed coffee, but neither of them were in the mood.

Mason's phone rang again. The number was unknown. "Chief Slade."

"This is Simon Harris. Where is my sister?"

Mason closed his eyes for a second. He guessed Pete had finally called Tessa's brother. "We're looking for her. I've talked to the last person known to have seen her, and I've put out a 'be on the lookout' for her vehicle. And I've been in touch with the local and county police. She's not turned up."

Simon's voice was angry as it came over the line. "I just got an earful from Pete about vandals destroying property, a vandal coming back but being chased off, a police dog guarding the house, Tessa getting a job, and you dating my sister. You want to explain any of that to me?"

Mason tried to speak calmly and professionally, but it wasn't easy. "Look, Simon, your sister didn't want to report the vandalism, but I had her fill out a report anyway. Unfortunately, I couldn't find the culprit. And yes, I drove her home from the town fair and chased off the vandal as he was making a second attempt. I chased him but had no luck apprehending him. And your sister got a job, which is none of my business, though it is at my sister's shop. And my dad's dog is watching the house in case the vandal comes back. He's a retired police dog. And yes, I guess you can say I'm dating your sister. We had dinner a couple of times. But I haven't seen her since Thursday, and I'm doing everything I can to find her."

"I'm on a flight headed your way, but I won't get there until late afternoon. The earliest arrival is five. Find her."

Mason didn't bother to be offended when Simon hung up on him. Truth was, he had a bad feeling, and usually, his bad feelings were right.

Laine hugged Mason from behind. "I take it that was Tessa's brother."

"He's on his way. I imagine the flight from Indiana is a few hours. I can't deal with him right now. I'm going to go back to the office and start calling hospitals and checking in with other local police. Someone has to have seen her."

"I'll call if she shows." Laine released Mason.

"Let Mom and Dad know what's going on."

"I will. Be careful, Mason."

Mason kissed the top of his sister's head and left. Though there wasn't a lot he could do, he needed to do something, even if it included calling in every favor owed to him.

Chapter Twelve

Mason was back at the station when Alicia popped into his office. "No one in town has seen her. But I just got a hit on your car. It was just signed into evidence. You might want to call Chief Peterson. His department impounded it for evidence. The guy I talked to wouldn't tell me why."

Mason gathered his stuff and headed out of town. Chief Peterson had the distinction of being Chief of Police for Willow Lake. Mason knew the man well and had pitched in from time to time when help was needed. In small towns, you got to know your neighbors well. Instead of calling, Mason headed to the Willow Lake Police Department.

When he got there, the lobby was a flurry of activity. He flagged down one of the cops he recognized and asked where Peterson was. The man waved him to Peterson's office.

Mason knocked on the door but peeked his head in. When Peterson waved him in, he closed the door behind him.

Chief Calvin Peterson was a small man, only five-five, with graying hair and a belly that he claimed was the result of his wife's fantastic cooking. The locals loved him, and he had a sharp mind. So while not an intimidating presence, Mason knew not to overstep his boundaries.

"Hi, Mason, what can I do for you?"

"A friend of mine is missing. My deputy told me that your department logged her car, my car actually, into evidence this morning. I'm hoping you can tell me where she is or if you've seen her."

Calvin nodded and knew exactly what he was talking about. "A blonde woman? Petite?"

Mason wished he could feel relieved but couldn't. "Yes. Her name is Tessa Harris. A friend of hers reported her missing this morning. I've been trying to locate her."

Calvin pulled up a screen on his computer. "You said she's a friend of yours too?"

"Yes. I loaned her my car. She was out with my sister last night. She was supposedly walking back to the car the last time anyone saw her."

"The initial report filed says we have a Jane Doe. There was no ID on her. She was admitted to the county hospital after being found battered and unresponsive. I just got an updated report with a name, Tessa Harris."

Mason hopped to his feet and started to head quickly for the door.

Calvin stopped him. "I'm coming with you. This is not your jurisdiction or your case. And you can fill me in on the details I can see you're hiding from me."

Mason didn't stop as he headed out to the SUV, Calvin right behind him. "There had been a series of incidents, just vandalism. But it's a bit of a stretch to imagine that there is no link between her vandal and her attacker."

Calvin climbed into the passenger seat and didn't even get a chance to buckle up before Mason tore out of the parking lot. "She a local?"

"No. Or she was when she was young but moved away. She's back in town fixing up her aunt's house to be sold."

Calvin's mind was in high gear. "Harris, huh? Why does that sound familiar?"

Mason knew Calvin was only a little younger than his dad. He probably remembered the Harris case. "Her father, Randy Harris, was arrested and convicted of arson and insurance fraud."

"That's right. No one was sad to see him locked up. So the daughter? Troublemaker?"

"No, the opposite."

"Mmm. Well, I guess I'll get to see for myself, so long as we don't get arrested for speeding."

Mason's gaze dropped to the speedometer and slightly lifted his foot.

Calvin was very matter-of-fact when he spoke again. "I'm guessing it's a good thing this didn't happen in your jurisdiction. You seem a little too close to her to handle the case."

Mason didn't deny Calvin's claim. But he wasn't going to sit on the sidelines, and he was sure Calvin already knew that.

They checked in at reception. Calvin flashed his badge and explained the situation. They were sent up to the fifth floor.

Calvin kept his voice soft as he spoke to the nurse at the desk.

Mason asked the only question he had. "Is she going to be okay?"

The nurse whose tag said "Poppy" asked, "Friend or family?"

"Friend. And cop. Her brother is on his way, but he's coming from Indiana. He won't be here for a couple more hours at the earliest."

"She's been hurt pretty bad. I can't go into the details with you since you're not family, but she should be downgraded this afternoon. You two can go in and see her, but she's on pain medication and something to help her sleep, so she's not been awake much. And when she is awake, she has been very uncooperative. All we got out of her was that her name was Tessa, and she wants to leave."

Mason found he could smile after all. "That sounds like Tessa."

Calvin let Mason go in alone and remained in the hall with the nurse. Mason's breath caught when he got a good look at her. Her face was bruised and swollen, and there was a small bandage on her left cheek. As he got closer, he could see bruising around her neck. There were scrapes on her arms, and her left arm was in a cast. From her chest down, her body was covered with a blanket. Monitors were beeping beside the bed. She had a catheter, but thankfully no breathing tube or anything else designed to keep her alive when her body couldn't do it on its own.

Mason took her hand, careful not to disturb the IV, and bent to kiss it. He didn't dare touch her anywhere else. Until he knew the extent of her injuries, he didn't want to do anything to hurt her.

A short while later, Calvin came up behind him. "I just got off the phone with Simon Harris. He'll be here in a couple of hours. Don't expect a warm welcome."

Mason set Tessa's hand down, keeping her palm in his hand. "I don't expect one. But hopefully, we can at least get a full report from her doctor."

"I don't imagine we'll be able to take her statement today. I'll have my deputy come back tomorrow. I checked, and the crime scene photos have been uploaded. I've had them sent to your inbox."

Mason felt relieved that he wasn't going to have to ask or fight the chief. "I owe you."

"The way I see it, most likely the perp is from your town, if the theory is that your vandal became violent. You'll know them better than me. We'll run point on the assault but will give you full access. I'm going to head out. One of my men is picking me up."

Mason nodded gratefully that Calvin was going to keep him in the loop and got his own ride back to the station. "I'll be in touch."

Calvin gave him a small salute and left.

Mason spent the next two hours with Tessa, willing her to open her eyes. But her lashes remained resting on her swollen cheek while Mason watched her breathing. He had pulled up a chair so he could sit near her, and he would hopefully be the first thing she saw when she woke up.

Mason was dozing when a voice startled him. The man in the doorway barely noticed him as he kept his eyes on Tessa. No doubt this was Simon. He'd changed since he was a kid, more so than Tessa had. He was taller, leaner, but well-groomed, and he wore nice clothing. His blond hair, the same shade as Tessa's, was disheveled. His blue eyes, also the same shade as Tessa's, held more than a hint of pain and anger.

Simon stopped in his tracks when he saw Mason. He'd been feeling unreasonable anger at the man since Pete had told him Tessa was missing. Pete had assured him Mason had been nothing but kind and polite to Tessa, but it didn't matter. Simon wanted to hit something, someone, and old animosity flared as he saw his childhood nemesis sitting with his sister.

Mason saw the anger in Simon's eyes and couldn't say he blamed him. But this was not the time or the place. His voice was soft when he spoke. "The nurse won't tell me much. I'm hoping you can fill me in."

Simon ignored him and went to his sister's side. His finger trailed across the cast on her arm, while his eyes assessed what he saw. "Who did this to her?"

Mason stepped away from the bed when Simon came around the other side. "I don't know. Yet. The official investigation will be coming out of Willow Lake's department. You'll want to ask for Chief Peterson. But I'll find him."

"Yeah, right. I'm supposed to believe that." Simon's touch was light, but he continued his examination of his sister.

"Despite what was, Simon, I promise I will find him."

Simon grabbed at his neck where his stethoscope would normally be and cursed when it wasn't there. "I need to find her doctor."

Mason didn't ask if he could follow; he simply did.

It took a few minutes, but Tessa's doctor, Dr. Howell,

came into the waiting room. Mason stood back while the two men shook hands.

"Your sister was brought in and admitted. At first, we feared brain swelling. She was also unconscious at first. When she is awake, she is not very cooperative. I can say she has a concussion, but so far, no brain swelling. She has a broken wrist, cracked and bruised ribs, a bruised trachea, thankfully not crushed, and an orbital bone fracture on top of the bruising and abrasions. It looks like she won't need surgery to fix that. The abrasions on her cheek are superficial but needed to be cleaned thoroughly and bandaged."

Simon rubbed a hand over his face, taking in all that the doctor had told him. "But she's been awake and coherent? No signs of neurological damage?"

Dr. Howell shook his head. "She refused testing, but her physical exam was fine. No signs of neurological damage. I'm not sure what her attacker's intent was, but if he intended to kill her, he failed. But I need to ask you a few questions about her medical history. We saw on her x-rays previous rib fractures that had healed. We also saw that her arm had been broken before. Was she in a car accident or attacked in the past?"

Simon spoke, forgetting Mason was nearby. "She was attacked some years ago. She sustained multiple broken ribs and a broken radius and ulna. Thankfully neither required surgery."

Dr. Howell made notations in his notebook. "I'd like to get copies of her records, but I'll need her consent."

"Good luck with that. The records of her previous

injuries are at a correctional facility in Texas. It could take weeks, if not longer. I can go over her medical history with you."

Mason remained where he was while Simon went off with Dr. Howell. Correctional facility? Mason glanced at Tessa's door. Figuring he wouldn't understand most of what Simon told Dr. Howell, and figuring it wasn't as important as Tessa, Mason went back to Tessa's room.

A short while later, Simon came back to the room to find Mason standing beside his sister's bed. "Why don't you go home, Chief Slade? There isn't anything you can do here. Or anything you will do."

Mason turned. "And what exactly does that mean?"

Simon's fists clenched. "It means exactly what it sounds like. I watched while my sister was arrested and convicted of a crime she didn't commit while her boyfriend got off scot-free. I watched how, when a job site was robbed, she got the blame for it. I've seen how the police treat my sister because of that conviction. So don't sit here and pretend for one minute that you or that Peterson guy is going to do a damn thing about this."

Mason clearly remembered the day Tessa had told him practically the same thing. "I'll tell you what I told your sister. I uphold the law; I don't break it. And no matter who they are, or what they have or have not done, part of upholding the law is to help those who have been harmed, wronged, or victimized."

Simon narrowed his eyes, then gave in when he saw sincerity in Mason's steady gaze. "If I have my way, that conviction will get reversed. So what are you going to do about this? And what are you doing dating her?"

"For your first question, when I leave here, I plan on going over the report filed. Peterson forwarded me the crime scene report and photos. Then I'm going to go ask for alibis for anyone I think might have done this, though that list is small. As for your second question, it's none of your business."

"I'll get the truth out of Tessa."

Mason shrugged. "Then she can tell you. But what I will say is that I like your sister, I care about your sister, and I screwed up the other day before she was attacked. She's currently not speaking to me, though I hope to change that."

Simon felt a slight tug of empathy. "Tessa's good at the silent treatment, though she's not one to hold a grudge. Depending on how badly you screwed up, that will determine how long she refuses to talk to you. I made her so mad once that she didn't speak to me for a week."

The brief moment of humor ended, and Simon once again rubbed his face. "I need to call Sarah and let her know what's going on."

"Congrats on the new baby. I'll stay with Tessa."

Simon contemplated the fact that Mason knew his wife was pregnant. "She must really like you. She normally doesn't discuss family with outsiders. All right, you stay with her, and I'll be back soon."

Mason took a seat. Though he wanted to go get his laptop, he didn't want to leave Tessa alone. Instead, he pulled out his phone so he could at least review the report that was filed.

"Mason?" Tessa winced at the hoarse sound of her

voice.

Mason jumped to his feet. He took Tessa's hand. "Tessa."

Tessa closed her eyes when Mason leaned down and placed a soft kiss on her lips. She tightened her fingers on the hand that was holding hers. "My head hurts."

Mason pressed a light kiss to her temple. "Do you remember what happened?"

Tessa gave a short nod. "I wish I didn't."

"You should rest your voice."

Tessa's nails dug into Mason's hand. "Don't you want to know what happened?"

Mason felt his throat constrict. "I can see what happened. And I do want to know, but not right now."

Tessa ignored him. "He came out of nowhere. He told me I should have listened."

Mason leaned closer to hear her better. "Did you recognize him?"

Tessa shook her head. "He wore a mask. And I didn't know the voice. He cried."

Mason heard Simon coming up behind him. "He cried?"

Tessa looked past Mason. "Simon."

Mason stepped back and let Simon take his place.

"Tessa. What happened?" Simon brushed a lock of Tessa's hair back.

"You shouldn't be here. You should be at home with Sarah and the children."

Simon took her hand and kissed her knuckles. "Sarah and the kids send their love. Right now, you just need to rest and worry about getting better."

Tessa tried to sit up but was feeling too weak. "I want to go home."

"I know. And I'll take you home as soon as you're better." Simon's eyes stung as he looked down at his sister.

Tessa curled into her brother's touch and fell back asleep.

Mason silently left the room. He was no good to Tessa here. He needed to find out who did this to her.

* * *

Two hours later, Mason was engrossed in the report and images Peterson had sent. He had gone to Tessa's house to let out Rexford and had been met by a pretty angry Pete. Mason could understand Pete's anger. He felt it simmering in his own blood. He wanted to get his hands on the person who had dared to touch Tessa.

But all he could do was read the files and hope he saw something the original officers didn't see. He was still waiting on the background check to come back on Tessa. He didn't want to run it through his department, so he was waiting on Peterson, who insisted on running it himself after Mason told him what Simon had said.

From what the officers who processed the scene could surmise, the perpetrator had come from the side alley and grabbed Tessa from behind. There were marks on the ground where Tessa's sandals had skidded and left rubber behind. There wasn't much evidence at the scene, certainly no usable prints, but there was some blood that didn't belong to Tessa.   The officers seemed at a loss as to determine how the perp left blood at the scene, but given where Tessa lay, they didn't believe it was hers.   There had been no blood on Tessa that wasn't her own, and there were no defensive wounds.

What Mason really wanted to do was question Tessa, but he didn't dare yet.   Every time he closed his eyes, he could see the swelling of her face, the cuts and bruises left on her soft skin.   He knew she needed him to be detached, to concentrate on finding who did this.   But he was afraid that if he got near the person responsible, he would be more than a little tempted to retaliate.

Mason had dozed for a time when the sound of his computer ping woke him.   The ever-present knot in his stomach tightened while he opened the file Peterson sent. The background check was very thorough.   It had all the current statistics he already knew about Tessa.   But at the age of twenty, the records clearly stated Tessa had been arrested and convicted of drug possession and intent to distribute.   Twenty-year-old Tessa had been in possession of a large quantity of methamphetamines.   She accepted a plea deal and was sentenced to three years in prison, of which she served two.

He read the file through, then read it again.   There were no drugs found in her system, and there had been no equipment found in her possession needed to make the drug. And though records showed the equipment was never found, the police had proof that some of the equipment one would use had been charged to her credit card, which had been maxed out before her arrest.   It seemed young Tessa had a lot of debt, debt that distributing the drug would have helped her pay. In her original statement, she denied all charges, claiming she didn't know the drugs were in her car. But when the police raided her apartment after the arrest, the local police found more of the drug in her apartment.

Mason guessed that at some point her lawyer told her that her best option would be to plead guilty to a lesser charge, rather than risk being found guilty and getting a lengthier sentence. She spent the next two years at a women's prison in Texas. During that time she'd been a model prisoner. Prison records said the attack she sustained was perpetrated by a couple of women who had a prior history of violence and assaulting other inmates. Records also showed that no further action was taken because Tessa denied the two women were the ones involved.

Mason closed the lid of his laptop, his stomach sick. He couldn't reconcile the woman he knew, the woman he'd slept with, with a drug dealer. Simon had said he was trying to get the conviction reversed. Mason was interested in knowing on what grounds Simon wanted to appeal the conviction. The cops had a pretty clear-cut case against her. But Mason also knew that sometimes the facts pointed to an innocent person. Mason just couldn't believe Tessa was, or had ever been, that type of person. There had been nothing in her childhood behavior, or in her behavior post-prison, that would convince him to believe Tessa would make or sell drugs.

Chapter Thirteen

Mason was stretched out on Tessa's couch when lights came through the uncovered living room windows. His watch told him it was a little after two. He sat up and looked outside. He watched as Simon climbed out of a rental car. Not wanting to startle him, Mason turned on the porch light and opened the front door. Rexford came to stand next to him, sensing that Mason wasn't worried about the man approaching the porch.

Simon scowled at Mason, but his eyes stayed on the large dog. "Why am I not surprised to find you here?"

"Given what happened, I wanted to be here in case the guy came back." Mason gave Rexford a quick command that had the dog going back to his bed in Tessa's room to sleep.

Simon looked around the living room while Mason closed the door. Simon trailed to the back of the house and turned on the kitchen light. "She does amazing work."

Mason had not been surprised to see the kitchen completed when he'd arrived. Tessa had completed the room, including the new light fixture, new outlets and covers, and all the tile had been grouted and sealed. The light color of the walls, trim, and ceiling complemented the tile she'd chosen.

Simon brushed past him to the bedroom, keeping his

distance from the dog. He went to the closet and pulled out a bag.

Mason only had one question. "How is she doing?"

Simon set the bag on the bed and started going through drawers and adding garments to the bag. "Her labs were much better, and her condition downgraded. The doctor is hopeful she'll be able to go home in a day or two. But she won't be able to travel for a while yet. The broken orbital bone and concussion will keep her in bed. And she's going to have a heck of a time functioning with her dominant arm in a cast."

It hadn't gotten past his notice that Tessa was left-handed. "But she woke up again?"

Simon slammed the dresser drawer. "Yes, she woke up again. And the first thing she asked was where you were. I told her you had to work. I don't know how true that was, but she was crying, and it made her feel better."

Mason had wanted to stay, but when she had told Simon she wanted to go home, it had hurt. Hurt because home was in Indiana, far away from him. "I'm sorry. I actually was working. I'm going to find out who did this to her."

Simon went to the bathroom and grabbed some toiletries. Then he dropped the items in the sink, his head bent. "I promised her I would take care of her, protect her."

Mason understood how Simon felt. If one of his sisters had been hurt the way Tessa had, he didn't know what he'd do. Instead of offering him some trite platitude, he gathered up the items and let Simon have a moment to himself. He added the items to the bag and zipped it up.

Simon came and stood in the doorway. "So what are you going to do?"

Mason sat on the edge of the bed. "I'll need to question Tessa. She said the man spoke to her. If we can find the man, she might be able to identify his voice in a lineup. But right now, I need to find out the motive. Why would someone do this to her?"

Simon had been asking himself that same question. "It doesn't make sense. I was the one who made enemies, not Tessa. And I can't believe this has to do with our father. He's been gone for years, living who knows where. When Tessa offered to fix up the house so I could get more money for it, it seemed like a good idea. After all, it had been almost twenty years since my father was arrested. Who would hold such a grudge that he would harm his daughter in retaliation?"

That was the problem. Mason couldn't think of a single person. "It would have to be someone who lived here back then. But not someone so old that he couldn't have perpetrated the attack."

Simon looked out the window. "I suppose that eliminates old man Degrassi. He couldn't have pinned and beaten Tessa. She would have been able to fight him off. And she would have recognized his voice."

Mason had an idea of who he could talk to. "I was thinking maybe I'd talk to the mayor. He was not a fan of your father, and he might know who else held a grudge against him."

Simon remained where he was, watching Mason closely. "You said you had a list of people you needed to get alibis for."

Mason's list was a short one, but the first one was Boyd Thomson. His deputy was holding a mean grudge against Tessa. He also would have been strong enough to hurt Tessa without getting a scratch. And though Tessa would have recognized Boyd's voice, that didn't mean he hadn't tried to disguise it. But Mason wasn't going to share that with Simon. He didn't need Simon going after a cop with no evidence. Simon was looking very on edge at the moment.

Mason picked up the bag. "I do have a list, and if I make an arrest, you'll be the first to know. In the meantime, are you staying here?"

Simon scowled but allowed the change of subject. "I had the same idea you had. But I doubt anyone will be making an appearance. I don't particularly want to stay here. Too many bad memories. I got a room at the hotel where Pete is staying."

"Let me take the bag to Tessa."

Simon eyed Mason. Then he swore. "Fine. She wants to see you anyway. I still can't believe Tessa got involved with you, of all people."

Mason gave a quick whistle to Rexford. "I'm going to drop Rexford back at my parents' house and then I'll take this to her."

"Tessa told me your dad retired and you took over as police chief. I don't suppose you told your parents about Tessa."

Mason smiled at him. "As a matter of fact, I did. Your sister spent an afternoon with my parents and my sisters."

Simon, forgetting about the dog, took a step toward Mason. When Rexford growled, he stopped. "Your father arrested me more than once, though I found out later he didn't actually press charges. One time it was for fighting with you. Another time it was because I was defending my sister. I can't say I'm a fan of your old man."

Mason patted the dog. "No, and he wasn't a fan of yours, but he had a pretty good idea of what went on in your home. It can't have been easy having Randy Harris as a father. But Tessa is very proud of you and what you've accomplished."

Simon didn't know what to say to that. But besides his wife and children, Tessa was the most important person in his life. "Tessa always made me feel guilty when I got in trouble. She'd always look at me like I'd disappointed her. It got to the point that I couldn't take it anymore. It was either straighten out or continue to disappoint her. You need to find out who did this to her."

Mason set Tessa's bag on the kitchen counter. "I do have something I want to talk to you about. What if this isn't about Randy? You said you wanted to get her conviction overturned, but in my background check, I don't see any evidence that supports an appeal. Could this attack have something to do with her arrest?"

Simon's answer was immediate. "No. I can't see how this could be tied to her appeal. Tessa thinks it's a waste of time and money, but I don't. She took the rap for her boyfriend. He set her up. But last I checked, he was in Texas and wouldn't care one way or the other where Tessa was. And right now he's in jail pending trial. Seems he doesn't have enough money to make bail."

"Timothy?" He asked, though Mason remembered well the name of the boy Tessa had run off with.

"Yes. They went to Texas and moved in with his brother. Tessa was working two jobs, and Timothy had been working full time. After a few months, they moved into their own apartment. But Tim's brother kept coming around. Tessa didn't like him but didn't want to cause any trouble between the brothers. Then Tim started disappearing, not coming home after work, taking off in the middle of the day, stuff like that. Tessa thought he was cheating on her, which he probably was. She told him to move out. Two weeks later, Tessa got pulled over, and the cops found meth in the trunk of the car. It wasn't even her car, but Tim told the cops she had stolen it. Then during the investigation, Tessa found out that her credit card had been maxed out and that there were charges for equipment to make meth. Two days later, while she was in jail, the cops raided her apartment and found a huge stash of drugs. The drugs were inferior, but they matched the drugs in the car. And though no equipment or cash was found, the cops didn't care, and neither did the DA. No further investigation was done. Tim played the betrayed boyfriend to the hilt, claiming he had moved out because Tessa was acting erratically."

Mason remembered the blood test result. "No drugs were in her system, so that didn't exactly explain the supposed erratic behavior. But she pleaded guilty anyway."

Simon's jaw clenched while he spoke. "Her public defender was green and didn't care one way or the other what happened to Tessa. Neither of us had enough money to hire an attorney. It broke my heart when Tessa said she was pleading guilty. But now I have money. I hired a private investigator to look into both Tim's and his brother's activities. Tim's brother has been arrested several times for possession and distribution. He even served a few years in jail. Tim is not the boy Tessa remembers. And this past year, Tim was arrested for drug possession. If he has any conscience left, he'll admit the drugs were his, and I can get her sentence reversed."

Mason felt some of the knots in his stomach ease. "I don't know if you'll be successful in reversing her sentence, but if there is anything I can do to help, let me know."

"For now, just take that dog with you and go see Tessa. She'll be glad to see you."

Mason gathered up Rexford's things and settled the dog in the SUV. Simon looked ready to drop, so Mason simply said good night to him and let the man go.

Mason's first stop was his parents' house. Since it was the middle of the night, he made sure to call out who it was when he came inside.

Donald entered the kitchen in a pair of flannel pajamas. "What happened?"

Mason smiled when his mom shuffled into the kitchen behind his dad, belting her robe. "Everyone is fine. Sort of. The family is fine. But something happened to Tessa."

Eleanor leaned against her husband. "What happened to Tessa?"

Mason set Rexford's things down. "She was attacked the other night. Someone worked her over pretty good.

She was out with Laine and walking back to her car when someone jumped her outside Laine's shop. Laine stayed the night with her friend, so Tessa was alone. Simon got into town this afternoon after the guy helping Tessa remodel the house called her in as missing."

Eleanor went to fix coffee while Donald sat at the table, now in full cop mode. "Was the attacker caught? I take it Chief Peterson is on the case?"

"The attacker wasn't caught. Tessa has been unable to tell me what happened, but I'll be heading over there soon. I hope to get the story out of her in the morning. Peterson sent me the crime scene photos and the reports. Then he sent me Tessa's background check."

Donald recognized the look in his son's eyes. "And what did the background check find, son? I told you to run it."

"I don't regret not running it. And if this hadn't happened, I wouldn't have."

Eleanor laid a hand over her son's fist. "What did it say?"

"She has a record and spent a couple of years in prison. But I don't believe she's guilty."

Donald slammed a palm on the table. "You don't want her to be guilty. It's not the same thing."

"Dad, I know Tessa. She wouldn't have done what she was accused of." Mason went over the story as the report told it while they drank the coffee his mother had made. Then he told his parents about the appeal Simon was working on and what the private investigator had found.

Donald was silent for a time. "All right, I agree, you

might be right. But you could also be wrong. Tessa was young; she could have been desperate. And unless those men testify that she wasn't a part of the plan, I don't see how the conviction will get reversed. But I know some good cops down in Texas. I'll see what I can do."

"Thanks, Dad. I should get going. And you two should be heading out for your trip. I'll be back to get Rexford tomorrow."

Eleanor cleared the table. "Don't be silly. We can't possibly leave with this hanging over you. Call me in the morning and let me know how she's doing. Your father will see what he can dig up."

Mason hugged both his parents. "I should feel guilty and tell you both to go anyway, but I could use Dad's help. I want to talk to Alex and see if he remembers anyone from back in the day who might have held a mean enough grudge against Randy to attack his daughter all these years later."

Donald yawned and nodded. "If anyone remembers who had a grudge against Randy, it would be him. But Alex isn't going to appreciate being questioned in regard to Tessa's assault."

Mason didn't care. "It's not like I think he did it. But unless it turns out this does have something to do with her arrest all those years ago, I just don't know why anyone would do this. And I'm going to discreetly question Deputy Thomson. I don't think he had anything to do with this either. I may not like the guy, but he's still a cop. And nothing in his record makes me think he'd do this."

Donald relented. "And other than being tied to Randy, why would anyone else attack Tessa? All right, I'll make an appointment and we'll go see Alex. Just don't get carried away. He's not only the mayor; he's also a friend. And I know him well enough to know that he wouldn't attack Tessa in revenge against her father. He'd go find Randy himself first."

Mason had no doubt Alex probably had, too. Mason had been in high school, but the fights between the two men had been legendary, at least locally. "Thanks, Dad."

Eleanor pulled out an insulated cup and filled it full of coffee for Mason. "I don't suppose you've gotten any sleep tonight?"

"I don't suppose I have. I'm going to bring a bag to Tessa and check on her. I'll probably doze there for a little while. Then I'll need to check in with Peterson. He'll want to be there when I question Tessa about the attack. And at some point, I need to go into the station. Maybe make that appointment for later in the evening."

Donald yawned and nodded. "For now, your mother and I need to get back to bed. We're not as young as we used to be. I'll call Alex in the morning. Knowing your mother, she'll be by the hospital to see Tessa."

Eleanor gave Mason a peck on the cheek and headed off to bed.

Donald watched his wife's retreat, then turned back to Mason. "Things seem to have gotten serious between you and Tessa."

"They did. Not sure how things got so complicated so fast. But there's something about her. She got under my skin."

"And in your blood. It was like that with your mother.

I couldn't pinpoint what it was exactly that fascinated me about her. She was pretty, but so were a lot of other women. She was funny, but again, so were others. But something about the combination that is your mother had me standing up and paying attention. I married her before anyone got too close."

Mason shifted uncomfortably in his seat. "I don't know that I have marriage on my mind."

Donald smiled knowingly. "But you don't want her to leave."

Mason gave up. "No, I don't want her to leave."

"I can't say she's the woman I'd have picked for you. But she's loyal to her family and friends. Laine is an excellent judge of character, and she likes Tessa very much. But the townsfolk might not take too kindly to their police chief consorting with a woman who has a drug conviction on her record."

"No, I don't suppose they would. And I think that Tessa, in her own way, was trying to warn me. We argued because she didn't want me staying the night and having people see my car in her driveway. She also had told me flat out to run a background check on her before I took her to dinner."

Donald shook his head. "Which you didn't do. I can help with Alex, but I can't fix the rest of this. Only you can decide what is more important to you. Only you."

Mason squeezed his father's shoulder and picked up the coffee his mother had fixed for him. "You're right. I'm going to head to the hospital. I'm sure Tessa would like her own things."

"Good luck." Donald walked Mason out. He shook his head again and closed the front door. His son never did go for easy. And heaven help this town if they stood between Mason and something he really wanted. Donald wasn't unaware of the sacrifices Mason made for this town. Donald had made his own while he was chief. But he'd been happily married with three children. Mason hadn't settled down yet, but if he wanted to do that with Tessa, Donald had a feeling his son might just choose the woman over the town.

Chapter Fourteen

When Mason arrived to find Tessa settled into a different room, he was grateful when he saw that most of the monitors had been removed. Tessa still had the catheter, but the heart monitor was gone, as was the blood pressure cuff and the pulse oximeter. The IV was still putting fluid and medication into her system, but she was slightly curled up on her side, the side that didn't have cuts and bruises. Her left arm with the cast rested on her stomach.

He set her bag down and took the opportunity to look her over. Once assured she was fine and was breathing evenly, he stretched out in the reclining chair. He could have groaned; it felt so good to lie down. His back ached and his head hurt from lack of sleep and too much caffeine. It was now five in the morning, and he needed to close his eyes, even if for just an hour or two.

He wasn't sure how much time had passed, but the sun filtered through the blinds. When he sat up, he saw Tessa's eyes were open, and she was watching him.

Mason stretched as he rose. "How do you feel?"

Tessa watched him as he came to her bedside. "Like someone beat me up."

In the light of day, Tessa's face looked worse. The bruise blooming around her left eye had deepened in color.

It would be a while before the color faded. But her gaze was alert, though he had no doubt she still had a headache, and her voice sounded a little better than it had yesterday. "Simon packed you a bag. I also tossed my tablet in there, in case you want to read or something."

"I just want to go home."

Mason's heart ached at her words. "You can't go home yet. Not until you're better. You can't travel with a concussion and cracked ribs."

Tessa waved her right arm, her agitation plain to see. "Not Indiana, just home. Sylvia's or your house, or wherever. I don't care. I just want to leave here."

The ache faded and he went to Tessa's side. Tears were trickling down her cheeks. He carefully gathered her to his chest. "As soon as the doctor says you can go, I'll get you out of here. I promise."

Tessa wrapped her good arm around Mason's waist, ignoring the pain in her ribs. She felt weepy, and she couldn't seem to stem the tears. "I'm sorry I didn't call you back."

Mason kissed the top of her head. "I'm sorry I was a jerk."

Tessa pulled away so she could look at his face. "You weren't a jerk. I just don't want anything to happen to you because of me."

Mason kissed her lightly, then again. "Nothing is going to happen to me because of you. You're the best thing to happen to me in a long time."

Tessa cupped his neck with her good arm and brought his mouth back to hers. She smiled when Mason's lips brushed over her bruised forehead and cheek instead of her mouth. But when he kissed the corner of her mouth, she turned her mouth up to his. He kept his touch light, but she wanted more. She traced his bottom lip with her tongue, and she felt Mason shudder against her.

Simon's voice broke them apart. "Now that is something I really don't want to see."

Energy spent, Tessa leaned back against the raised mattress. "Morning, Simon."

"I'm glad to see you are at least feeling better and awake. I talked to your doctor. They're going to get you out of bed today and get that catheter out. If all goes well, you can probably get out of here tomorrow."

Tessa's face fell. "Not today?"

"No, not today." Simon waved into the hallway. "Chief Peterson is here. I'd like to be here when you go over your story."

Tessa's hand blindly reached out to Mason's. Her grip was weak, but she held onto him as if he could give her strength. "Guess it's best to get it all out at once."

Mason squeezed Tessa's hand. "I need to know what happened. What he said. Peterson is taking point on the case. The attack happened in his jurisdiction, not mine. But I swear I'll find the man who did this."

Chief Peterson stepped into the room, declining to comment on Mason's statement. "If you are up to it, I'd like to go over what happened and get your official statement."

Tessa wasn't sure she was up to it. She was tired, her head was pounding, her face, ribs, and back hurt. But if there was anything in what she remembered that could help them find who did this to her, then she needed to go over it.

Mason took her hand and held it. "I'm right here."

Tessa swallowed, trying to ease her throat. That still hurt, too. "I left Laine at Mauve's apartment. She'd had a little too much to drink, and Laine didn't want to leave her alone. I had only had one drink early in the evening, and I needed to get back so I could let Rexford outside. There were other people around until I got near Laine's shop. I was near the car when someone knocked me down from behind. Then he had a scarf or something around my neck. I couldn't breathe. He said he'd warned me that I should have left. The scarf loosened and I could breathe again, but he had me pinned. Then I think he hit me in the back. I sort of remember rolling over. Then he was talking again, asking me why I didn't listen. And he sounded like he was crying. He had a mask on, but I swear there were tears in his eyes. Then he hit me again and I couldn't breathe, and I started to pass out. But before I passed out, I saw him hit the ground with his fist, like he'd missed my face. He was saying something else, but I couldn't make out the words. I don't remember anything else."

Peterson pulled a sheet of paper out of a folder he was carrying. "I guess we know how his blood got on the concrete. But why the tears? Why hit the ground? The medical report shows he most likely kicked you a couple of times in the chest and back. He must have gotten up and done it while you were unconscious."

Mason scowled and crossed the room to snatch the report. He glared at Peterson. If she didn't remember, he didn't need Peterson feeding her memories.

Tessa closed her eyes. "He was taller than me, but I guess that's not hard to do. He was white. I only got the impression that he was slender, not muscular like Mason."

Peterson rose, ready to head out. "The description isn't great, but it's better than nothing. We can see if anyone remembers seeing a slender white male near you, or perhaps following you. I'll need to talk to Laine and Mauve. It's not likely anyone saw him, but we could get lucky."

Mason handed Peterson back the report. "Laine should be at her shop. I talked to her yesterday. She can tell you where Mauve's shop is."

Peterson tipped an imaginary hat and took his leave.

Simon opened up the bag. "Want me to help you change into your nightgown? I packed your blue one."

Tessa closed her eyes again. "Too tired."

Simon felt her forehead and was reassured when her temperature was normal. "All right. You need to rest."

Tessa opened her eyes again. "You should be home with Sarah and the children."

Simon kissed her forehead. "You sound like a broken record. That's what you said last night. I'm not going anywhere."

Tessa closed her eyes again and drifted off.

Simon turned to see Mason staring out into the parking lot. The man was furious and trying to hide it. "I'll be here with her all day. I won't leave her side."

Mason's jaw clenched. He turned his head to look at Tessa. "I shouldn't have left her."

Simon released Tessa. "Want me to kick your ass?"

Mason scrubbed his palms over his face. "I should

probably let you, but for now, I'm more help to Tessa in one piece. I need to go. Peterson will question Laine and Mauve. I need to track down those alibis I mentioned. And I'm going to talk to an old enemy of your dad's."

"Still think this was some kind of retaliation?"

Mason didn't know what to think. But he had to start somewhere. "Tell Tessa I'll be back tonight. I'll keep her company while she sleeps. And don't be surprised if my mother shows up later today with my sisters in tow after Laine closes her shop."

Simon took the seat Mason had vacated earlier. "I'll be on the lookout."

Mason gave him a curt nod and started to leave.

"And Mason?"

"Yeah?"

"Find the man who did this to her."

"I will. I promise."

Simon leaned back after Mason left.

"You like him, don't you?"

Simon sat up at his sister's voice. "I don't want to."

Tessa gave him a weak smile. "I'm glad. I like him too."

Simon came to stand beside her bed. "Yeah, except the part that worries me is that I think you're in love with him. After Tim, I didn't think you'd ever let another man get close to you."

Love? Tessa's head was feeling a little swimmy, but she couldn't deny Simon's claim. She was pretty sure she was in love with Mason. There was much to admire about him. He was a good man, one who cared about others. He loved his parents, his sisters, and got along well with everyone he met. He was fair and just. And he was handsome and sexy, and she didn't want to imagine going back to Indiana without him.

But love wasn't going to be enough. "He doesn't know about Tim or jail. He won't love me back."

"You never told him?" Simon realized that he was the one who had let her past slip.

Tessa tried to shake her head but was too tired. "Not good enough."

"You get that out of your head right now. He'd be lucky to have you."

Simon always defended her. He'd been her protector, the one to keep her safe. "Love you, Simon."

Simon's throat tightened. "I love you, Tessa. Now just rest."

* * *

Though Mason knew Thomson and Degrassi would have alibis before he interviewed them, he was still ticked off. Degrassi didn't have the kind of money one would need to hire someone to attack someone else. Thomson would know how and could probably afford it, but Mason just couldn't see him paying someone else. Thomson had a temper, and if he had been enraged enough to hire someone to attack her, he'd have been more likely to do it himself.

But Mason couldn't help but feel the attack was very personal. Tessa said that it was twice that the man cried. It just didn't make sense. And why punch the ground? To be thorough, he had checked both Degrassi's and Thomson's hands for broken bones or bruising, but it was obvious neither man had attacked her.

Peterson had called him back and told him that neither Laine nor Mauve had been of any help. They hadn't seen anyone watching them. They'd had dinner and then gone dancing. Laine said she hadn't been drinking; only Mauve had been. Like Tessa, she admitted to having one drink before dinner. Peterson had asked around the restaurant and the club, but no one had anything to share. Most didn't even remember the women being in the club.

Timothy was a bust as well. He'd finally gotten in touch with the local police, and they had confirmed that Timothy was being held without bail. Drug possession and assault. Seemed he got a little rough with his girlfriend, and she pressed charges.

That just left Randy. Tessa didn't know anyone else in town, though most knew of her. Sylvia wouldn't have had any enemies who would do this. Perhaps it was time to hunt the old man down. Tessa said they hadn't seen her father since his arrest, but that didn't mean Randy wasn't keeping track of his kids.

"It's after five." Donald hovered in Mason's doorway.

Mason glanced up. "Didn't realize it was already so late. Alex waiting for us?"

Donald nodded. "He's up at his house. Asked if we'd stop by there."

Mason grabbed his laptop and his jacket. He hadn't bothered to tuck his gun away, so he was still wearing it. "Let's go."

When they arrived, Alex greeted them both with a

friendly handshake. "I thought you were leaving tomorrow for your trip."

Donald glanced around. Looked like they were alone. "We have to postpone it. I'll let Mason here tell you why."

Alex poured himself a drink. "Rumors have already made their way to me. Degrassi pitched a fit, saying you harassed him about attacking Tessa Harris."

Mason declined the glass Alex held out to him. "I believe I questioned him on his whereabouts. Completely different thing. And someone did attack Tessa Harris. She has broken bones, bruises, and cuts. She was unconscious when she was found and taken to the hospital. And while I don't think Degrassi is the one who did it, I wouldn't be doing my job if I followed assumptions and not facts."

Alex waved them to take a seat. "All right, calm down. So why exactly do you want to talk to me about Tessa?"

Mason took a deep breath to calm himself. "The only reason I can think of that someone would have attacked Tessa is because of her father, Randy. The messages left on her property told her to get out. Tessa's account of the attack is that the man who attacked her told her she should have listened and left. There's no doubt the same person who vandalized her property is the one who attacked her. But she's not from around here. She was never in any trouble growing up. I can't think of anyone who would be holding a grudge against her."

Alex swallowed his drink in one shot. "So you figure this is about Randy. He was not without enemies. And there are probably a few people, people like Degrassi, who still hold a grudge. But I can't think of anyone who would do something like this to his daughter."

Mason prodded further. "Actually that is what I'm hoping you might remember. You got into a few fights with him over the years. Almost every fight Randy was in was because he was up to no good. He stole from people; he liked to hit on other men's wives. If stories are to be believed, he was successful with some of those wives. Who else in your circles back then might have done this to her because of Randy?"

"I suppose any one of the men who worked at the mill Randy worked at could be worth talking to. But that old mill shut down ten years ago. Most of the men who worked there left town to find work elsewhere. Our economy took a big hit that year. It wasn't until the mayor of Willow Lake started offering incentives to shopkeepers to come open shops and turn the town into a tourist spot that things started turning around again. Even that old house of Sylvia's will fetch a nice penny thanks to people wanting to live near the lake but who can't afford to live in the lake town anymore."

With some prodding, Mason took down a few names that the mayor remembered. "All right, thanks."

"Keep me up to date on the investigation. I don't like the thought that someone in my town was hurt, even someone like Tessa. And I don't like the thought that someone in my town is capable of this much violence."

Mason's fist clenched at the "someone like Tessa" comment, but kept his mouth shut.

Donald shook Alex's hand again. "We'll keep you informed. Peterson is running point, but my boy here will find him."

Alex slapped Mason on the back. "I knew you were the right man for the job when you were brought on before your father retired. And Donald, don't forget to call me for that fishing trip when you get back from your vacation."

Mason took a deep breath when they stepped outside. He saw Monty and waved at him.

"Hi, Chief. What are you doing here?"

Mason smiled at the kid. "Just needed to talk to your dad about some town business. Nice bike."

Monty patted the handlebars. "Gonna get me a real motorcycle one day."

Donald laughed. "Good luck with that. I used to try to talk your old man into funding a motorcycle for me when I was chief. Thought I'd look pretty cool riding through town on a Harley. Of course, the Mrs. would have had my head."

Monty nodded knowingly. "Yeah, my mom would have a fit if I had one. Probably skin my hide."

Mason saw Monty's expression turn serious. "Something up?"

Monty shuffled his feet. "Is it true someone attacked Ms. Harris? There were rumors at Margie's after school today."

Mason's eyes narrowed. "Yes, it's true. You wouldn't happen to know something about that, would you?"

Monty's eyes widened. "What? No, I don't know anything. I just remembered you hanging out with her, is all."

Mason couldn't imagine what sixteen-year-old Monty would know about Tessa's attack, but he looked nervous.

"If you do hear anything, or any of your friends, be sure to let me know."

"Sure will. I'd better get inside. Dad says we're picking Mom up from work and going out for dinner. Landon's supposed to be there."

Donald waved the boy off. "Tell your mom and brother we said hi."

Monty waved and quickly went inside.

Donald kept his eye on the door Monty had closed. "That was weird."

Mason agreed. "Who knows what goes on in his head."

"He was always a bit odd. But a good kid."

Mason drove his father back to the house. "Where's Mom?"

"She left to pick up Laine and Cyndi around the time I left to find you. I imagine they're at the hospital. Want some dinner? Your mother fried some chicken last night."

Mason's belly rumbled, and he followed his dad to the kitchen. No one turned down his mom's fried chicken.

Donald set the plate of leftovers on the table and pulled out a container of homemade potato salad. "Your mom and I were thinking we don't think Tessa should go back to her aunt's house. And she shouldn't be alone. We were thinking she could stay here. That way she won't be alone, and you won't have to worry about her while you're at work. We're not going anywhere until you find the man who did this. But I think it's going to be harder than you think."

Mason took a large bite of the chicken and swallowed before answering. "I'll run it by her. I was thinking of taking her back to my place, but then she would be alone when I wasn't there."

"Good, then it's settled. We'll put her in Laine's room. And I assume you're going to want to use your old room while she's here."

Mason's eyebrow raised at his dad. "You're not very subtle, you know. But yes, if Tessa is here, then I'll be here."

Donald heaped his plate with chicken and potato salad. Then he handed the bowl to Mason. "Eat up. You're going to need it."

Chapter Fifteen

"Stop fussing. This is the best option." Mason helped Tessa into the SUV.

Tessa winced and quit fighting Mason when he tried to fasten her seat belt. Instead, she used her good arm to tug the hem of her nightgown down to cover her legs. The scabs on her knees and shins were not pretty. "How did you talk Simon into this?"

Mason leaned down and kissed Tessa. He then closed the door, rounded the SUV, and hopped into the driver's seat. "Easy. He had three choices. He could let you stay at your aunt's house by yourself, he could let you stay at my house alone, or he could let you stay with my parents. You can't travel, so your leaving is not an option."

Tessa crossed her good arm over her chest. "I'm not leaving. I'm finishing the house. Simon sent me out here to finish it, and I'm going to darn well finish it."

Mason stifled a grin at her mutinous expression. "I'll leave that to you and Simon to argue over. Personally, I'd rather have you at my house. Sneaking down the hall to your room with my parents watching our every move is going to present a bit of a challenge."

Tessa felt her cheeks heat. She was tired. Her body hurt in places she'd never believed could hurt. And yet desire curled in the pit of her belly thinking about Mason sneaking into her room. "You don't have to worry about that quite yet. Simon is going to stop by. I need your help convincing him to go home. He's at the house with Pete right now, since you were so adamant about picking me up. I shudder to think what Simon is doing with the house. He is not a handyman by any stretch of the imagination. I just hope he isn't painting anything."

Mason drove sedately as they headed toward his parents' house. It had taken a bit of convincing to get Simon to agree to let Tessa stay with his parents. Simon wanted to set her up at the hotel. And while she'd have access to room service, it didn't sit well with Mason to let her stay by herself. The minute Tessa was feeling up to traveling, Mason had no doubt Simon would try to convince Tessa to come home. And while he understood Tessa would be safer hundreds of miles away, Mason wasn't ready to let her go.

Tessa closed her eyes and leaned the seat back. "Should be interesting having Simon at your parents' house."

Mason took his eyes off the road long enough to see the fatigue on Tessa's face. "Dad has promised to be on his best behavior. Mom is looking forward to meeting him. Everything will be okay. I promise."

"You sure are making a lot of promises lately."

That hadn't gotten past Mason's notice either. Seeing her, desiring her, had him wanting to make all sorts of other promises Tessa probably wasn't ready to handle.

Tessa opened her eyes and glanced at Mason. "Thanks for springing me. I don't think I could have spent another night there."

Mason nodded but didn't comment. Tessa had not been a model patient. She had refused almost all treatment and kept demanding to go home. When Mason told her doctor he was taking her to his parents' house to recover, the doctor finally released her. Mason knew that a good part of her was concerned about the cost of the hospital stay and the fact that the health insurance she did have wasn't going to be of very much use, given the nature of her injuries and the high cost.

"Right now, you just have to focus on getting better."

Tessa grunted and lifted her broken arm. "This is what ticks me off. The rest I can handle. But it will be weeks before this cast is off. I'm not going to be very efficient painting one-handed."

Mason had no doubt Tessa would cover her cast in plastic and get on with the job at hand. However, her cracked ribs would keep her from doing anything too strenuous. But he had enough sense to keep his mouth shut. He had a feeling this was her way of coping with what had happened to her. Part of him was glad she wasn't simply crying, but the anger he could see simmering just below the surface had him worried.

Tessa closed her eyes for the rest of the drive. When the car pulled into a long driveway and stopped, she opened them again. The house was two stories and sat on a good piece of land. There was a beautiful willow tree in the front that shaded the house. The siding was a pale yellow and the roof and shutters a gray-blue. The brightly blooming flowers in the front yard that filled the space around the porch added color. Flower boxes also hung from the porch, adding more color. The colors might not be to everyone's taste, but Tessa thought the house was adorable.

"Let me help you out."

Tessa barely heard Mason, so she just nodded. When he helped her out, she wrapped her good arm around his neck. "I like it."

Mason glanced at the house before grabbing the duffle bag from the back seat. "Mom decorated it. The inside is just as bright as the outside. She loves color. Dad kept telling her they won't be able to sell it unless she paints the house in neutral tones, but so far, she's been holding him off."

Once inside, Tessa smiled. The walls were bright, though the colors didn't seem garish to her. It was like being inside a garden. The walls were a similar yellow to the outside. Bright pops of color in the furniture and decorations broke up the yellow color that could have been an eyesore, but somehow fit the house. "I would keep it. It's very inviting and cheery."

Eleanor came to greet them. "Thank you, Tessa. I was going for cheery. For a long time, the walls were simply white. It got to be depressing, staring at the stark walls that had turned dingy over the years. Donald thought I was crazy to pick such bright colors, but now he loves it, too."

Donald came in behind his wife. "Mason, why don't you get her settled. You guys can compare decorating tips later."

Eleanor came around Tessa's other side and helped Mason get her up the stairs. It didn't get beyond Tessa's notice that Donald was right behind them. She could have wept in relief when her back hit the recently turned-down bed.

Eleanor brushed the bruises on Tessa's cheek. "Laine helped me redecorate her old bedroom into a guest room. I turned Cyndi's room at the end of the hall into my sewing room. Mason's room is next to yours; the bath is across the hall. Our bedroom is at the opposite end of the stairwell."

Tessa was already half asleep. "I can't thank you enough for letting me stay here."

Eleanor tucked a strand of hair behind Tessa's ear and tugged the sheet up to her neck. "You just rest now. We can chat later."

Donald and Eleanor left the bedroom, leaving Mason alone. He set her toiletries on the dresser and put her clothes away. He doubted she'd do more than rest for the next couple of days, but he wanted her surrounded by her own things. He kissed her briefly and left.

He found his parents in the kitchen, which was where he expected them to be. "She's already asleep."

Donald poured his son a fresh cup of coffee. "Someone did quite a number on her."

Eleanor brushed a tear away. "The poor dear. She has to be in pain."

Mason stared down into his coffee. "It could have been much worse. Right now, it's the crime scene that doesn't make sense. It looks like the perp spent some time punching the parking lot concrete instead of Tessa's face."

Donald just shook his head. "You've definitely got a puzzle on your hands. I've seen some strange things over the years, but premeditated attacks are generally carried out without hesitation or remorse on the attacker's part. Tessa is very lucky to have gotten away with what amounts to minor injuries."

Eleanor scowled at her husband. "I doubt Tessa is feeling lucky right now."

Mason agreed with his father. "Dad is right. She's very lucky. As far as the doctor can figure, her arm broke when her assailant tackled her. He could have choked her to death, but he didn't. There was no major damage to her trachea, though her voice is still not back to normal yet. The orbital bone break was probably from only one or two blows. The doctor said if he had hit her more than that, there would have been more damage and more broken facial bones. She didn't lose any teeth, and the rest of her face doesn't show signs of trauma. The cracked ribs are most likely from a kick to the chest, though again if they had been repeated, she'd have more than cracks. The doctor said he felt like the perp was hesitant or had tempered his attack. So while I agree Tessa is probably not feeling lucky right now, it could have been much worse."

Donald pulled his wife to his side. "If the man punched the ground, then he has to have at least torn his knuckles up pretty badly."

Mason pushed his coffee back. His stomach was feeling a bit sour. "Which is great if I had a suspect. I can say that it wasn't Degrassi, and it wasn't Boyd. And there are no witnesses to the attack that Chief Peterson or I have been able to find. If it weren't for the fact that Tessa remembers her attacker saying she should have listened and left town, we wouldn't know it was the same person who vandalized her house."

Donald held out a chair, and he and Eleanor took a seat. "What about her dad? Found him yet?"

"Not yet, but to be fair I haven't looked that hard. And I haven't talked to Tessa about finding him. But a cursory check shows his prison release documents, and I was able to track some deposits from Sylvia when she sent him money from time to time. No one else in the family has seen him. Simon's and Tessa's accounts don't show any money transfers, though I suppose either of them could have sent him cash. But Tessa says no one has seen him, and I believe her. I'm just not sure what motive Randy would have after all these years. But I'll be paying him a visit."

Donald gave his son a stern look. "Let me know if you need me to come with you. If he did this, I wouldn't mind helping to put him back behind bars."

Eleanor knew the rest of Tessa's story. "What about Timothy? That was a dead end, too?"

Mason had felt uncomfortable telling Tessa's story to his parents, but he knew trying to keep something like her ex-boyfriend and her prison record a secret would have been impossible. He knew his father well enough to know he'd already been looking into Tessa's past. "In this case, he's innocent. He was in jail at the time Tessa was attacked. And he's been in Texas. There is no evidence he ever made his way here or would even have known Tessa was back in her hometown."

Donald had taken the news of Tessa's prison record pretty hard, given how fiercely his son defended her to him. Tessa could end his son's career. "If I were you, I'd do my best to keep his name out of your investigation. Chief Peterson won't spread gossip, but if anyone at the station finds out about Tessa's arrest, it will be public news by morning."

Eleanor laid her hand on top of Mason's clenched fists. "What did Tessa say about her arrest?"

Mason kept his eyes down. "She didn't. I didn't talk to her about it."

Donald's angry voice filled the kitchen. "For heaven's sake, why not?"

Mason didn't have an answer. He supposed that at the heart of his reasons was fear. If Tessa knew he knew, she might very well bolt. She certainly would have found an excuse not to come with him to his parents' house. He needed her to trust him. Until then, since it wasn't relevant to this case, he would keep it to himself.

The doorbell rang before anyone could argue with Mason's choice. Before his parents could get up, he headed for the door. He knew who would be on the other side. "Hi, Simon. Your sister is resting."

Simon slowly entered the house, giving it the same look over that Tessa had given it, though for different reasons. "This is one place I never expected to set foot in."

Donald and Eleanor met him at the door. Donald gave him a good once-over before extending his hand. "I guess I never expected to have you set foot in here, either."

Simon shook Donald's hand. "Chief Slade."

"Just Donald these days. My days as chief are over. This is my wife, Eleanor."

Simon shook her hand. "Ma'am."

Eleanor broke the awkward tension. "Would you like some coffee? Tessa is upstairs resting. I was going to make her some tea and a snack if you'd like to carry it up to her when I finish fixing it."

Simon reluctantly nodded. "Coffee would be great."

Simon took the chair offered and attempted to relax. "The town hasn't changed much."

Donald took a seat across from him. "Not much. It's grown a little. Mason tells me you have a wife and a couple of kids."

Simon took an appreciative sip of the coffee Eleanor set before him. "Thank you. And yes, my wife's name is Sarah. Our son Adam is four, and our daughter Lilah is two. We'll be adding a third early next year."

Eleanor added cream to her coffee. "Mason also said you were a pediatrician in Indiana."

Simon glanced over at Mason, who was hovering in the doorway. "I imagine Mason investigated me quite thoroughly. But yes, I'm a pediatrician in Indiana. When I left the army, I went back to school. I'd enjoyed working as a medic. But I find it easier to work with children than adults. I met Sarah while I was finishing up my residency. Tessa followed me to Indiana, as did our mother. I hadn't planned to get married and do the father thing, but I've been very blessed."

Eleanor gave him a huge smile. "Nothing like a good woman to settle a man down."

Simon finally relaxed in his seat. "Yes, ma'am. There is nothing I wouldn't do for Sarah and the children."

Eleanor set about fixing a tray for Tessa. She idly

listened as the men chatted.

Simon let Mason lead the way while Simon handled the tray. "It's nice of your parents to let her stay here."

"They know I care."

Simon stopped outside the bedroom door. "I'm starting to believe you do. Promise me, Mason, that you'll take care of her. She's been through a lot. She deserves better. She tried to keep me on the straight and narrow. She was the one who cried tears over our father's arrest. She's the one who still visits our mother and makes sure she's comfortable. There is a lot of love and compassion inside her. Nothing and no one will ever make me believe she did the things she was convicted of. It's not in her."

Mason gripped the door handle. He looked Simon in the eyes. "I don't believe Tessa is that person. And I meant what I said before; if there is anything I can do to help you prove that, you let me know."

Simon's hands trembled a bit as he held the tray, but he held on. "Be sure to tell her that."

Mason opened the door. Tessa was still asleep, but it was obvious she was having a bad dream. He came to her side and gently woke her. "Come on, Tessa."

Tessa's eyes opened. "Mason?"

Mason kissed her lightly. "Simon's here."

Tessa looked beyond Mason and smiled at her brother. "You didn't paint, did you?"

Simon laughed and set the tray down on a table that had been placed beside the bed. "No, I promise I didn't paint anything. You must be feeling better."

Tessa did feel a bit better, though her dream left behind

a layer of fear. Most times when she slept, she dreamed of the attack. But she didn't want Simon to know that. "Sarah and the kids are okay?"

Simon held the cup of tea to Tessa's lips. He didn't respond until she'd taken a couple of sips. "They're fine. Sarah sends her love. She's half tempted to pack up the kids and hop on a plane. I assured her it wasn't necessary."

Tessa gripped his hand. "Simon, please go home. You need to be with your family."

Simon turned her hand in his. "I am with my family."

"You know what I mean. You need to get back to your wife and kids. And you need to get back to work."

Simon looked over at Mason. "I do need to get home. And I think I'm leaving you in good hands."

Tessa looked over at Mason and smiled. "I'm in very good hands."

Simon gave her a pained look. "Please, no details. Mom asked about you, and I gave her an abbreviated version. She says she hopes you get better soon."

Tessa supposed that hoping she would get well soon was more than she expected from her mother. Janine found it difficult to show her children any affection, though she was apt to display more with her grandchildren. Sarah had a way of getting Janine out of her self-imposed shell. Sometimes Sarah even got a laugh out of Janine, though it was a rare occurrence. But with Sarah's and the children's influence, Janine did come for birthdays and Christmas with some coaxing. Tessa figured her mother's well-wishes were a good sign.

Simon visited for a little while before Tessa started

getting tired again. "I have a flight out tonight. Tessa, call me anytime day or night if you need anything. And I want one of you to call me if anything happens. And don't worry about the house. Pete is staying on to finish up the work. His painting skills are at least better than mine."

Tessa's eyes were drooping, or she would have argued. "I love you, Simon."

"I love you too, Tessa. You get some rest. Call me."

"I will."

Mason stepped aside as Simon left the room. He followed the man downstairs. "I'll keep you informed."

Simon held out a hand. "Tessa really does like you. I guess I do too."

"Same here."

Simon said his farewells to the Slades and took his leave.

Chapter Sixteen

The windows were dark, and the house was quiet when Tessa woke. She vaguely remembered Eleanor coming in and trying to get her to have something to eat. Tessa's only recollection was some mumbling that she didn't understand, so it was a sure bet Eleanor hadn't understood her either. But the message that she was too tired to eat must have gotten through. Tessa could see a tray near the bed with something covered. Tessa thought about it, and her stomach revolted at even the thought of food. Even the tea, though it had tasted nice, had been too much for her stomach.

Tessa stretched a bit but winced. Her ribs hurt, though they felt better than they had. But even trying to roll over on her side caused pain. She wasn't by nature a back sleeper, so the forced position made her crabby. In fact, just about everything made her crabby right now. She hoped Mason found the man who did this to her, so she could take a crowbar to his ribs and see how he liked it.

But first and foremost, what she really wanted was a shower. And even that was denied her. Her left wrist and hand were in a lightweight cast, and she couldn't get it wet. She would need to take a bath instead, but Tessa figured that where there was a will, there was a way. She gingerly climbed out of bed in search of a fresh nightgown. She found it and a small bag of her toiletries. Thankful that she didn't have to borrow shampoo, Tessa headed to the bath.

Tessa closed the door before turning on the light. The bath was down the hall from Mason's parents, so she didn't have to worry about disturbing them. She filled the bath with water almost hot enough to burn before setting her things within reach. Thankfully the knobs and shower head were on the left side of the tub, so she could drape her left arm over the edge without bumping into them.

The soaking part was nice. It had been a long time since she'd had the luxury of spending time lying in the bathtub. Normally Tessa was too busy to take the time. Even her showers were rushed in the hope of keeping her water bill low. But when it came time to wash up, Tessa found it much more difficult than she thought. She was trying to wash her hair when she heard a light knock on the door. Frustrated and near tears, she glared at the door. "Go back to bed, Mason."

Mason had no intention of doing that. He opened the door. Tessa was sitting in the tub, her arm draped over the edge, and shampoo was dripping into her eyes. Without saying a word, he slipped into the room, closing the door behind him. He pulled the shower sprayer down and knelt next to the tub.

Sniffling a little, Tessa turned her back to him as best she could. She sniffled again when she felt Mason wiping the soap from her face and pulling her hair back so he could wash it.

Mason washed and rinsed Tessa's hair, then added some conditioner. He then soaped up a rag and washed what he could reach. He pulled the plug from the tub and then washed the rest of her. He then rinsed the conditioner out of her hair, gave her body a second rinse, and helped her out of the tub.

Tessa let Mason dry her off after he wrapped her hair in a towel. "You're awfully good at this. I probably don't want to know how many women you've bathed."

Mason smiled behind Tessa's back. "You could have asked me for help."

Tessa looked at the curtains in the bathroom, but it was still dark outside. "I didn't want to disturb anyone. I just wanted to wash my hair. What time is it?"

Mason helped her into her nightgown, trying to ignore the bruising that covered her torso. The anger he would deal with later. Right now, she needed his help. "It was just shy of three when I came knocking."

"In that case, how good are you with a comb and a hair dryer?"

Tessa let Mason take care of her. He managed to comb the tangles out of her hair and blow dry it. By the time he was finished, her body was aching and she was yawning.

Mason set down the brush and placed a soft kiss on her hair. "I should put you back to bed."

Tessa opened her eyes to see Mason now standing in front of her. This was the first time she'd been completely alone with him besides the ride over to his parents' house. She reached out a hand to touch his jaw. He hadn't bothered to shave, and the stubble on his cheeks was rough against her palm. "Stay with me for a while?"

Mason couldn't resist touching his lips softly to hers.

He lifted his head and smiled into Tessa's upturned face. "Anything you want."

Tessa let Mason take her back to the guest room and settled against him when he climbed under the covers with her.

Thirty minutes later, Mason was stroking her shoulder but knew she wasn't asleep. "Something wrong?"

Tessa pulled away. "I'm wondering why I'm here."

"It's the safest place for you. We've been over that."

She knew that was true, but that wasn't what was bothering her. "It might be safest for me, but what about your parents?"

Mason leaned on his elbow so he could look down at her. "Are you forgetting my father was the police chief before me? He can handle anything that might come this way."

Tessa's gut clenched, but she had to say it. "Unless the source of danger is right inside their house, a danger they're protecting."

Mason sat up. "What does that mean?"

It was an effort to sit up, but she managed. "Me. I'm talking about me. You might have ignored me before and not done a background check, but after what happened, I know you finally did. It would be procedure."

Mason would have eventually brought up her arrest and imprisonment, but it hadn't been his intention to do it tonight. But since she brought it up, he pushed. "Okay, yes, it is procedure. And yes, I did. Peterson found your arrest in Dallas. I read your prison record, though your brother mentioned it at the hospital. He assumed I knew. What I read was lean on the details, as was your brother."

And that's why Tessa didn't understand. "Then why am I here? You know what I am."

Mason got angry. "And what exactly are you, Tessa? Are you a drug dealer? A thief?"

Tessa felt tears sting. "No."

"Then what exactly is the issue?"

"I shouldn't be here."

Mason thought back to their earlier argument. "Because of what the good townsfolk would think?"

Tessa bunched the blanket up to her chest. "Do you really think you can keep it a secret? Small towns can't keep secrets."

Mason cupped her chin and kissed her. Then for good measure, he kissed her again. "Let me worry about it."

Tessa leaned into Mason, unable to fight her urge to be closer. "I guess you could always pretend that you didn't know after I'm gone."

Mason didn't want to think about it. In the short time he'd known her, he'd become attached. Her leaving wasn't an option. He eased her back down so she was lying flat. Knowing she was way too sore, he simply lay down beside her and eased her into his embrace.

Tessa was no longer tired. "I suppose you want to know the whole story."

He did, but wasn't going to push her. "You should rest."

Tessa was quiet for a time, but sleep was going to be impossible. She had to know what he would do after she told him the whole story. "After Daddy was arrested, things got worse. I know that sounds crazy since he was the reason for most of our problems, but it did. We moved back in with Aunt Sylvia. Mom completely withdrew and hardly left her bedroom. Simon started getting into trouble more than he used to. Money became a bigger issue than before. Simon was stealing anything he could get away with. Later I found out he was pawning it. That's how he paid our school fees and got me new clothes. And then when he left and joined the army, he sent money home to me and Aunt Sylvia."

Mason kept his fingers stroking her neck, even when he tensed. "I hadn't thought of the money."

Tessa closed her eyes. Not a day went by back then that she hadn't thought about money, but that wasn't the important part of her story. "After Simon left, I got so lonely. It was hard to make friends; impossible really. Except for Timothy. His dad worked as a garbage man and his mom worked in the school cafeteria, so he got picked on a lot. As we got older, we just sort of fell into a relationship. When we graduated, he wanted nothing more than to get away. He wanted me to go with him. It seemed like such a grand thing to do. Getting away sounded like heaven. So we packed up and took his rattletrap car and headed to Dallas. His brother let us stay with him. I found a job, two actually. I had a part-time job in an office during the day and then worked at a restaurant at night. Tim had a harder time of it. Finally, he got a job at the garage where his brother worked."

Having been a cop in a big city, he had a pretty good idea of what was coming next. "I take it the garage was a front for something else."

Tessa looked at Mason, but she couldn't tell what he was thinking. "Yes, it was. I had no idea. We moved out of his brother's apartment and into our own. He kept telling me business was slow, but then he showed up one day with a new car. Well, a used car but nice. I knew we couldn't afford it. It was the first time he told me to mind my own business. Things went downhill pretty fast from there. Looking back, I can't believe how stupid I was. He called me all sorts of names, so I threw him out, but he kept coming around. He used the apartment while I was at work, though I never confronted him about it. I knew he would deny it, but things would be out of place when I got back. Things like the toilet seat being up or the fridge missing half its food. And he used the parking space at the apartment building to store his car because he didn't have anywhere to park it at his brother's place."

When she stopped, Mason prompted her. "Then what happened?"

Tessa took a moment to gather her thoughts. "Tim's brother, Parker, set me up. He called me and said Tim had been hurt. I still cared about him, so I grabbed Tim's spare keys and took his car. I ended up getting pulled over. I didn't understand what was happening. The police yelled at me to get out of the car. They grabbed and handcuffed me. I wasn't resisting, though I was definitely panicked. They tore the car apart. They found meth. The next thing I knew, I was at the police station. I was being charged with stealing a car, drug possession, and intent to sell. The police got a warrant and raided my apartment. They found more meth hidden. In the end, my very incompetent public defender told me I had two choices. He said I could plead guilty and get a lesser sentence, or I could plead innocent and get a longer sentence. Told me it was my choice."

Mason swore. "So you pleaded guilty."

"My lawyer had no intention of defending me. He said the evidence was stacked against me and there was no point. He refused to listen to me that they weren't my drugs. They had to be Tim's or his brother's. I kept telling him he should investigate Parker. At first, I pled innocent. But then I realized the prosecution had an easy case. They showed I had the drugs, had the car, and Tim and his brother were pointing the finger at me. In the end, I changed my plea, hoping for leniency. Case closed."

"Simon said he wants to appeal your case."

Tessa gave a short, harsh laugh. "While I was still in prison, Tim's brother was arrested for drug possession and intent to sell. He was also running a chop shop out of his garage. Tim somehow managed to keep clear of the police when Parker was arrested. But Tim wasn't able to keep himself clean. Two years ago, he was arrested for grand theft auto. Tim wasn't into the drug scene, but cars he knew, and he had no qualms about picking up where his brother left off."

"You don't think Simon has a chance?"

Tessa shook her head. "It doesn't matter anyway. I served two years and had just turned twenty-three when I was released. Being found innocent years later isn't going to change the fact that I spent those years behind bars, that I had to live through the trauma of the arrest and the trial. Simon thinks that because Parker and Timothy were key witnesses, if they could now be discredited, there is a chance a lawyer would look over my case and try to get the verdict reversed. I told him to stop wasting his money. He has a wife and kids and school loans. What is done is done. A reversal doesn't make it all better."

Mason took her hand. "What happened in prison? Simon said you'd been hurt."

Tessa pulled her hand free and rolled away from him. "A couple of women took a dislike to me. They busted my ribs and broke my arm. I was told I should be grateful they didn't slice up my pretty face. I spent some time in the infirmary. After that, I spent a lot of time isolated for my own protection. It's funny how protection looks a lot like solitary confinement. I don't want to talk about it anymore."

Mason scooted until her back rested against his chest. "I'm so sorry, Tessa."

Tessa glanced back at him. She hadn't believed he would believe her. She thought he would turn his back on her. She felt her eyes sting and her throat close. She turned her head away. "It seems so long ago now. In the years since, I've found a great job and have Simon and his family. It's enough that I have them and I'm free. So don't let Simon rope you into his scheme. Just leave it in the past."

Mason wrapped an arm around her waist. "Do you think either of them could have anything to do with what is happening now?"

Tessa shuddered but shook her head. "Parker is in prison. I'm not sure about Tim, but it seems ridiculous to think he would have something to do with this. I've not seen or heard from him since the trial. In the end, he was following his brother's lead. Had he been on his own, I don't think any of it would have happened. Why? What are you thinking?"

"Why don't we talk about it in the morning?"

Tessa wasn't going to be put off. "It is morning. What?"

Mason recognized the tone in her voice. She was going to get defensive, which was the last thing he wanted. He relented. "I'm thinking there are only two logical scenarios. Either this has to do with Tim and what happened between the two of you. Or this has something to do with your father."

Tessa shivered. "People hated my father. It's not outside the realm of possibility that people hate me. And I can't help but think that if it weren't me here, but Simon, then this would have happened to him. So all in all, I'd rather it was me."

Mason rolled her onto her back and loomed over her, his leg sliding between hers. "And I'd rather it was not you. And I'm not letting you out of my sight, or that of my father, until we find out who did this."

Tessa shifted under him. She couldn't help the desire that was curling in her belly, despite the pain in her ribs. "But motive? Just because you hate my dad doesn't mean you go around beating up people associated with him."

Mason couldn't help but feel the tiny shivers in her limbs with Tessa lying under him. "I hate to say this, but the next step is locating your father."

And though she agreed, seeing her father again was the

last thing she wanted to do, outside of ever setting foot inside a jail again. Tessa wrapped her arms around his neck. "How about we talk about something else? Or rather, do something else?"

Mason's pupils dilated in response to Tessa's words. "As much as I'd like to do that something else, you're hurt."

Tessa pouted, but the pout was meant to tease. "I bet if you tried really hard, you could figure out how to make love to me and not hurt me."

Mason nibbled on her neck, pushing the collar of the nightgown out of his way as he went. "Before this happened, you were refusing my phone calls."

Tessa tightened her arms around Mason's neck. "I had decided I was going to call you. I missed you. And sometimes I can be unreasonable."

Mason wasn't going to do something stupid like agree with her. Instead, he ran his hands up her legs, then up her sides, taking her nightgown with them. He tossed it on the floor beside the bed. Though he'd seen the bruising more than once, it still angered him. He let his lips softly kiss the discolored skin.

From there, Mason got creative, keeping his touch light and his body just a breath away from hers, so as not to put any pressure on her chest or belly. Tessa had never been teased and tasted like this before, and she had to bite her lip to keep from making any noise, overly conscious of the fact that Mason's parents were down the hall. She was sure they knew she and their son were lovers, but knowing it and hearing it were two different things.

By the time Mason slid between her thighs, Tessa had

completely forgotten about his parents. Admittedly her experience with men was limited, but she knew there was no one else like Mason. And as she peaked, with Mason braced above her so he wouldn't hurt or crush her ribs, she knew there would never be another man for her. For better or for worse, at that moment, in the darkness of his parents' guest room, Tessa knew without a doubt she was in love with Mason Slade.

Chapter Seventeen

Tessa was drained the morning after she told Mason about her arrest. Thankfully he had to go back to work, and she was given a couple of days to rest. She knew he was looking into where her father was. If he had found him, he hadn't said. And Tessa hadn't asked.

But now it had been a few days since she'd gotten out of the hospital, and she was feeling better. She was also feeling restless. Laine had told her not to come into the shop until the doctor cleared her. Tessa had no intention of seeing any doctor again for a long time. But she wasn't quite ready to go back to work yet.

Laine had stopped by a few times after work, just to chat and cheer her up. She had even bought her a new blouse and skirt to replace the ones that had been ruined in the attack. Tessa was still embarrassed by the outburst she'd had in front of Mason's family. When she had realized her new clothes were gone, she'd shed one too many tears. Both Laine and Eleanor had understood and had been sympathetic. Mason had looked like he wanted to be anywhere else but there.

Even Cyndi visited her. Mostly they talked about Cyndi's pregnancy, while Tessa shared a few stories of Sarah's pregnancies and Simon's over-protectiveness. The two women had shared a few laughs and even a couple of tears. Cyndi had also shared that news of the attack had reached the locals. Most were horrified that someone in their town would do such a thing. Had Tessa not been lying down, she might have fallen over when Mason had brought her mail from her aunt's house. In it were cards wishing her a speedy recovery; some included apologies for what had happened in their town. One card in particular from the mayor had her gaping. He had issued a dinner invitation as soon as she was feeling better.

When she had shown the card to Mason, he had gotten an odd look on his face. But then he had shrugged and told her that his father's friendship with the mayor extended to Mason. The last thing Tessa wanted to do was have dinner with her father's old enemy, but she had a feeling the mayor might be persistent if she refused his invitation. So instead of declining, she told Mason to extend her acceptance on a day that was convenient for him. Mason had come back saying they were invited to dinner in a week's time.

But right now all Tessa wanted was to see the progress Pete had made on the house. He'd called her a couple of times, but she was too used to being involved in her projects to sit on the sidelines. It had taken some doing, but she'd convinced Mason to take her to the house after work. So now here she was in the Slades' living room, watching the evening news with Donald, waiting for Mason to get off work.

"Anyone home?" Mason called through the house.

Tessa, who wanted to bounce out of her seat, had to take her time. She met Mason in the hall. "Hi. You're off early."

Mason leaned down and gave her a brief kiss. "Slow day. Of which I am grateful. So I knocked off early so we could see the house, then get back here in time for Mom's famous spaghetti dinner."

After having spent almost a week eating Eleanor's cooking, her mouth started to water. "Then, by all means, we should hurry."

Mason kissed her again, this one lingering. "Let me change, and we'll go."

Eleanor came around the corner as Mason headed up the stairs. She smiled at Tessa. "My son is smitten with you, you know?"

Tessa blushed. Yes, she was aware. Tessa could think of a few more adjectives to describe him too, like virile or lusty, but she certainly couldn't say that in front of his mother. "He's a good man. You raised him well. You must be so proud of him."

Eleanor waved Tessa into the kitchen for a minute. "His father and I are very proud of him. A mother worries, of course, given what he does for a living. He spends all of his time caring for others. I'd like to see someone take care of him, though he would deny that he needs to be taken care of."

Tessa nodded. "Everyone needs someone to care about them and take care of them sometimes. You do that by feeding him."

"Noticed, huh? Well, I can always trust Mason to stop by for dinner if invited, unless he's working. He rarely misses a Sunday dinner. Speaking of which, are you up to it?"

"Sunday dinner?"

Eleanor picked up her spoon and stirred the pot that was simmering on the stove. "Yes, we have family dinner most Sundays. Our last one was canceled, with you being hurt. But if you're feeling up to it, I'd like to have everyone over."

Tessa couldn't remember the last time she'd attended a Sunday dinner. She was more apt to show up at Simon's apartment after work, usually after dinner so she could rile up the kids before bedtime. But despite her qualms about getting any more involved with Mason's family, she found herself agreeing. "That would be nice."

Eleanor beamed. "Wonderful. I'll call everyone tonight and let them know we're on for dinner."

Tessa realized everyone included Laine's and Cyndi's husbands. Everyone would assume she was Mason's girlfriend, not that Mason was doing anything to discourage that belief. Their kiss in the hallway was just one example. He constantly showed her affection in front of his family. But she liked it too much to ask him to stop.

"Ready?" Mason followed the voices to the kitchen.

"Yes." Tessa was quick to respond and leave the kitchen.

Mason helped her into the SUV. "Mom coddling you too much?"

Tessa fastened her seat belt and adjusted it so it didn't dig into her ribs. "No, she's good. She's having everyone over for Sunday dinner. She wanted to make sure I was feeling up to it."

Mason patted her knee. "Are you feeling up to it?"

Tessa was feeling much better, minus the cast on her arm. "Yes, I feel up to it. It's just a little awkward, I guess. I think they think I'm your girlfriend."

Mason smiled. "You're that and a whole lot more."

Tessa could attest to the "whole lot more." Mason snuck into her room pretty much every night. The only night he hadn't was when he'd been called out to a nasty car accident. "I guess I never thought about it. But your parents aren't blind. Nor are they deaf. They probably hear you sneaking out of your room at night."

Mason knew she had that right. He'd run into his dad the other night on his way to her room. At first, Donald had simply shaken his head at his son. Then he'd seemed to think about it for a second, apparently came to some conclusion, saluted his son, and went back to his room. Mason doubted his dad had shared the story with his mom, but his mom had already given him her approval of the relationship building between them.

Pete was outside unloading some supplies when they pulled up. Tessa let Mason help her out of the SUV.

Pete came over and gave her an awkward hug. "How are you feeling?"

Tessa looked over at the house. The roof and siding were done, and the new windows were installed. The house looked exactly like she'd imagined it. And to top it off, the landscaping was done. The new plant beds were in, and the grass was starting to grow. "I'm okay. Sore some, but good. The house looks great. The yard looks great, too."

Pete gave it a once over. "Not too bad. Inside is looking good, too. Go on and check it out."

Tessa didn't have to be told twice. She let Mason walk her to the house. She stepped inside the cool interior. "And the air conditioner was installed."

Mason was glad for that. The evening was still too hot for his liking, and he didn't want Tessa in the heat for too long. Although he did miss her in her tank top and shorts. But like Tessa, he was curious about the house. The living room was patched and ready for painting. The kitchen was completely done. As they strolled through the rest, it looked like all the patching had been done, and all the rooms were ready for paint. The bathroom had also been redone, the taping, sanding, and priming all completed on the new walls. The floors were not done yet, and the new tub, sink, and toilet had not been installed, but the room looked a sight better now that all the old peeling paint and cracked tiles were gone.

Tessa stroked her hand over the wall. "I can't believe how much he got done."

Mason wrapped his arms around her from behind. "He had a little help. There's a young man in town who's a new carpenter apprentice. He jumped at the opportunity to help. Pete said the kid has promise."

Tessa turned in his embrace and placed her hands on his cheeks. The day's stubble tickled her palms. "You do so much for me. And I do so little for you."

Mason dragged her closer. "It's not a contest. And you do plenty for me. You did my laundry yesterday, though I told you not to. You heated up dinner when I came home late. And you sat up with me when I wasn't ready to sleep yet."

Tessa couldn't help but think they were such small things in comparison. He found someone to help fix up the house when she couldn't. He was there for her when her house was vandalized. He put her up in his parents' house to protect her. He was hunting down the man responsible for hurting her. Washing some clothes and nuking dinner weren't the same thing.

Mason leered at her, trying to break the tension. "And trust me when I say later tonight, I'll be sneaking into your room for some truly amazing sex. You've ruined me for other women."

Tessa pressed her breasts against his chest. "Yeah?"

Mason walked her backward and pressed her back against the wall. "Definitely yes."

Tessa nibbled his lower lip while he took the opportunity to fondle her breasts.

The front door slammed, and the pair broke apart. Tessa blushed while Mason groaned.

"Look good?" Pete called from the living room.

Tessa straightened her blouse and stepped into the hall. "The bathroom looks great. Everything looks great. I can't tell you how much I appreciate you taking care of the work."

Pete shrugged. "Nothing to it. Tomorrow, I need to finish up the master bedroom, then I just need to tile the bathroom floor. After that, it's all up to you to finish the painting. I can do the ceilings and install the fixtures if you want."

What Tessa wanted was for her arm to be out of the cast so she could do it herself. But Simon was waiting on her to put the house on the market. "Go ahead and paint the ceilings and put in the new light fixtures. And that will leave you with just the tub, toilet, and sink. I'll make Mason help me with the painting. I'll call Simon tonight and let him know he can start talking to the realtor."

Pete stacked up the paint cans he had brought in and went back outside.

Mason brushed back some stray hairs on Tessa's cheek. "I can help you paint, huh?"

Tessa smiled brightly at him. "I can paint one-handed. I just can't pour or cleanup. So when you're not working, you can help. I'll teach you the right way to paint. Pete is doing the hard part. Trust me, the ceilings are the hardest. And then, too, you can climb ladders and help do corners."

Mason sighed. Looked like he was going to be painting in his near future.

* * *

Sunday dinner was loud and raucous. So a typical Slade family night. The family had stayed later than usual, but by nine, the house had cleared out. Mason was glad when he got to say his last good night. Tessa might not be tired, but he was exhausted. He'd gotten called out after he and Tessa visited the house. And the next couple of days had been much of the same. He'd been at work most of Sunday morning but had made it home just in time for dinner. And tonight he'd finally gotten a current address on Randy Harris. The bastard was just across the state line, which was only a few hours away. His theory that Randy was involved just got a lot more plausible. Now he had to break it to Tessa.

He stripped out of his clothes and found the worn pair of flannel pants he had been wearing while at his parents' house. Usually, he slept nude except for really cold winter nights. The flannel was half of only two pairs he owned.

There was a light knock on his bedroom door, and he had no doubt who was on the other side. He opened it and gestured Tessa inside. His parents were probably still awake, and Tessa still wore the dress she'd worn to dinner.

Tessa sat on the edge of the bed. "You look exhausted, Mason."

Mason seconded that with a huge yawn. "The last couple of days have been brutal."

Tessa patted the spot beside her. "You wouldn't think small towns would keep the police so busy."

Mason stretched out on the bed instead of sitting. He almost groaned in relief. "You'd be surprised. But we also help other local and county police when needed. We were needed."

Tessa knew from experience that was all Mason would say. He didn't go into detail about what he had been working on. He had told her that he liked to shut it off when he got home, not rehash it. She could respect that.

Tessa gently pushed Mason until he rolled over onto his stomach. She gently massaged his neck, shoulders, and back with her good hand. It certainly wasn't a hardship to look at Mason from behind.

Mason groaned out loud and relaxed further into the mattress. "That feels amazing."

Tessa worked on the muscles of his back until he fell asleep. He had already folded the covers back, so all she had to do was cover him up. She lay down next to him, planning to stay only for a few minutes. Instead, she fell asleep.

A loud knock on the door, followed by a bright light, woke the pair. Tessa abruptly sat up, confused about where she was. She saw Donald at the door. Then she felt Mason stirring beside her.

"Your sister Cyndi called. She's at the hospital. She was having some bleeding. She told your mother the doctor assures her she and the baby are okay, but they're keeping her. Your mom and I are heading over."

Mason threw the covers aside. "Let me get some clothes on. Tessa and I will be right behind you. Did you call Laine?"

Donald's glance flicked over at Tessa. "Your mother is calling her. We'll take two cars in case you get called in."

The bedroom door closed. Mason tossed his flannel pants in the closet and tugged on a pair of briefs and a fresh pair of jeans. He was grabbing a shirt when he noticed Tessa hadn't moved. He dropped the shirt and came to her side. "Are you okay?"

She took a deep breath and nodded. "Sorry. When he burst in and the lights turned on, I got scared."

He gathered her against him. She was shaking. "Come on. We'll go get your clothes. You'll be cold in that dress."

Tessa climbed out from under the covers, not remembering when she had covered herself up. "Are you sure you want me to come? This is a family thing."

Mason knew now was not the time, but if he had his way, she would be family before the year was out. "Yes, I'm sure. Come on."

Tessa waited while Mason tugged on a t-shirt and grabbed his socks and shoes. When she got to the guest room, Mason was the one who gathered her clothes. She quickly changed, then grabbed a pair of sandals after running a brush through her hair.

By the time they got downstairs, his parents had already left. They were both quiet on the drive over. When they arrived, Cyndi had already been settled into a room.

Tessa stood behind the group gathered. She had stood back and watched as Mason kissed his sister's forehead. Cyndi's husband, Tyler, was beside her bed, holding her hand. Laine and Russell weren't far behind their arrival.

Cyndi, looking very tired, was relaxed in the bed. "All you guys didn't have to come. I'm fine. Just a scare, is all."

Eleanor shushed her. "You just rest."

Cyndi glanced at the group. "I can't do that with everyone watching."

The crowd retired to the waiting area. Eleanor and Tyler were the only ones to stay behind. Laine and Russell sat next to each other, Laine resting her head on her husband's shoulder. Donald took up residence at the windows. Mason paced.

Tessa took a seat across from Laine and Russell.

Laine glanced at her dad, then Mason. She then turned to Tessa. "Should you be out of bed?"

Tessa gave Laine an absent nod. "I'm fine. I should be able to start work again on Friday. Hopefully, next week, if

Mason can spare some time, I'm going to start painting the house."

Donald came and sat next to Tessa. "Hopefully Mason can find the man who did this. And if it turns out it was your father, I'll have a go at him myself. Right after Mason."

Tessa frowned. "What?"

Mason stopped pacing. "I meant to tell you before I fell asleep. I found your dad. I'll be paying him a visit."

Tessa shivered, but it wasn't from being cold. "You mean you and I will be paying him a visit."

Mason was going to speak when Donald jumped in. "That's not a good idea, Tessa. You need to let Mason handle this. If your father did have something to do with this, you don't want to be anywhere near him."

Tessa's jaw ached from clenching it. "If he did have something to do with it, then I have the right to confront him."

Laine's voice was husky when she spoke. "I don't think we should be arguing about this right now. Not here."

Tessa settled back into her seat. She was startled when Donald patted her hand and winked at her.

Mason resumed his pacing.

A short time later, Eleanor found the group. "She's sleeping. The doctor came in and everything looks okay. She said this can happen sometimes. Cyndi will need to be on bed rest for a while, but the doctor said she doesn't expect any further complications."

The family released a collective sigh of relief. Laine and Russell left first. Eleanor and Donald visited with Tyler for a short while before they left.

Mason had stopped pacing and was now standing by the windows watching the sunrise.

Tessa came and placed a hand on his shoulder. "We should go. You have to work soon."

Mason kept his eyes on the horizon. "You're right. You do have a right to confront him. I've got some paperwork to tackle, but we can leave around lunchtime."

Tessa put her arm around Mason's waist. "Your sister will be okay."

Mason let out a pent-up breath. "I see a lot of bad things, Tessa. Sometimes it's hard not to see the bad in every situation. Thanks for coming and being with me."

Tessa felt her eyes sting. "I wouldn't be anywhere else."

Chapter Eighteen

Despite his words at the hospital, Mason did try to talk Tessa out of coming with him. In the end, it was futile, just as he'd known it would be. Under other circumstances, it would be nice to go for a drive with Tessa. Other than their first date, they hadn't had a chance to repeat the experience. Tessa hadn't said anything, and she seemed content with their relationship as it was. It had been amusing when Tessa finally realized on the drive home from the hospital that his dad had caught them in bed together. Never mind that they both had clothes on. He'd told her it could be worse, but she hadn't seen the humor in his words.

Tessa spoke, hoping to break the tension. "I looked up the house. It looks a lot like the houses I grew up in. A bit worn and a lot shabby."

Mason thought about her aunt's house and the type of house her father would have bought. "I take for granted the house I grew up in. It's always felt like home; it felt safe, the way a home should feel. Dad was always tinkering with something when he wasn't working. No matter where I was or what I was doing, it was always a pleasure coming home. Mom would have dinner ready. My dad did his best to be home for dinner, though he was missing more times than not."

"I like your parents' house. Four bedrooms, two full

bathrooms with a half bath off the kitchen. The yard is a nice size, big enough for playing games and running around, but not so big that it would be difficult to maintain. And a nice two-car garage, heated according to your dad. And your mom turned the kitchen into a cook's dream. And I always thought it was best when the eating area was attached to the kitchen instead of in its own space."

Mason turned onto the county's main highway. "It's hard to think about them selling it. Laine wants to buy it, but she's overextended with her shop. Cyndi and Tyler bought his grandparents' house."

"So why don't you buy it?"

Mason glanced over at Tessa. "Thought about it. Seems like a lot of house for one person. Want to marry me, and we can buy it and fill it up with kids?"

Tessa knew heat infused her entire face. The thought of getting pregnant by Mason was a highly erotic thought. She could easily imagine what their kids would look like.

Mason wasn't unaware of her reaction. "How about we table that thought for now and talk about it later?"

Tessa knew she should laugh it off. He wasn't serious. Was he? He didn't look like he was joking. She shifted uncomfortably in her seat.

Mason wasn't ready to let the subject completely drop. "Don't you ever think about having kids, a family of your own?"

Tessa kept her eyes on the scenery flying by. "Sure. Before prison. I guess in the beginning I thought Timothy and I would build a family. That dream was crushed pretty fast. After prison, I wasn't ready yet. When I was finally ready to try dating, I found out that the type of men who are attracted to ex-cons are not the type I want to settle down and raise a family with. Simon is always harping on me; he tells me I need to get out more. When I stopped trying to find my own dates, he tried setting me up a few times. But it didn't work. Everyone who knows Simon knows his sister is an ex-con. He met Sarah before I got out of prison. They got married after I was released. So it wasn't a secret why they were waiting."

"And the men he set you up with?"

"They were nice enough, but they were uncomfortable around me. His friends look at him with pity when I'm around. Needless to say, I don't spend much time with him and his friends. One friend of his went so far as to tell me that Simon should be given an honorary sainthood for taking care of me. Let's just say dating got old really fast. And it's not like I can keep it a secret."

Mason placed a hand on her knee. "I know, and it bothers me, but not because I think you're guilty. I know what goes on inside prisons. You survived it and are a better person for it. But even if you were guilty, I'd still be with you."

Tessa eased around in her seat so she could face him. "I guess that's what I don't get. You're a police chief. I'll reflect pretty poorly on your judgment. When the townsfolk find out, they're either going to demand that you be fired, or they're going to rebel and dishonor your authority."

"I've been thinking about that. I'm well-liked. So is my dad. When we both stand at your side, the town will have no choice but to accept you. People can change. In time, people will start to remark on how wonderful it is that you turned your life around."

Tessa was still embarrassed that Donald caught her in Mason's bed. She hadn't meant to fall asleep. "Did your dad say anything to you? I mean, your parents have been great. They're nice people. But now that they know, they can't be thrilled you're sleeping with me. They probably can't wait until the day I pack my bags and leave."

"Actually, neither said anything. Yes, they both know. But they got to know you over the past few days. Dad's on Team Simon."

"Team Simon?"

Mason couldn't help but smile. "Yes. Team Simon. The team that wants to prove you were wrongly convicted. Dad knows people. He's already been in contact with Simon and the lawyer he hired."

Tessa's hand fisted in her lap. "I told him to stop wasting his money."

Mason laid a hand on her fist. "Older brother prerogative. He can spend his money any way he wants. And don't look to me to discourage him. I believe in justice. And I also believe in righting wrongs. What happened to you was a gross miscarriage of justice. If I can help get the conviction overturned, I will."

Tessa opened her fist and turned her hand so that she was holding his. "No matter what I say?"

Mason really wanted to kiss her but kept his eyes on the road. "Yep. You're going to have to get used to having other people care about you besides Simon and Sarah."

If Tessa wasn't already in love with him, she would have fallen for him at that moment. Her heart swelled with emotions she couldn't name. It took her a while before she could speak again. When she did, she got back to the point of their drive. "What exactly are you going to do? Go in there and demand he confess?"

Mason was amused. "I think I can do better than that. The trick is to be subtle; to take him off guard. Then get him to confess."

"Dad never did understand subtle. Your dad can probably count the number of times my dad was arrested for his not-so-subtle behavior."

Mason squeezed her hand and took his back. "The mayor can probably attest to that fact, too. Just let me do the talking."

Tessa didn't have a problem with that. She still was unsure of what she was doing, confronting her father. She hadn't told Simon or her mother that they had found Randy. No matter the outcome, she wouldn't tell her mother. Simon would demand the truth, and Tessa would bet her next paycheck that Mason would be cooperative.

Tessa was relieved when, during the rest of the drive, they chatted about everyday things. Mason told her about some of the police work he did while living in Salt Lake City. Tessa told him about some of her more eventful painting and remodeling jobs she'd done. After a few hours, they were pulling onto the street her father lived on. The neighborhood could have been a clone of the one she'd grown up in.

When they finally pulled up in front of her father's

house, Tessa couldn't help but comment. "This looks like every other run-down, worn-out house we ever lived in when I was growing up. I'll take my tiny studio apartment over this any day."

Mason came around and took her hand. "Agreed. Let's get this over with."

Tessa couldn't say she was surprised when a dark-haired woman with an obvious dye job answered the door in response to Mason's knock.

A lit cigarette dangled from her aged lips. "What?"

Mason took his credentials out of his wallet. "I'm looking for Randy Harris."

A shocked expression came over the woman's face. "I don't know what kind of game you're playing, but it ain't funny."

Tessa took a small step forward. "I'm Tessa Harris. I'm looking for my father."

The woman squinted, seeing Tessa for the first time. "Now that is funny, given how long it's been since he saw you."

"Is he here?"

"Missy, I can't say I'm happy to be the one to tell you this, but your daddy is dead."

Tessa wavered on her feet for a moment. "Dead? When?"

Mason put an arm around Tessa and addressed the woman. "Mind if we come in?"

The woman flicked her cigarette into the bushes and waved them inside. "Suppose. But you have no rights as far as I'm concerned."

Mason led Tessa to the small loveseat in the worn living room. "We just want to know what happened."

The woman shrugged. "Guess it's okay to tell his daughter. He was killed two weeks ago. Someone shot him. Police haven't been around much, and I doubt they're trying hard to find his killer. You're a cop? How come you didn't know?"

It was a good question. Mason hadn't read or seen anything that hinted at his death or shooting when he'd gone looking for Randy's whereabouts. "Can you tell us the specifics?"

The woman shrugged. "Randy worked the night shift at the warehouse outside of town. Cops said he went on his break around one. Randy always went out for a smoke. When he didn't come back, one of his coworkers went looking for him. Cops said they found him not too far from where the smokers hang out, shot twice in the chest. No one heard anything. No one saw anything. Like I said, I haven't heard anything from the cops since. They questioned me, questioned some folks at the warehouse, and a few of his friends. No one knows why."

"Do you have an alibi for that night?" Mason went into cop mode.

"Now, the local cops asked me the same thing. I was with some friends down at the bar down the street. The opposite side of town from the warehouse, in fact. People saw me. Gave me a nice alibi."

Mason nodded. "Do you know who would benefit from his death?"

"Me, for one. I don't have him hanging around,

mooching money off me anymore. He drank every penny he made. And I suppose his wife might if there were any money, which there ain't."

That surprised Tessa. "You know about my mom?"

"Course. He said he couldn't marry me because he was already hitched. Said he had a couple of kids too, that he hadn't seen in years."

Mason took Tessa's hand and rose. "Thank you for your time. Your name?"

"Nancy." She looked at Tessa. "And tell your mama there ain't nothing here for her. She better not get to thinking she's entitled to his money or his stuff. It's mine."

Tessa leaned into Mason. "You don't need to worry about it. There is nothing of his that anyone in the family would want."

Tessa let Mason help her into the SUV. When he settled into the driver's seat, she turned to him. "So now what? He can't possibly be the attacker."

"We make a stop at the police station. First rule is to always verify what you're told."

Since that made sense, Tessa dropped silent. She wasn't sure what she was feeling about her father. Certainly not grief. But perhaps a bit of sorrow at his wasted life. She'd have to tell her mom. Or perhaps she'd chicken out and tell Simon first and let him tell their mother. Tessa supposed Janine wouldn't care one way or the other, other than to know she was now a widow.

When Mason and Tessa arrived at the local police department, Tessa decided to stay out in the waiting area while Mason went and spoke privately with the detective who was working the case. The day of her arrest was still a vivid memory for her. The less time she spent here, and the closer to the exit she was, the better off she'd feel.

Mason thanked the receptionist again as he made his way to where Tessa was waiting. "Why don't we get something to eat? Then we can chat."

Mason found a decent place to eat on the other side of town. After they ordered, he told Tessa what the detective told him. "Nancy had most of the story. The detective has no leads. There were no cameras, no witnesses, and no one heard the shots. The coroner confirmed the time of death was around one in the morning, the time Randy was on his break. It wouldn't have taken but a couple of days following Randy around to know his routine. The noise in the warehouse would have drowned out people inside hearing the shots. The bullets pulled from the body were pretty damaged, but the coroner thinks if he had a weapon to compare it to, he could match it. But the detective said the case is already cold. He has no leads and no motive."

Tessa swallowed the food that had lumped up in her mouth. "How come the detective didn't question me? I'm family, I'm nearby, and I'm an ex-con. I could simply hate him and come and shot him."

"Except you were with me at the time of his death. Having a cop vouch for you is a pretty airtight alibi."

Tessa couldn't help but smile at him. "You sure do come in handy."

Mason's eyes darkened. "And I'll be happy to show you how handy later. But the detective has hit a wall. Nancy does have a solid alibi. Nothing was taken, so robbery is out. And given your attack, I just can't see this as having been random. I told the detective what happened, but he's not interested in tying your attack to his victim."

"Guess I understand that. Randy was not exactly an upstanding citizen. And at the end of the day, unless someone comes forward, the detective doesn't have much in the way of evidence."

Mason finished his coffee. "No. He doesn't. Sometimes crimes are just not solvable. And you can't waste time on them when there are so many other cases to deal with. It sucks, but it's the way it is."

Tessa looked out the window of the restaurant. It was already getting dark outside. "So the next step is what?"

Mason wasn't sure yet. Randy was a dead end, literally. Tessa ruled out her ex-boyfriend and his brother as suspects. He had to trust her judgment on that. It did seem a bit farfetched anyway. And it wasn't an option to sit around and wait for the guy who attacked her to return. "I say we get a hotel room and get a good night's rest. I'm not feeling up to the long drive back, and I'm sure you're not either."

Tessa hadn't wanted to admit she was still sore. And she was exhausted. The half cup of coffee she drank wasn't going to keep her going. She was glad Mason had insisted they pack an overnight bag, just in case.

Mason drove them a few towns over, stopping at a nice hotel they had passed on the way in. Tessa took a hot bath while Mason called his family to check in on Cyndi. She could hear through the closed door that she had been released from the hospital.

Tessa came out wearing a soft cotton nightgown, her hair pinned up. "I should call Simon."

Mason nodded and went to take a shower.

Tessa told Simon the story as quickly and concisely as possible. There was no point in speculating about the reason he'd been shot. She knew Simon would come to the same conclusion that Mason had. And he had told her he'd let their mom know. Grateful she wouldn't have to tell Janine, she hung up. Simon was better at dealing with their mother than she was. Probably because, with the children, Simon spent more time with her than Tessa did.

"How'd he take it?"

Tessa realized she was sitting and staring at her phone. "Same as I did, I guess. I can't pretend I'm broken up about it. But it's odd to think he's dead. And I guess it's a little sad that he never tried to make something of his life."

Mason, sensitive to her mood, came and sat behind her. He lightly rubbed the tension from her shoulders. When she sighed and leaned against him, he eased her down on her belly so he could reach the rest of her back.

Tessa didn't protest when he eased her nightgown over her head and off. Then she felt him move off her for a moment to toss aside the towel he had wrapped around his waist when he'd come out of the bathroom. When he came back to her, his fingers continued to massage her neck and shoulders before moving down her back.

Mason kept his touch light, keeping his weight off her so as not to hurt her ribs. But as he massaged her soft skin, he couldn't help it when his fingers trailed down her back to her hips and over the curve of her backside. Pressing his hands into the mattress beside her body, he bent to place a soft kiss behind her ear. Then a soft kiss on her neck. He kissed a trail down her spine.

She arched herself into him, the light massage turning into something more intimate. She loved the feel of his lips and tongue on her skin. "Mason?"

"Don't move."

Tessa turned her head but stayed where she was when Mason left her. When he came back, he had put on a condom. When he climbed back onto the bed, he knelt between her thighs, positioning her hips to accept him into her body. Her fingers gripped the fabric of the blanket beneath her, anchoring herself when he slipped inside. She felt one arm wrap around her lower belly as he surged into her over and over. She buried her face in the mattress, muffling the sounds she knew she was making. Her climax hit the same time his did when he surged into her one last time.

She felt Mason collapse half on, half off her. His breath was wet on her temple. Her own breath was still coming in gasps from the aftereffects of his lovemaking. She couldn't help the tears that stung her eyes. She knew she shouldn't, but she couldn't hold back anymore. "I love you, Mason."

It took a moment for Tessa's words to register. At first, he thought he had imagined them. But then he saw her biting her lip, as if trying to hold in her words. He carefully turned her over. "Do you mean that?"

She didn't want to look him in the eyes, but he gave her no choice. His fingers were on her cheek, easily holding her face to his. "Yes, I do."

Mason sat and hugged her to him. "Thank goodness. I thought I was going to have to work a lot harder for you to admit that."

Tessa pulled back. "You knew I loved you?"

Mason grinned at her. She almost looked outraged. "I had hopes. And you've made me very happy. I love you too, Tessa."

She gaped at him for a second. Then she gave him the same grin he was giving her. "I'm glad."

After a quick trip to the bathroom, Mason pulled Tessa to her feet, then pulled the covers back so they could settle under the sheets. She curled up against his side. His fingers trailed over her skin, simply enjoying the feel of her beside him. He stroked her arm and her breasts before settling his hand on her hip. He fell asleep with her tucked securely to his side.

Chapter Nineteen

When Tessa woke up in the morning, Mason was behind her, his hand resting possessively on her breast. Holding his hand in place with the fingers outside her cast, she used her other hand to return the favor. She knew the instant he became awake.

"Feeling playful this morning?" Mason's fingers plucked her nipple while her fingers lightly stroked his morning erection.

"Feeling happy. I've never been in love before. I guess this is how I imagined waking up with the man I love each morning." Tessa's grip tightened on his hand to move his fingers to her other breast so it could receive the same treatment.

Mason heard the teasing words, but they sobered him. Carefully easing away from her, he settled her onto her back on the bed. "Never been in love before? Not even with what's-his-face?"

Tessa responded to his serious tone. "I didn't love Timothy. I guess I used him. But he used me, so I guess we were even in that sin. I wanted to love him. I wanted us to be the perfect couple. But deep down I knew I didn't love him, and he didn't love me. It didn't take long to realize there was no chance of us being the perfect couple. But I did care about him. We were friends. I just couldn't get beyond that. I imagine you've been in love before."

Mason figured he deserved the question being turned on him. And he knew she deserved an honest answer. "When I was new to the police force, there was a woman. Her name was Helen. She was a rookie cop, too. Our relationship got as far as living together. I did love her, at least as much as a man focused on his career could be. She said she loved me too, but she was just as dedicated to her career. She got a job offer out of state. She asked me to go with her. But I was doing well with the department and didn't want to start over. So she left. It hurt for a while. I didn't date anyone else for some time. Then the hurt just sort of drifted away. I seriously dated a few other women but didn't love them. And I certainly didn't feel this strongly for Helen."

Tessa pulled Mason down to her so she could kiss him, her legs wrapping around his hips. "Her loss is definitely my gain."

Mason accepted her sultry invitation. Afterward the pair climbed out of bed, showered, had a quick breakfast in the hotel café, and got back on the road.

Tessa was much more relaxed now that they were heading back home. It was funny, really, to think of Willow Landing as home. "So the next step?"

Mason had been contemplating that next step. "We'll stop in and talk to Chief Peterson. See if he and his team have made any progress."

Unfortunately, he hadn't. His men questioned neighbors and business owners in the neighborhood but had nothing to add to the investigation. Walter on Mason's team didn't find anything new either. With no other leads, Mason dropped Tessa off at his parents' house and then headed back to the station.

Mason hated it when things came to a halt like this. He'd already created enough of a stir when he'd questioned Degrassi and Deputy Thomson. News of Tessa's attack had been met with mixed emotions. Some people felt bad and wished they could help. Others figured the Harris woman got what she had coming.

The rest of the week yielded no other leads either. Tessa, with Pete's help and supervision, finished painting the house, finished the bathroom, and installed the new lighting. She called Simon and told him to get the real estate agent out there and get the house listed. The sooner it was sold, the better she'd feel.

Now that the house was listed, Tessa knew she should be heading back to Indiana. Her little apartment was waiting. Her small, lonely apartment. Mason hadn't said anything other than congratulations the night she told him the house was finished. Then he had kissed her and sent her off to bed. Thirty minutes later, when his parents were in bed, he had snuck to her room and made love to her. He teased her because she insisted they needed to sleep separately under his parents' roof, and he had respected that request. In turn, they didn't sleep much most nights. After making love, he would stay for a while, sneaking out in the early morning. She was tired, so she knew he had to be.

Tessa was in the guest room getting dressed for her dinner at the mayor's house when there was a knock at the door. She opened it to find Mason on the other side, already dressed in a dark navy suit.

Mason dropped a kiss on her upturned lips. "See you're not ready yet."

Tessa was standing in her underwear and slip. "I have a dress I bought at Mauve's store. But I was having issues with my makeup. Having only one hand makes things difficult."

He thought she looked beautiful and said so. He helped her into the navy dress that matched his suit. Then he led her downstairs, and his parents waved them on their way.

Tessa straightened the skirt of the dark blue dress, as thrilled with how it fit now as she had been when she bought it. "I wish we didn't have to do this."

Mason took his turn straightening his tie. One nice thing about wearing a uniform was no tie. "It's hard to turn down an invitation from the mayor. We can have dinner, a quick drink, and use your injuries as an excuse to duck out early."

"Mason, tell me the truth. Do you think you'll find the guy who did it?"

Mason sighed. "Had to ask it like that, didn't you? Honestly, Tessa, I don't know. We have his blood from the pavement, but not much else, other than your description. It could be anyone. But I'm going to do everything I can to find him and keep you safe."

She knew he hadn't had any other leads but hadn't been able to help asking. Every day she was living in limbo. She loved Mason, so much so that she knew she'd give up anything, even her home, to be with him. And she believed him when he said he loved her. But when she suggested moving into his house, he told her he preferred her staying at his parents' house so she could be supervised by his dad when he was at work. And he never mentioned what would happen if they didn't catch the man, or what would happen even if they did.

But she didn't have any more time to discuss it. The mayor's house loomed before her. Objectively, she knew it was a nice house. It was Victorian in design but darker than she preferred. But something about the house set her on edge.

Mason wasn't oblivious to her sudden tension but knew the best thing would be to get the night over with. He slipped a borrowed shawl over her shoulders and led her up the steps. The doorbell was answered almost immediately. A maid in a gray dress led them to what Tessa figured was the room where the mayor liked to entertain guests.

Alex Griswold came over and shook Mason's hand. Then he took Tessa's. "I'm so glad the two of you could come."

"It's nice to meet you, Mayor." Tessa extracted her hand.

"Alex, please. Ah, and here is my wife, Daria."

Tessa shook the woman's hand, but she got the distinct impression that the woman was not happy to see her.

Alex offered them all a drink, handing Mason a glass of scotch and Tessa a glass of white wine from the bottle his wife had opened for herself.

Alex sat across from them after his wife excused herself to check on dinner. "I can't tell you how sorry I was to hear what happened to you, Tessa. It's disturbing to think something like this happened in my town."

Tessa wasn't sure how she was supposed to respond to that. She was tempted to apologize, but then forced it down. And technically, it hadn't happened in his town, but she figured the point was moot. "I imagine whoever it was simply thought he was doing the town a favor."

Alex nodded. "I had some unpleasant thoughts myself when I heard a Harris was back in town. It's no secret that your father and I were not friends. At least, not when he left."

Mason took a sip. "How do you mean?"

Alex leaned back in his seat, a man very comfortable in his surroundings. "Randy and Janine were friends with my wife and me for a time. Tessa, you would have been too young to remember. But eventually, the friendship soured. Randy couldn't seem to hold his liquor. He made a lewd pass at my wife. I couldn't stand by while he made unwanted advances. We came to blows over it at a bar."

Mason remembered that well. It was one of the many times his father arrested Randy Harris. But he didn't like the way Alex was bringing up old news. "I'm sure Tessa isn't interested in old history."

"Of course. Any luck in finding the attacker?"

Mason wasn't any happier with that change in subject. "No. And neither has Peterson. There wasn't much evidence, and not much to go on. I had a lead, but it was a dead end."

Alex refreshed his drink. "What lead?"

Mason knew the mayor would find out anyway. "Randy Harris. But when I went to talk to him, I found out he had been murdered two weeks before."

"Murdered?"

Mason thought the shock on Alex's face was real. "It came as a surprise to me and Tessa, too. He was shot twice and died at the scene. No leads. So he wasn't alive when Tessa was attacked."

Alex sat back down. "Guess it would have been too easy. But he was an obvious suspect. I didn't realize he lived nearby."

Mason gave him a brief rundown.

"It's a pity. We were friends once, after all."

A commotion in the hall interrupted the conversation. Monty slid to a halt inside the room when he saw Mason and Tessa. His eyes landed on Tessa for a moment before sliding away to Mason.

"Hey, Monty. How's it going?"

Monty found his voice. "Good, Chief. I had football practice with some of the guys. Tryouts for the team are next month."

"It's a sure thing." Mason noticed Monty wouldn't look at Tessa, and he seemed nervous.

Alex stood and slapped his hand on his son's back. "No doubt. He's the best player the team has. Go on up and get washed up for dinner. We've got guests."

Monty bolted from the room.

"How's Landon doing?" Mason watched with troubled eyes as Monty left the room.

"Good. It's nice having him home for summer break. He'll be heading back to college soon. Speak of the devil."

Landon Griswold came in and said hello. "Nice to meet

you, Tessa. And good to see you again, Chief."

Tessa felt a shiver down her spine but didn't understand why. She glanced around, but other than Alex and Landon, no one else was in the room. She was grateful when they all headed to dinner.

Tessa ate some of the food set before her, but the Griswolds were getting on her nerves. Daria kept glaring at her, and she had no idea why. Monty just chatted on and on about football. Landon was a typical politician, every word and phrase properly articulated, but phony all around. Alex was the consummate host, and he never let the conversation falter.

Alex dabbed his lips with his napkin. "But I've dominated the conversation. How is your family, Tessa? I hear you live in Indiana with your brother now."

Tessa didn't want to answer him but didn't want to be rude. "I live in Indiana. My brother does too, with his wife and two kids. My mom lives there. She likes being a grandmother."

"And you fix up houses?"

Tessa glanced at Mason. He gave her an encouraging smile. "Mostly I paint them. Indoor and outdoor. I've started venturing into renovations, but I've got a lot to learn yet. Aunt Sylvia's house is done and on the market. It will be nice to have a family living in it again."

"My condolences on your aunt's passing."

"Thank you."

They all adjourned back to what Tessa figured he called the library. Though the books on the shelves all looked chosen for their size and coloring, not for their content.

Monty eventually excused himself to do his homework.

Tessa nudged Mason, hoping he'd get the message that she'd had enough fun.

Landon settled in across from Tessa. "So your mother lives in Indiana. What about your father?"

Tessa didn't like the way Landon was looking at her. She couldn't put her finger on what it was about him that bothered her. He seemed sincere. He seemed like a very nice man. But something was bothering her, and he made her uncomfortable.

Mason patted her knee as he answered Landon for her. "Condolences are needed in this case as well. We learned that Randy Harris is dead."

"No one will miss that vile man." Daria rose. "Excuse me. I need to check on Monty. He says he is doing his homework, but he's most likely playing video games."

Alex also rose. "I imagine you're more than ready to rest, Tessa. Again, I am sincerely sorry for what happened. I have faith Mason will find him."

When Tessa and Mason were once again outside, Tessa let out a pent-up breath. "Here's your hat; what's your hurry?"

Mason smiled. "I got that feeling, too. For a while, I didn't think he was ever going to stop talking."

Tessa pulled the shawl around her shoulders. She wanted nothing more than to get back to the warmth of Mason's parents' house. "Probably why he's a politician. Landon takes after him in that, though they don't look alike."

Mason started up the vehicle. "Monty favors his dad.

Landon favors his mother. I've no doubt Landon will fill his dad's shoes one day. That might be the day I retire."

"Don't want to work with him?"

"There has always been something off about him, if you know what I mean."

"Yeah, I got that vibe. Do you think you'll retire?"

Mason thought about it. "Sure, one day. I figure once I can't be effective as chief anymore. I have always felt like my dad retired too early. Though I think my mom had something to say about that. She wasn't happy when I wanted to be a cop. She'd rather I had been a doctor or a lawyer."

"Typical family hopes and dreams, I suppose. Except in my house, we just hoped Simon would graduate high school before being arrested."

"He became the doctor. I don't have that in my blood."

"Me either. Don't know where he gets it from. I wanted to be a princess when I grew up."

That got a laugh out of Mason. "Complete with a prince to whisk you off to his castle, no doubt."

Tessa set a hand on top of his. "I'm willing to settle for a police chief with a house."

Mason took a deep breath. "We haven't talked about our future."

Tessa dropped her hand. "No, we haven't. The house will no doubt sell fast. Want to move into a tiny apartment with me in Indiana?"

"I want you to stay, Tessa. And if you're honest, I think you want to stay."

"I want to stay. I just don't know how it would work.

The small-town police chief and an ex-con. And I would miss Simon, Sarah, and the kids."

He ignored the ex-con statement. He'd deal with that if it ever became an issue. "Think Simon longs to move back to Utah?"

Tessa's head dropped on the headrest. "No, I don't think so."

"What if I promise to take you back for birthdays and a couple of holidays?"

"I think the townsfolk might be a little upset with you. I'm guessing your vacation time is close to nothing."

"A week once a year if I'm lucky. Last year I managed two weeks."

Tessa didn't have the perfect answer. But she did have one. "How long do you think we can conduct an affair in your parents' house? Because I was thinking that if you bought their house, we could conduct it indefinitely."

Mason pulled into the driveway of his parents' house. He looked at Tessa. "You're serious."

She shrugged. "I love you, Mason. I can't go home unless you come with me. Or you kick me out."

Mason pulled her into his arms, not an easy feat maneuvering her across the front seat, but he managed. "I love you, Tessa. And if you're serious, I swear I'll make them an offer tonight."

Tessa kissed him, shifting so she could wrap her arms around his neck. She pulled back when the front porch light came on. She giggled. "I think we have an audience."

Mason saw the curtains flutter. Probably his mother. "Definitely. So you want to buy a house with me?"

Tessa's arms tightened. "Yes. But how about we find my attacker first? Because even if we bought the house, your parents would have to stay until he's found."

Mason knew she had a point. "You seem to have faith that I'll find him. Because, Tessa, it's not looking good."

Mason found sleep difficult, even with Tessa wrapped up tight against him, this time in his bed. Something about dinner with the Griswolds wasn't sitting well with him. Monty had certainly acted strangely. The kid always had a wave and a smile for him. But he'd been tense all through dinner. His chatter about football had been only half-hearted, and he kept jerking his gaze away from Tessa. But Mason couldn't imagine what Monty would know about Tessa. He would have heard about Randy Harris, as small-town gossip was invasive. But what would that have to do with Tessa directly? Monty was just a kid.

"You're thinking; I can hear it." Tessa placed a small kiss on Mason's chest.

"I thought you were sleeping."

"What are you thinking about?"

Mason placed a kiss on her hair. "Just cop thoughts. They keep me up sometimes."

"If we're going to do that buy-a-house-together thing, you might want to learn to share some of those cop thoughts from time to time. Might help you sleep better."

Mason knew most of his cop thoughts would never be voiced, at least not to Tessa. But in this case, it involved her. "Monty was weird tonight. I'm trying to figure out why."

Tessa knew what he meant, but he wasn't her attacker. "I don't know him well, but he seemed tense. But Mason, he's just a kid. And there is no way he attacked me."

"But what if he knows who did? Sometimes witnesses can be jumpy, especially if they don't want to talk to the cops. Maybe he was somewhere he wasn't supposed to be or doing something he wasn't supposed to be doing, and he saw something."

"Okay. So how do you go about questioning the mayor's son without causing harm to your job?"

It was a good question. But he'd long ago made himself a promise that he wouldn't be intimidated. "With tact."

Tessa sat up to look down at him. "And are you good at that? Because I can't personally attest to that as being a trait you possess."

Mason pulled her down on top of him, careful of her cast. "This from the woman who says I'm handy to have around."

Tessa shifted to sit astride him. "It wasn't your ability as a cop I was referring to, or your personality traits."

"No?" Mason's hands streaked up her thighs.

"Nope. I'll show you what I meant. Maybe then you can sleep."

Afterward, sated and exhausted, they both fell asleep.

* * *

Tessa took Rexford with her when she went to visit the house the next morning. Pete was packing up the last of his tools and had donated the leftover supplies that couldn't be returned.

Tessa gave Pete a brief hug. "I couldn't have done this

without you. It looks amazing."

Pete shrugged off her gratitude. "You know what you're doing. You could always get into interior design. You know what looks good together. I heard the agent already has some interested people coming to look at it."

Tessa was sure it would go quickly. "She's had some curiosity seekers, too. People want to see what Tessa Harris did to Sylvia's house."

Pete pet the dog, then gave the house one last once over. "I'm glad I don't live in a small town anymore. And, before I forget, Simon says to call him."

"All right. Bye, Pete."

Tessa watched as Pete drove off. It was a long haul back to Indiana. She took out her phone and called Simon.

Simon answered on the first ring. "I hear all is well, and Pete is on his way."

"Yes, Pete just left. The agent is bringing the first batch of buyers over tomorrow. I'm going to give the house a quick dusting and polish before I head out."

Simon's voice came through the line. "When are you headed back home?"

Tessa hadn't talked to Simon much in the past few days. And she hadn't told him that she was staying. "Simon, I love you."

The line was quiet for a moment. "You're not coming back, are you?"

"At some point, I'll have to get my stuff, unless you feel like packing up my apartment, but no. I'm staying with Mason. He loves me, Simon, and I can't come back."

"I knew when I saw you in the hospital that he did.

And it was written all over your face that you loved him when you talked about him. But Tessa, a cop?"

She was still a bit amazed herself. "Yes, a cop."

Simon sighed into the phone. "All right. But we'll have to fly in for the wedding, preferably before your new niece or nephew comes. Two kids on a plane will be hard enough. Keep me posted. And let me know the moment Mason finds that bastard who attacked you."

Tessa promised as she hung up. She and Mason had not talked about marriage. She supposed that in a small town it would be difficult to simply live with him, especially with his job. It was something she took for granted. You fall in love; you get married. He'd be handsome in a tux.

Knowing daydreaming wasn't going to get her anywhere, she patted her leg for Rexford to follow while she went through the house one last time. The old couch was gone, as was the table in the kitchen. Laine had come over and packed up her stuff when she'd gotten out of the hospital, so none of her personal belongings were here, either. The old bed was also gone, a gleaming wood floor now in its place.

"It's a very nice house. You should be proud."

Tessa spun on her heel at the sound of the voice. Alex Griswold stood behind her. "What are you doing here?"

"Sorry to startle you. I ran into your real estate agent at the diner, and she mentioned you were out here today. I wanted to apologize for last night. I figured this was my best chance to talk to you alone."

"Why don't we do that outside?"

"Sure." Alex headed back out.

Tessa gave a sigh of relief and followed him out with Rexford on her trail. "There isn't any reason for you to apologize."

Alex leaned against his sports car. "Maybe. But I feel bad about Daria."

Not following what he meant, she walked over to Mason's car and let Rexford into the passenger seat. "Daria was fine."

"We both know that's not true. She was rude last night. She doesn't like your mother, and I'm afraid she took her hostility out on you."

"Up until last night, I didn't know my mom even knew you. Don't worry about it."

Alex straightened but didn't come closer. "Tessa, I wasn't truthful with you last night. Your dad and my wife had an affair. But Randy wasn't serious and wasn't going to leave his wife for her. At first, I didn't know. I picked that fight at the bar, knowing full well Donald would arrest Randy and not me. Randy was always getting into some kind of trouble or another. No one expected me to be the cause."

Tessa didn't know why he was telling her this. "Why did you stay married to her?"

"I wanted to be mayor, for one. I couldn't let an infidelity stop that from happening. Daria said she was sorry, that it had been a mistake. And she was pregnant with Landon. I couldn't let someone else raise my son."

Tessa closed the car door. "It's old history, Alex. There's no need to drag it up. You and Daria must be happy. And Randy has been gone for a long time."

"When you said he was dead, I thought someone might think I did it. I guess I just wanted to be upfront about the affair. And if I'd wanted Randy dead, I'd have done it the day of the fight."

Now she got it. He was trying to cover his butt. But she honestly didn't care, nor did she believe Alex killed Randy. "Like I said, it's old news. No one is going to think you came after him all these years later."

"Thanks for listening, Tessa. And good luck with the house."

"Thanks." Tessa got into her borrowed car and headed back to Mason's parents' house. Alex had frightened her, but his voice was wrong. He wasn't the man who had attacked her. Something kept nagging at her, but she couldn't put her finger on it.

Chapter Twenty

Mason sat outside the high school watching the boys practice. Monty wasn't ever going to make it in pro football, but no doubt he had talent.

"Hey, Chief."

"Yo, Chief."

Mason waved at the boys who shouted out to him as he headed closer to the field. He waved at Monty when the boy noticed him.

"Hi, Chief. What's up?"

"I need to talk to you. Can you spare a minute?"

Monty looked back over at the guys who were taking a break. "Yeah, sure. What's up?"

"What do you know about the vandalism and the attack on Tessa Harris?"

"What? I don't know anything."

Mason put an arm on Monty's shoulder and led him from the crowd. "See, the thing is I don't believe you. Guilt can do funny things to a person, like not allowing them to look at someone. At dinner last night, you couldn't look at Tessa. Now I'm asking myself why. Do you know who vandalized her house? Did someone at school or around town say they did it? Did you see who attacked her?"

"No, man. I don't know what you're talking about. I didn't hear anything. I've got to head back."

Mason let him go. The boy had been sweating, and his eyes had darted around nervously. Mason needed to start asking more questions. The first person was going to be Monty's friend, Ray.

Thankfully, Ray was a good kid, and he had a future ahead of him. A little pressure, and Ray would crack.

It was late when Mason got home. The house was dark, and he was sure Tessa had already gone to bed. He stripped off his shirt and headed to his bedroom. When he got there, he smiled at Tessa curled up under his covers. He quietly left the room and took a quick shower. When he got back, he slipped into bed beside her.

"Mason?" Tessa fumbled to turn on the bedside lamp.

Mason kissed her and turned it on himself. "Sorry I'm so late. We had an emergency."

"Must have been a big one. It's after one."

Mason didn't elaborate. "You should go back to sleep."

Tessa rubbed her eyes. "Actually I wanted to talk to you. I had the oddest conversation with Alex Griswold today."

Mason didn't think he was going to like this. "What did he want?"

Tessa gave him an abbreviated version.

"Guess a man can go a little crazy when he finds out his wife's cheating. Especially with a guy like Randy. But I doubt anyone would consider him a suspect in Randy's murder all these years later. Then again, I don't like coincidences."

"Do you think he could be involved?"

Mason rubbed a hand over his face. "I don't know,

Tessa. I've known Alex for a long time. I can't picture him murdering Randy Harris and then coming and attacking you. That affair was a long time ago."

"What happened with Monty?"

"He denied he knew anything. I was going to track down his friend Ray, but then I got called in. Tomorrow I'm hoping to catch up with him. If Monty were up to no good, Ray would know about it."

Tessa shivered and settled back under the covers, seeking Mason's warmth.

* * *

The next morning, Tessa got a text from the real estate agent asking her to meet at the house. She kissed Mason goodbye before heading over. She took Rexford with her again, as it made Donald and Mason feel better having the dog with her when she went to the house by herself.

It was a little after nine when she got there. She saw Degrassi outside, and she wasn't surprised when he scowled at her and went back inside. She felt sorry for the new owners of the house for having to put up with that cantankerous old man. But not sorry enough to warn them.

She waited a little while, then sent a text back. The agent apologized and said she was running late. She told the woman she'd wait inside where it was cooler. She wished she could have afforded to stage the house to entice buyers, but she hoped that the tile work and the updated kitchen and bath would be enough to get the asking price. She'd chatted again with Simon last night, and she had sent him pictures of the final result. He'd been more than pleased and told her it had been worth every penny he had invested in the old house.

Almost an hour went by, and Tessa was getting hungry and was tired of waiting for the agent. Rexford was still in the car, but she couldn't leave him there all day. She sent a text back saying she was heading out and would stop by her office some other time when it was convenient. She stepped out of the house and locked the front door.

"Hi, Tessa."

Tessa jumped at the sound of that low voice. She felt a shiver go down her back. She turned to face her attacker. "Hello, Landon."

* * *

Mason found Ray outside the local ice cream shop. "Hi, Ray. I need to have a quick chat with you."

Ray warily eyed Mason. "Monty said you might come by."

"Did he? What did he say?"

Ray glanced around but didn't see Monty. They were supposed to be meeting up. "He said you were talking crazy."

Mason gestured for Ray to follow. "Let's take a walk. Now I know Monty either had something to do with vandalizing Tessa's house, or he knows who did. Now it's possible he just knows who did and is protecting his friend."

Ray started to sweat. "No. I had nothing to do with it."

"But you know who did it, don't you? Look, Ray, you

can either tell me the truth, or I'll haul both you and Monty down to the station for questioning. Even a small infraction will keep you from the college of your dreams."

Ray's head dropped. "Monty said he had to do it. Said he had to protect his family. I went with him, but I told him I couldn't go through with it. He called me names. Said if I were a real man, I'd step up. So I sprayed some words on the house like he told me. But then I realized he'd damaged Tessa's car. I told him we were going to get caught, but he laughed at me. Said some secrets can be kept forever. I told him you'd find out it was us. He said he felt bad and all, that you would waste your time looking for us, but he said without evidence there was nothing you could do."

"Who was he protecting? You said he had to protect his family. His dad? His mom? Who needed protection from Tessa?"

"That's the part I didn't get. He said it wasn't Tessa he was protecting them from, but Tessa's dad. He said that her dad might show up. He said where one Harris was, soon the rest would follow. It was all crazy talk."

Mason tried to tie it all together. If Monty thought he was protecting his family, which member would that be? Everything pointed back to Alex, but Mason just didn't see it. He pulled out his cell phone and called Tessa. He wanted to call his dad, but his dad would be just as biased as he was. Tessa would be more objective.

But her phone went to voicemail when he called. He knew she was headed over to the house to sign some paperwork with the realtor. Maybe if he hurried, he'd catch her there. He wasn't too far away.

* * *

"I told you to leave. You just wouldn't listen. I didn't want to hurt you; really, I didn't. But you didn't give me much choice, just like you aren't giving me a choice now."

Tessa started slowly walking backward down the porch. "Maybe if you had come by in person instead of vandalizing my house, we could have had a civil talk."

"I didn't vandalize your house. My little brother Monty did that. Poor kid was all worked up. I told him Randy would come and try to steal our mother away. I explained to him about the affair Mom had with Randy. Monty was beside himself. He wanted to go confront our mother, but I told him it wasn't her fault. It was Randy's fault. And you had to go so we could make sure Randy didn't come."

Landon stepped out of the shade of the trees, and Tessa saw his face, feeling that same shiver again. His face was twisted with anger. She'd seen that look before on the face of a different man. The face of her father. "This wasn't about your mother at all, was it? This is about you. You and Randy."

Landon pulled out a gun and waved it at her. "I knew you'd figure it out eventually. What gave me away?"

Tessa took a large step back, almost falling backward off the porch step. "Your face just now. When Randy came home drunk, sometimes he'd be in a rage, usually because he'd been in a fight and lost. He'd have that look on his face. You're not Alex's son, are you?"

"I am his son!" Landon pounced on her, grabbed her by

the shoulders, and shoved her against a nearby tree.

"You're not his son. You're Randy's." Tessa barely choked out the words.

He shoved the gun in her face. "No one will ever know. I'll be the next mayor. I'll run this town. And I won't let you stop me. I knew if Randy saw me, he'd know the truth. I couldn't let that happen. You should have left. But you didn't, and I knew you'd eventually figure it out, too."

Tessa struggled in his grasp, but he was stronger than her. Knowing it was going to hurt, but not having any other weapon, she brought up her cast and hit him across the temple. He yelled from the pain and let her go. Tessa sprinted for the car to get to Rexford. She could hear the dog barking and clawing at the door. She was halfway across the drive when she saw Mason's SUV pull up.

Mason saw Tessa's disheveled appearance, and then saw Landon near the house with a gun in his hand. He didn't hesitate. He jumped from the SUV, weapon drawn. "Stop right there, Landon."

"No, I won't let you ruin this." Landon turned and tore off through the woods, dropping the gun in his wake.

Mason was right behind him. He barely heard Tessa shouting for him as he ran. He could see Landon a few yards ahead of him. He shoved back branches and bushes as he ran. Rexford caught up with him and then passed him. "Good dog, Rexford. Attack."

Rexford gained speed and jumped on Landon as the man tried to cross a small creek.

Mason continued to run, watching as Rexford took Landon down. Landon fell into the water. Landon struggled to get up, but Rexford jumped onto his back. "Rexford, guard."

The dog growled and stood on Landon's back as the man's struggles ceased.

Mason caught up, pulling his handcuffs from his belt. He followed into the water, his uniform and shoes getting wet in the process. "You're under arrest, Landon."

Mason yanked him to his feet and cuffed him while he read him his rights. Landon was blubbering, but Mason couldn't make it out. He half-dragged Landon back to his SUV, picking up the gun on his way. He shoved him into the back seat before calling for backup to come out.

Tessa ran over to Mason and hugged him to her, ignoring the fact that water was soaking into her clothes.

Mason buried his face in her hair. "Are you okay?"

Tessa was shivering but fine, though her wrist ached inside the cast. "I'm fine. What are you doing here?"

Mason released her and leaned up against the car, taking a moment to catch his breath. "I met with Ray. He told me Monty vandalized your house. Said he did it to protect his family. But that didn't make sense. So I came here hoping to catch you before you left. Thank goodness I did."

Tessa came forward and wrapped her arms around his waist again, resting her head on his chest. They stood that way until a car arrived. But instead of Walter or Alicia from the station, it was Alex and Monty who pulled up.

Mason set Tessa behind him. "What are you doing here, Alex?"

Alex ignored Mason. His eyes were on Landon. "I

heard the police band. I was on my way to the station to see you."

Monty came to stand beside his dad, his head hanging.

Mason confronted Alex. "The truth, Alex. What are you doing here? You knew Landon attacked Tessa, and you said nothing."

Alex flinched in reaction to Mason's anger. "I swear I didn't know. Monty came home last night, and I heard him tell Landon that you knew Monty was the one who vandalized Tessa's house. I didn't hear Landon's response. But Landon left the house in a hurry, and he didn't come back. When I asked Monty what happened, he told me he'd vandalized Tessa's house because Landon told him they needed to chase Tessa away. Said because he was a minor, the punishment would be lighter if caught. Then I started to piece it together after I caught Daria crying in the bedroom. She told me Landon found out the truth."

Mason kept his hand hovering over his weapon. "What truth?"

Tessa came to stand beside Mason. "That Randy is Landon's father, not Alex."

Monty's head shot up. "What?"

Alex pulled Monty to him. "It's okay, son."

Monty pulled away. "How is any of this okay? Why didn't you say anything?"

Alex looked away from his son to Mason. "Daria was pregnant. I was thrilled. Our first child together. She was three months pregnant when I found out about the affair. Daria swore she was already pregnant before the affair began. I wanted to believe her. I wanted that baby to be mine. And I didn't want Randy anywhere near my wife and child. So I told myself the child was mine. I believed it for a time. Then as he got older, I didn't only see Daria's features or mine; I started to see Randy in his face as he matured. I had a doctor run a test without their knowledge. Landon wasn't my biological son. But by then, it didn't matter. I wished I hadn't had the test done. But I did confront Daria. We had a bitter argument. She left for a time. When she came back, she was pregnant with Monty. I ran a paternity test the minute he was born. He was my son. So she moved back in permanently, and we both swore never to talk about it again."

Mason looked over at Landon through the window of the SUV. "When did he find out?"

Alex's eyes followed Mason's. "Not long after Tessa came back to town. Daria got drunk. She feared Randy might be right behind Tessa. She was desperate that no one would know. I don't know what she told Landon exactly, but during that conversation, the truth came out. Daria told me Landon was furious at first, then calmed. She didn't want me to know she told him. But after dinner with you and Tessa, I started to get suspicious. Daria was acting irrationally. Monty was sulking. Landon just kept harping on how he was going to be the best mayor this town ever had. So last night, I confronted Daria. Then this morning, I confronted Monty. I didn't know where Landon was, but I needed you to find him before he did something stupid."

Mason pointed to the gun on the seat of the SUV. "Like kill someone?"

Alex paled. "Where did you get that?"

"I found it on Landon. And I bet when I run the ballistics it's going to match the bullets found in Randy Harris. I'm sorry, Alex. You need to call a lawyer."

Alex was on the phone when Alicia arrived. Landon was transferred to the squad car. Mason put the gun in an evidence bag and let Alicia head back to the station.

Alex and Monty were behind them.

Mason took a moment to call his dad and tell him what happened. News of the mayor's son's arrest wouldn't be kept secret for long, and Mason didn't want him to hear it from anyone else.

Tessa stared after the car. "They never had to worry about Randy. Even if he had shown up after all this time, there was no way he would have claimed Landon as his own. Randy must have suspected the kid might be his years ago."

Mason grabbed Tessa to him. "I need to go to the station. And you'll need to fill out a report. Then when I'm done booking Landon, I'm going to have to charge Monty and Ray with vandalism. It's going to be a long day."

Tessa kissed Mason and let him go. "I'm not pressing charges against Monty and Ray."

"Tessa, that's a nice gesture, but..."

Tessa stopped him. "They deserve a second chance. Let it be."

Mason didn't argue. He led Tessa to the SUV and headed to the station.

* * *

Tessa left the station after her statement had been made. Donald picked her up and took her back to the house to get Mason's car. Once back at the Slades' home, she went to the guest room intending to take a nap, but she had been too restless to sleep. Unable to be still, Tessa took Mason's car and just drove.

She had gone a few miles when she realized she was not far from Willow Lake. She parked the car on the side of the road and walked the short distance to the shoreline. She picked a dry spot and sat down.

She was still reeling from the day's revelations. She found her attacker, found her father's murderer, and found and lost a brother all in the same day. Mason was right about small towns. The truth couldn't be hidden forever. But this truth had sat dormant for many years. She couldn't help but feel this truth should have remained buried.

She'd have to tell Simon. She'd let him decide if they should tell Janine or not. But Tessa couldn't figure that her knowing would make any difference, any more than knowing her husband was dead made any difference. But with her husband's death came a kind of freedom. Finding out her husband's illegitimate son killed her husband might be a different kind of chain.

Tessa also imagined Alex would not be reelected mayor. Tessa could admire the man for raising Landon as his son, knowing that he wasn't his. But in the end, was keeping the secret more important than honesty? Tessa didn't have an answer for that.

Tessa laid her head on her knees, and her heart ached with loss, for herself and for the others. But with Randy's death, she too felt a new kind of freedom. Part of her always wondered if Randy would show up in their lives one day, ruining their futures. Just the thought of Randy anywhere near Simon's precious children was enough to make her shudder.

Tessa looked up, resting her arms on her knees, the ache in her wrist less than what it had been earlier. She hadn't told Mason for fear he'd drag her back to the hospital. Right now she imagined he was up to his eyeballs in paperwork and lawyers. The case against Landon would be sealed as soon as the ballistics tests came back, though that would take time. There would be Mason's testimony, her testimony, and that of Alex and Daria. Tessa also wasn't sure Alex's marriage was going to withstand what was to come. And for Monty, she could only hope he got the love and support from his parents he needed. For all intents and purposes, he'd lost his brother today.

But for her, Tessa Harris, the future was bright ahead of her. She stood up, brushed the sand from her backside, and went back to the car. There wasn't much she could do for Mason right now, other than being there for him. So she drove back to the house to have a chat with his parents.

* * *

It was with a heavy heart that Mason returned to his parents' house. Landon's attorney was trying to get started on bail, but Mason highly doubted he'd be successful. Being a small town, Landon was transferred to a larger facility a few towns over where he'd await arraignment. So, for now, the excitement was over. Alicia finally went home to her husband, and all Mason wanted to do was get home to Tessa.

Throughout the day, thoughts of her interrupted his work. He had Walter take her statement, keeping her only as long as necessary. He'd called his dad and asked him to come get her so she could leave. He knew how she felt about police stations, and he didn't want her tainted with any more bad memories than necessary.

It was only a little after eight when he came through the door.

Donald greeted him with a hug. "I know that wasn't easy for you."

Mason hugged his dad back. "Better me than you."

Donald wasn't going to argue the point.

Eleanor came in and hugged her son, as well. "I'm so proud of you Mason. I hope you know that."

He kissed his mom's cheek. "I know."

Tessa came into the doorway that led to the kitchen. She smiled at him. "I've got dinner for you."

Eleanor let her son go. "Tessa came back and cooked up a storm. Your dad and I ate already. We're going to head up to bed."

Mason watched as his parents went upstairs. He looked at Tessa. "It's only eight. A little early for bed."

Tessa waved him into the kitchen. "It's their not-so-subtle way of giving us some privacy."

Mason glanced at the kitchen table. It was covered in food. "My mother wasn't kidding."

"It was easy to do in such a nice, big kitchen. I went

with Italian tonight."

Mason took a seat. "Like our first date."

Tessa beamed at him. "Exactly. I have cheese lasagna, chicken marsala, and bruschetta. And a nice red, or so I'm told, to calm our nerves."

When Mason tried to help, Tessa pushed him back into his chair. He sat contentedly, sipping the glass of wine she poured him, as she bustled around the kitchen. She fixed him a large plate, and he ate every bite.

Mason relaxed in the chair. "I could get used to this."

Tessa laughed, but there was a hint of nerves in the laugh. "Me, too. We found my attacker. I'm free to go home with you, or go back to Indiana, or stay here. This afternoon I went to the lake and thought about the future. So I took the next step."

Mason tensed. "What next step?"

Tessa came over and sat on Mason's lap. "When I was younger, I was confused by the phrase 'you can't go home again.' I understood what it meant, that when you do go home it isn't the same; things have changed. But in some ways, I felt like I hadn't changed, and that home would always be what it was before, because I would always be trapped by parts of the past. But I get it now. I can't go home again, and I'm so grateful that it's true. But I can go to a new home, one not tainted by the past. And that's what I want. I want to stay here. So I asked your parents if we could buy the house."

Mason's arms tightened around Tessa. "And what did they say?"

Tessa kissed him lightly at first, and then kissed him

again as if they'd been apart for months instead of hours. When she'd satisfied that immediate need, she pulled back. "They said yes."

Mason rose so he could set Tessa on her feet. Then he dropped to one knee. "Marry me, Tessa."

Tessa knelt in front of him, her eyes filling with tears. "I love you, Mason. I want nothing more than to marry you, buy this house, and raise a family."

Mason kissed her again, lifting her into his arms. He carried her upstairs to his bedroom. "I love you, Tessa. Welcome home."

Epilogue

Tessa's wedding day dawned bright and clear. She spent the night at Laine's house with Eleanor, Laine, Cyndi, Sarah, and the kids. Mason had stayed at his parents' house, soon to be their house, with Laine and Cyndi's husbands, Simon, and his dad for company.

She was zipped up in a beautiful white ball gown that Laine and Cyndi had helped her pick out. For a brief moment, Tessa felt like the princess she'd teased Mason she'd wanted to be. And there was no doubt in her mind that he was her perfect prince.

Cyndi's doctor had released her to go back to normal activities, and the first item on the list had been a dress. The second had been talking to the local minister, who had agreed to marry them. So they were getting married in the church Mason attended as a child. The third had been the reception. The town hall had a large room, and Alex had insisted they use it for the wedding reception. Tessa had stopped by on the way to the church for a sneak peek. Cyndi and Laine had decorated it in various hues of blue and silver, with white flowers on every table.

One order of business that Tessa had been against was Mason, Simon, and Donald talking with the attorney Simon had hired to get her conviction overturned. She'd repeatedly told them to stop, but they hadn't listened to her.

She had been stunned when Mason came back and said a judge was looking at her conviction. Donald knew some people and had pulled some strings to get her case heard. The attorney was confident a reversal would be forthcoming. But regardless of the outcome, Tessa was happy. And if it made her family, both old and new, happy to do this for her, then she decided to stop fussing and let them.

Tessa glanced at the clock. "It's time."

Sarah, who was now looking pregnant, handed Tessa her bouquet. "You look beautiful, Tessa. And I adore your Mason. He's perfect for you."

Laine piped in. "Just don't tell him that. It will go to his head."

Cyndi, also now looking pregnant, chided her sister. "Come, now. It's his day, too. A little flattery won't hurt."

Laine smiled at her sister. "Ever the peacemaker. Let's go get our brother married."

Laine and Cyndi were first in the procession. Then Sarah. Tessa took a deep breath and rounded the corner. She saw Mason first, looking as amazing as she had imagined him in a tuxedo. He had a large, perfect white rose pinned to his jacket. Donald stood beside Mason, with Russell and Tyler next in line. She caught Eleanor's eye from the first row and gave her a huge smile.

Then Tessa noticed the church. She was stunned to see it was packed with Willow Landing's townsfolk. She saw Walter and Alicia. She saw Alex and Daria and Monty. And then she saw Margie from the diner and John Baxter from the hardware store among the crowd. Both were smiling at her. She didn't see Degrassi or Boyd in the sea of faces, but that didn't surprise her. And she was quite pleased they weren't invited and putting a damper on her wedding day.

"Ready?" Simon took her arm to walk her down the aisle.

Tessa wrapped her arm in Simon's. She paused to kiss his cheek. Then she let him guide her down the aisle to where her future awaited.

Simon turned her over to Mason. She looked up into the face of the man she loved with adoring eyes. "I love you, Mason."

Mason returned the look. "I love you, Tessa."

She put her arm in his and turned to the minister; they vowed to love and cherish each other until death do us part.

<u>Books by Elizabeth Castle</u>

Single Titles:
Going Home
This Kind Of Love
Chasing Hope
The Babe & The Librarian (novella)

The Heart's Way Series:
For Now and Always
Ask Me To
Say You Love Me
Forever Love

Bennett Family Series:
This Time Love
A Bride For David
(novella)

All Of Me Series:
All Of My Days
All Of My Nights

Cantwell Quartet Series:
Falling Slowly
Unraveled
Hidden Away
Entangled

Contemporary "Retro" Romance Series:
Loving Jordan

Visit elizabeth-castle.com for newsletter signup and up-to-date releases.

www.ingramcontent.com/pod-product-compliance
Lightning Source LLC
Chambersburg PA
CBHW020743310726
48969CB00002B/397